*If you can't be
acknowledged as the
daughter of a prince, the
least you can do is marry one.*

When Elizabeth, youngest of the notorious Royle sisters, comes face-to-face with her future husband, a man she's seen only in her dreams, she nearly swoons—especially when she discovers he is a prince. But her ecstasy is short-lived as she quickly learns that the man she longs for is betrothed to someone else—a princess, no less. Most women would give up, but Elizabeth is a Royle, after all.

Refusing to surrender her dreams of a royal wedding, Elizabeth takes the position of lady-in-waiting to the fiancée, determined to get close to her perfect match. But the lover she desires is not who he seems . . . and only once she discovers the true man behind the crown will she find the perfect love she's been longing for all her life.

By Kathryn Caskie

HOW TO PROPOSE TO A PRINCE
HOW TO ENGAGE AN EARL
HOW TO SEDUCE A DUKE

Kathryn Caskie

How To Propose To A Prince

An Avon Romantic Treasure

AVON

An Imprint of HarperCollinsPublishers

This is a work of fiction. Names, characters, places, and incidents are products of the author's imagination or are used fictitiously and are not to be construed as real. Any resemblance to actual events, locales, organizations, or persons, living or dead, is entirely coincidental.

AVON BOOKS
An Imprint of HarperCollins*Publishers*
10 East 53rd Street
New York, New York 10022-5299

Copyright © 2008 by Kathryn Caskie
ISBN: 978-0-06-112487-7
www.avonromance.com

First Avon Books paperback printing: March 2008

Avon Trademark Reg. U.S. Pat. Off. and in Other Countries, Marca Registrada, Hecho en U.S.A.
HarperCollins® is a registered trademark of HarperCollins Publishers.

Printed in the U.S.A.

10 9 8 7 6 5 4 3 2 1

For reader and amateur genealogist,
Rhonda Ring Marks,
who might well be a modern-day Royle sister.

How To Propose To A
PRINCE

Chapter 1

A Royle Wedding

It was raining . . . a bit.

Only a bit, her sister had said.

Elizabeth Royle looked down at the dripping embroidered skirt of her jaconet muslin walking frock and became instantly nauseous. It was surely ruined.

She and Anne had only been walking for two minutes and already she was soaked to her knees. The umbrella they shared had done nothing to protect her dress or azure crape mantle from the white sheets of rain sweeping down Pall Mall.

Her Bourbon walking ensemble would never be the same.

Ever.

Had her sister Anne not been leaving for her honeymoon in Brighton on the morrow, Elizabeth would have never agreed to shop with her for a few sartorial essentials on such a horrid day as this.

But she well understood her sister's need for the proper traveling attire. Elizabeth had long ago learned the great importance of appearing impeccably groomed and clothed at all times.

Why, a carefully chosen bonnet, for instance, could not only camouflage a mass of less than fashionable red hair, but protect bone-white skin from the sun and stave off the sprinkling of freckles across the nose and cheeks that would inevitably follow any accidental pinking of the skin.

So, who better than she could appreciate the value of a wardrobe specifically selected to highlight physical attributes while distracting the eye from other less than desirable features?

At least the outing this day had afforded her the opportunity, before Anne left on her journey, to begin to tell her sister about the man she intended to marry.

After all, it was possible that Anne would wish to delay her honeymoon in order to attend the nuptials. Though, Anne's postponing her journey would probably be more likely if Elizabeth had a date for the wedding.

Or, at least, her fiancé's name.

"Oh, heavens, Lizzy, that means nothing. It was just a dream," Anne said, rolling her amber eyes.

"No it wasn't. It was far more." Elizabeth stopped abruptly, causing an annoyed couple to unexpectedly veer off the damp pavers into the squishy mud edging the street.

"How so?" Anne's tone lifted with false interest, and she seemed to be trying ever so hard to extend the limits of her patience.

Elizabeth shoved a loose copper lock that dangled before her eye over her ear. "I swear to you, Anne, last night I wrapped a sliver of your wedding cake and put it under my pillow, exactly as Mrs. Polkshank had advised, and it worked—I dreamed of him, the man I would marry."

Frustrated, Anne peeled a mist-dampened curl of her golden hair from her brow, then grabbed her sister's arm and started her down Pall Mall again. "And he was a . . . *prince*?"

Heat surged into Elizabeth's cheeks. "Well . . . yes."

"Do you not see how preposterous this notion is? How are you so sure he is royalty? What did you see in your dream?" Anne raised a cynical eyebrow at her as they walked, but only waited a moment for a reply before prattling on. "And, I must remind you, it was just a dream—*a dream*, Lizzy."

"I—I did not see anything to indicate his royal standing. I just . . . felt it," Elizabeth tried to explain. How could she make Anne understand when she herself did not? She just *knew*.

"What did you see, then? It is entirely possible you are only misinterpreting what you saw, you know." Anne had obviously noted her embarrassment and sought to placate her.

"That he is gloriously handsome, though there is an air of controlled strength about him. I could see it in the purposeful way he moved. The way others moved about him, deferred to him." A smile touched her lips.

"What about his hair, his face? Has he got a long nose, a mole with a hair jutting from it, or a weak chin—some feature that might help you identify him in a crowd?" Anne grinned impishly.

"His face is beautiful. Perfect." She scowled at Anne. "And I would recognize him anywhere. His eyes are so unusual." Elizabeth bent and glanced upward, past the dripping brim of the umbrella. "They are as leaden gray as this sky, but a thin ring of summer blue surrounds them. I have never seen eyes like that—except in my dream."

Elizabeth drifted off, lost in the memory of those haunting eyes. Instinctively, she turned to the sound of a team of horses clopping past. She strained her eyes, but in the rain and the thick fog rising up from the street, she could see nothing but a huge shadow slowly passing them by.

"Lizzy! Keep walking. We're nearly to the draper's shop." Anne squeezed Elizabeth's arm and urged her along, chattering as they walked. "Tell me more about your gentleman."

"If you insist." She grinned. "His hair is thick, dark and wavy, and his skin is almost golden, as though he'd spent a goodly amount of time out-of-doors."

"Well, it's clear then." Anne laughed teasingly. "You are to marry a farmer." She paused for a moment, then fashioned an expression of mock concern. "Oh, dear, Lizzy. Your guardian won't much like that."

"Anne—" This was not amusing to Elizabeth at all.

"Gallantine and the Old Rakes of Marylebone will accept nothing less than a peer of the realm for the only unwed secret daughter of the Prince of Wales." She feigned a mournful sigh. "But ... if you dreamed of marrying a farmer, I suppose it must be true." This earned Anne's arm a hard pinch from Elizabeth.

"Please do not tease me about this. And, I told you, he is a prince, so I will be a princess. I am quite sure of it. All my grandest wishes are about to come true."

A barely concealed smirk twitched at Anne's lips. "A princess, hmm? Be careful what you wish for, Lizzy. I daresay, a princess's life is not all balls and baubles."

"I am not taking this premonition lightly, sister."

"Oh, it's a premonition now, is it?" Anne chuckled, obviously not understanding how vivid this presentiment had been to Elizabeth. "Please, promise you will not place all your hopes on this one dream."

"My dreams do come to pass . . . frequently, too." Elizabeth flicked an eyebrow upward in annoyance.

"Yes, they do, but only half of the time. And even then, you usually get half of what you see wrong. You'd do as well flipping a penny to determine your future."

Bah! Her sister was only repeating what Mary, the eldest (by mere minutes) of the Royle triplets said. "Well, continue to doubt me if you must. But won't you be a plucked goose when an offer is made and I marry before the summer ends."

"Before the summer . . . *this* summer? Oh, Elizabeth, you haven't even met your husband-to-be yet. There is no possible way you will find a wedding ring on your finger in just two months."

"Why not? You did, and Mary as well, and now she and the duke already have had a baby."

"Oh, sweeting, please do not set your heart on this course," Anne pleaded. "You will only be disappointed."

Elizabeth suddenly stopped, yanking her sister to a halt along with her. "Gorblimey. Anne, it's . . . him. Right there."

She raised her reticule before her to conceal the finger she poked in the direction of a fog-draped gentleman stepping down from the grandest carriage Elizabeth had ever seen.

But he looked even finer than the gilt carriage. Braided gold epaulets adorned the shoulders of his kerseymere coat. Several military medals were pinned to a red satin sash that swept dashingly across his broad chest to his lean hip. Two regimental-straight lines of gleaming buttons, too brilliant to be mere brass, ran down his dark blue coat.

"Surely you do not mean that nobleman?" Anne blinked the rain from her eyes and then stared as if assessing him. Clearly, she disbelieved that this man was the one Elizabeth would marry.

"Surely, I do. I am certain of it." Elizabeth tipped her head in his direction. "He is my future husband."

"Well, his skin is rather sun-kissed, I'll give you that much, but he is clearly not a farmer." A breathy chuckle slipped out from between Anne's lips.

Elizabeth glowered at her sister. "*You* said he was a farmer, not I!"

"I vow, I think we need a closer look to verify his identity as your future husband." Anne was making a game of this. "Come on, Lizzy, let's follow him."

"Yes, let's." Her sister's true motivation for following the gentleman did not matter a bit to Elizabeth. She knew for certain that if she could only observe him more closely, she would be completely sure, and convince Anne of the validity of her dream.

When Elizabeth turned to peer at him again, however, he was gone. "Oh, lud! Now we've lost him."

"No, we haven't." Anne inclined her head to the shop just four doors down Pall Mall. "He went into Hamilton and Company, just there."

Elizabeth widened her eyes to see through the fog and rain, and just glimpsed two liveried footmen entering a shop.

"Ah, Jeweler to the Crown by Royal Appointment," Anne added, her eyes gleaming mischievously. "He is definitely *not* a farmer."

Elizabeth paid Anne's ribbing no mind. She hastened her step, hauling her sister along with her. "Mayhap he has gone inside to choose a ring for me." She gave her sister a playful wink. "Have you considered that, Anne?"

The brightness in Anne's eyes dulled quite suddenly and her countenance became sober. "Not at all—and you should not, either." She exhaled as her frustration with Elizabeth grew. "Nonetheless, I should like to take shelter from the rain, so let us go inside."

But Elizabeth paused before the shop door. A steady stream of water poured from the Hamilton and Company sign above, pounding the umbrella she and Anne huddled beneath like a roaring waterfall.

Anne tugged at her arm. "Elizabeth, we are being drenched. Why do you delay? He is right inside. Come along."

Elizabeth trembled. If her premonition was true, her future lay just beyond, and yet, she could not seem to step over the threshold.

What if, like Anne claimed, it was only a dream—a vision she only had half right?

Before she could worry over it a moment longer, her sister pressed down the brass latch and the shop door opened. A bell sounded overhead as Anne dragged her through the door, noisily heralding their entrance to the startled shopkeeper.

The ebony-haired gentleman they pursued looked up from the glittering piece of jewelry he was holding in his hand and whirled around as well. His gray eyes instantly locked with Elizabeth's.

Anne leaned close and whispered. "Pity, it's a diamond and ruby brooch he's considering, Lizzy, not a ring for you." She exhaled. "Do you know, I can't recall if you liked rubies or emeralds. Which do you prefer?"

Elizabeth didn't answer. Didn't say a word. She could not. It was he.

Her prince.

The shopkeeper smiled up at Anne. "Good afternoon, Lady MacLaren, Miss Royle."

"Good afternoon, sir," Anne replied distractedly. "I see you are occupied, but worry not. My sister and I are in no hurry to be served. In truth, we would be most content browsing your cases and shelves."

"Absolutely, Lady MacLaren." The shopkeeper bobbed a quick bow. "But I shall have my son Bertrum attend to your needs presently."

Elizabeth wrenched her gaze from her intended and stared blindly into the glass case at a pair of amber drop earbobs, but she could feel the heat of his eyes still upon her.

"Come, Lizzy. Look at these tiaras. Why, they are fit for a princess. Stunning, simply stunning."

Tiaras? Her cheeks were blazing now and she hurried to catch up to her sister, who had wandered across the deep, narrow shop and was nearly pressing her nose against the glass for a better look.

"End these games at once, Anne," Elizabeth whispered hotly into her sister's ear. "You are not the least amusing and your antics are embarrassing me."

"I am only jesting, Lizzy." Anne grinned up at her, but when her gaze met Elizabeth's fretful eyes, she realized the extent of her sister's unease.

"Please, cease." Elizabeth's chest tightened like corset bindings as her nerves frayed further.

"I apologize. Really, I do. Though . . . these

tiaras are lovely, aren't they?" She turned and glanced over her shoulder momentarily, then smiled brightly and spoke quietly through her teeth. "Is it him?"

Elizabeth sucked her lips into her mouth and gave her head a nod.

"Are you sure?"

"Yes." She clasped her sister's wrist and drew her closer. "Oh, God. What shall I do?"

Anne glanced at the gentleman again, and Elizabeth hesitantly followed her gaze. Now he was examining a necklace dripping with graduated droplets of verdant emeralds and snowy pearls.

"First, remove your wilted hat." Anne whisked the soggy Bourbon bonnet, with its dripping white feather, from Elizabeth's head and shoved it under her own arm.

"Anne, you're crushing it," Elizabeth ground out between her teeth. "And he'll see my awful hair."

Anne didn't reply. Her eyes momentarily shot in the handsome gentleman's direction again, and then she quickly plucked four hairpins from Elizabeth's hair, sending a cascade of red curls tumbling down her back.

Before Elizabeth could protest, Anne had shoved her fingers through the bonnet-matted hair at her crown to restore the fullness of her bright curly hair. "Well now, much better."

Elizabeth pushed her sister's hands away and reached for her soaked hat, but Anne turned so she could not retrieve it.

"I am only trying to help. You want to present well, Lizzy, do you not?"

A twittering male voice called out from the rear of the shop. "Oh, dear Lady MacLaren and Miss Royle. How lovely you came to our humble establishment this day."

Startled by the intrusion, Elizabeth snapped her head around to see a young man in a close-fitting blue coat and tighter-still charcoal-hued pantaloons hurrying toward them, waving his hands excitedly in the air. "I am coming to your service, my good ladies. Do not fret!"

Elizabeth angled her head toward her sister. "How do the shopkeepers know our names?"

"They probably read them in the *Times*," replied a rich, resonant male voice coming from directly behind her.

Elizabeth's eyes widened. *Gorblimey.* She knew who was standing there, so close that she could feel the heat radiating from his body.

Anne covertly sunk an elbow into Elizabeth's side. "Turn around," she whispered almost undetectably.

Slowly, Elizabeth swiveled her head in his direction, following its momentum with her body a scant second later, until she faced him fully and met his piercing gaze.

She could not help but stare.

Lud, from such close proximity she could see a ring of clear blue edging the silvery gray of his eyes. She gasped and a shudder shook through her. Any doubt as to his identity evaporated in that instant.

This man standing before her had been plucked directly from her dream.

There was no question. He was the gentleman she would one day marry.

Anne whirled about, likely having heard her surprised reaction to the man. Her sister blinked with astonishment when she, too, discerned the unusual color of his eyes—exactly as Elizabeth had described. Anne clapped a hand to her chest. "I—I beg your pardon, sir, it seems neither of us had been aware of your approach."

"I do apologize, Lady MacLaren. I did not mean to startle you . . . or Miss Royle." He exhaled a ragged breath as though somewhat embarrassed. "Miss Royle had asked . . . and, well, I only meant to explain to her that your wedding, Lady MacLaren, was reported in the *Times*."

"And every other newspaper in the realm," the young shop clerk blurted. "I saw at least four caricatures of you both. It would be hard to mistake your faces. Why, Lady MacLaren, your betrothal ball at Almack's is still the talk of London."

"Bertrum!" Mr. Hamilton hissed, and poked a finger toward the storeroom. "There is a shipment to be inventoried. Please see to it at once." Hamilton, the elder, looked to his customers. "I beg your pardon. Do forgive my son."

Bertrum Hamilton, realizing he had forgotten his place, turned dejectedly on his heel and slowly started for the back of the shop when Elizabeth's would-be fiancé unexpectedly called out. "Young man."

Bertrum turned and met his father's reproachful gaze. Receiving a hesitant nod of consent, he approached them again, his head hanging low. "I beg your forgiveness, Your Royal Highness. How may I serve you?"

Your Royal Highness? Elizabeth gasped again, and looked immediately to Anne, whose golden eyes had gone wide.

"Your Royal Highness? No, no, you mistake me for another." A distinct ruddiness swept the gentleman's cheekbones.

"Have I?" Bertram's brows migrated toward

the bridge of his narrow nose. "I do beg your pardon . . . s-sir."

Elizabeth's prince turned from the clerk, straightened his back, and his chest expanded as he prepared to address the women. "Please excuse me, Lady MacLaren, Miss Royle, but your comment about the tiaras being fit for a princess caught my attention. And I believe you were correct in your assessment. The tiaras are beautiful."

"Yes, they are." Elizabeth beamed at the prince. A bead of water dripped from a tendril of hair and into her lashes, making them flutter madly. Gads, she must appear the veriest of ridiculously charmed misses.

His eyebrows lifted slightly and he returned a bemused smile. "When I approached, my dear ladies, I had only thought to request a small favor. I should not have even thought it, or spoken to you, but now that I have, I am duty-compelled to make myself known to you both. I am Lansdowne, Marquess of Whitevale." He bowed deeply. "I do hope you will forgive my earlier impertinence."

From the periphery of her vision, Elizabeth saw the young clerk roll his eyes disbelievingly.

Within a clutch of moments, Anne had politely introduced them both. "My lord, what favor did you wish to ask of us? It would be an honor to assist you in any way possible."

"I—I . . ." He gestured for the clerk. "That tiara, there. The one the ladies were viewing."

Young Bertrum Hamilton reached into the jewel case and lifted a glittering diamond tiara from a tuft of black velvet. "This one, my lord?"

"Yes." He took the jewel-encrusted tiara from the clerk and then held it out to Elizabeth. "Might you try this one on for me . . . for just a moment or two? Please."

Elizabeth nervously forced a polite smile and nodded. She reached for the tiara, but Lord Whitevale suddenly waved her hand away.

"Would you allow me, Miss Royle?" he asked.

Once more Elizabeth nodded mutely. Her hands were trembling so fiercely that she probably would not be able to position it upon her head properly anyway.

She did not say a word. La, she barely breathed, for fear she would shriek with excitement. Her heart pounded as he raised the glittering tiara and eased it into the curls of her red hair as he settled it atop her head.

Her dream was coming true. She knew it!

Well, half true at least. So, Lord Whitevale

was not a prince. But that was of no consequence. Here she stood with a sparkling diamond tiara on her head placed there by the man of her dreams.

Who would have ever thought such a wretchedly miserable day would become so brilliant? She lifted her lips at the thought, earning a reciprocal smile from Lord Whitevale—one that warmed her chilled body from the tips of her damp toes to the crown of her head.

Then, without warning, he gently plucked the tiara from her head and turned to the clerk. "Yes, this is it. Will you have this sent to Cranbourne Lodge this very day? And enclose this, will you?" He withdrew a letter from inside his coat and handed it to young Hamilton.

The clerk bowed. "Yes, Your Royal Highness—I mean, yes, my lord."

"My thanks, Miss Royle. You have made my decision for me," Lord Whitevale said. "I have no doubt this will suit her perfectly."

Her? It will suit her? Just who is he speaking of?

Utterly confused, Elizabeth peered up at him, waiting for an explanation, but he did not condescend to supply one. Instead he bid her and Anne good afternoon, then abruptly quit the shop and followed his footmen into the dense rain.

"Bertrum," Hamilton, the elder, whispered rather loudly. "Why did you insist on referring to Lord Whitevale as His Royal Highness?"

Bertrum did not bother lowering his voice. His tone told Elizabeth he meant for them to hear his words. "Because that is who he is. I saw his procession arrive two days ago. I was in the front of the crowd that had gathered for the spectacle and I saw him clearly. And here, look at the signet in the wax sealing his letter."

Abruptly, Bertrum pressed the letter flat to the glass case and held a small lamp to it before his father could snatch the missive away. "I knew it. Look at it closely. His signature is visible through the foolscap."

"I do apologize, ladies," Hamilton the elder stammered. "I assure you, this is not the way I conduct business. Every purchase is entirely confidential."

Elizabeth didn't care a fig about that. She pinned her new friend Bertrum with the gravest of gazes. "Who is he . . . really? Please tell me. I must know."

Appearing most proud of his deductive abilities, Bertrum lifted his chin. "That gentleman, Miss Royle, was none other than Leopold of Saxe-Coburg-Saalfield.

Elizabeth's legs wobbled as if to give out from

beneath her, forcing her to grapple for a nearby chair. "You do not mean . . . *Prince* Leopold of Saxe-Coburg-Saalfield?"

Bertrum grinned. "Indeed, I do."

Anne paled and she redirected her gaze to Elizabeth. "Didn't we hear chatter, at the Kirk musicale I believe, that Princess Charlotte has recently set her cap for Prince Leopold?"

"Oh, 'tis not just chatter, Lady MacLaren," Bertrum interjected. "The *Times* reported that there have been secret discussions in Parliament about just such a union between the families. Though, not all members agree. I, for one, would choose Prince Leopold for Princess Charlotte. Did you notice the size of him—why, he is a born leader if I ever saw one."

"Bertrum!" Hamilton the elder snapped.

A throbbing began in Elizabeth's head as she realized what this revelation truly meant to her. She brought her fingertips to her temples, hoping to rub away the ache. But she knew it was useless.

Her rival for her intended's affection was none other than the Princess of Wales.

Lord, help her now.

Chapter 2

The Clarendon Hotel
London

"Damned wretched of you to send me out in this bloody awful weather." Sumner Lansdowne, Marquess of Whitevale, added a final splash of brandy to each of the two heavy crystal glasses before him. He turned and handed one to his cousin beside him, then raised the other glass to his own lips and drank.

"'Twas all in the name of love." Leopold, Prince of Saxe-Coburg-Saalfield, silently chuckled into his glass before looking sidelong at Sumner. "Someone had to go out. Besides which, it was you who insisted that I remain in this gilded gaol of a hotel . . . where it is safe."

"You'd be a fool to venture into public after yesterday's event." Sumner leveled a grave gaze at Leopold as he brought the crystal to his mouth and slowly sipped the brandy.

"The bullet might have been meant for you, Sumner, have you considered that?" Leopold's left eyebrow arched as he posed the ridiculous notion. "Or, simply a reveler in the crowd firing his pistol into the air. Must you take this so seriously?"

"Yes, I must. And so must you, Leopold. Your life may well depend upon it. We have no choice but to exercise utmost caution during this mission . . . that is . . . during our stay in London."

"A mission, eh, cousin?" Leopold's lips twitched upward. "You make it sound like a military campaign. Need I remind you that I am in London to woo a woman, not to usurp the throne."

"And I am here to ensure you survive. That, cousin, is my mission." Sumner tipped back his glass and drew a long draught of brandy, then roughly wiped his mouth with the back of his hand.

As much as Leopold pretended to dismiss the danger of his presence in London, he was nothing if not brilliant and calculating. Sumner was well aware that he knew the risk to his own life by simply appearing, without royal invitation, to win the hand of the Princess of Wales—especially when another held so much support within the most powerful echelons of Parliament.

"Or you could dismiss these threats and enjoy yourself in London," the prince muttered.

Sumner slammed his glass to the table. "Leopold, we must proceed under the assumption that the shot was directed at you—and was quite possibly fired by someone associated with those who sent the threatening letters."

"Always my protector." The prince glanced down and pensively swirled the brandy in the glass. At least Leopold had heard him. "Look here, Sumner, I know you are only doing your duty, but this is extraordinarily difficult for me. I am used to driving the charge across the field, not cowering in the treeline."

"You are not cowering. You are being prudent."

"So you say." Leopold let his gaze trail across the room, where he fixed it to the great window centered along the east wall. It might as well have had bars over the glass.

Sumner exhaled, all too aware of how much it irked Leopold, a highly skilled soldier in his own right, to be watched over and ordered about by his cousin. To be forced to remain far from danger. But the occurrences over the past two months had made a personal guard for the prince a sad necessity, and Sumner was the only logical and practical choice. His reactions were swift, his English was perfect, his gun skills keen, and his loyalty to the Coburg family unmatched. The Coburg family knew that he would put Leopold's life before his own, which was precisely what he had been entrusted to do.

"Letters . . ." As though something had suddenly occurred to Leopold, he shifted his gaze to Sumner. "Speaking of letters, my good man, you included mine with the—what did you choose?—I suppose I ought to know so I can respond knowledgeably when she comments on my gift."

"A tiara." Sumner sighed beneath his breath, remembering the sight of the beguiling Miss Royle wearing it. "It was a tiara . . . fit for a princess."

"Ah, yes," he replied with a distinct air of bored disinterest. "I am sure you made a suitable choice. But, you did include the letter, did you not?"

"Yes, I *did*." Sumner nodded, amazed at how fluidly his cousin's attention had shifted from attempts on his life to Princess Charlotte. "And, I was promptly mistaken for you, *again*."

Leopold's expression darkened as Sumner eyed him from the roots of his dark hair to the tips of his gleaming boots. "Frankly, I do not see the resemblance. You are at least a hand's length shorter in stature." Sumner grinned as he took a lingering taste of his brandy.

"And with your warrior's shoulders and muscle-knotted arms," he went on, "you lack the elegance and refinement I possess in abundance." Leopold looked haughtily down his aristocratic nose at his cousin, then pursed his lips and waggled his dark eyebrows.

Sumner tried to stop the guffaw charging up his throat, but Leopold, always so formal in public, just looked so damned absurd. Carmel-hued spirits spewed out all over the twin rows of glasses positioned atop the satin wood table before him in a fit of laughter and coughing.

Sumner caught a glimpse of movement and glanced up at the two liveried footmen positioned just inside the door. "I do apologize, gentlemen," he said. "I am afraid my cousin is severely lacking in manners."

"I?" Leopold's eyes rounded. "*I lack in manners?*" The prince whirled around to look at the footmen and the maid hurrying into the room.

"He is to blame." Leopold turned back to face his cousin and rose up on his toes to look Sumner straight in the eyes. "I, sir, am the very model of a superbly mannered nobleman." He dropped back upon his heels and peered at the footmen as if to ensure they had heard him.

Not that it should have mattered to him in the least, but the constant mistaking Sumner for the Prince of Saxe-Coburg-Saalfield seemed to rankle Leopold to no end.

The maid, eyes demurely downcast, scurried over to tidy up the table, while the footmen settled the brandy-spattered glasses upon a tray for removal. When they had finished, the footmen bowed deeply and the maid dropped a low curtsy before Sumner, and then all three tipped their heads in acknowledgment to Leopold before backing out of the room.

"Did you observe that? Did you?" Leopold huffed. "Why is it that even when we are standing side by side, people assume that you are the prince and not I?"

"I told you," Sumner grinned before finishing his sentence, "it's my commanding stature." He clapped Leopold's shoulder and drew him toward the two gilded chairs positioned on either side of the hearth. "Which is why my plan will work perfectly."

"Very well." Leopold huffed a breath from his lungs as he sat down and leaned against the tufted backrest. "Tell me, what is in that clever military mind of yours?"

Cavendish Square
Lady Upperton's library

Elizabeth tried very hard to avoid looking into Lady Upperton's faded blue eyes as she accepted the dish of tea from her. She couldn't bear one more expression of skepticism from someone she cared about, and especially not from her own sponsor. "I know this is exceedingly difficult to believe, Lady Upperton, but I am quite certain he is the man I will marry. Even Anne is so convinced."

"Impossible." Lady Upperton lifted her own teacup to her lips and sipped from it while peering doubtfully over its rim at Elizabeth. "The word swirling Almack's card room last week was that Prince Leopold has secretly come to London to seek the hand of the Prince Regent's daughter, Charlotte . . . and that she is most amenable to the young man's attentions—especially after the debacle of an engagement her father had orchestrated with that skinny goose, William of Orange."

Elizabeth swished her index finger from side to side. "I do not believe it. The *Times* reported that Princess Charlotte is no longer in London. But Prince Leopold is. Anne and I saw him."

The foglike steam rising up from Lady Upperton's cup had a dreamlike quality about it, and it sent Elizabeth's mind spinning back to misty Pall Mall—and then to the moment when she peered up into the prince's silver eyes as he placed the tiara on her head.

No, he would not marry Princess Charlotte. He would marry *her.* She knew it in every part of her being.

Never before had she felt such an instant connection with another human being as she had with him. When she looked into his eyes for the first time, she'd had the oddest notion that he was the part of her that she had been missing all of her life. The piece that filled the aching hollow in her soul. But how could she ever make anyone understand this? There were no words to express the connection she felt with him.

"So, dear, you saw Prince Leopold?" Lady Upperton settled her dish of tea on the table before her and did her best to appear very confused. "Please do forgive me, sweeting. I thought you told me you had met . . . one *Lord*

Whitevale." She lifted her snowy eyebrows and widened her eyes expectantly—as if she did not anticipate what Elizabeth's reply would be.

Elizabeth tensed. Must she explain what had happened again?

"Lady Upperton, I told you, he only said he was Lord Whitevale, but the shopkeeper proved beyond doubt that in truth he was Prince Leopold. He showed us the royal seal, and the prince's signature was clearly visible through the vellum . . ." She dropped her voice to a murmur. ". . . when the shopkeeper held a lamp to it." Elizabeth chucked her chin. "I tell you, the gentleman I met in the shop is the man I will marry."

"Oh, Elizabeth." Lady Upperton sighed, momentarily resting her face in her tiny hands. When she looked up again, her exasperation was clear. "Put your fanciful hopes out of your mind, gel. If Prinny accepts Prince Leopold, a union between the two families is a surety." She leaned forward and placed her hand atop Elizabeth's. "You must accept this, my dear."

There was a shrill scraping sound yanking their attention to the cold hearth. There, a bookcase opened like a door and a dark secret passage became visible. The air suddenly was sucked from the room and into the mouth of the secret doorway, as surely as if the library itself had inhaled.

Lady Upperton's fluffy white eyebrows lifted again and a smile elevated the corners of her painted lips. "Ah, he's here at last."

From the darkness of the secret passage, Lord Gallantine's lean, aged form stepped through the door and into the candlelit library. He adjusted his auburn wig and then gave a firm tug to each bottle-green sleeve of his once fashionable coat.

He looked up at the two women and then fixed his gaze upon Elizabeth, and there it remained pinned as he approached.

His tone was not jovial at all. In fact, he seemed oddly aggravated with her. "What is this twaddle I am hearing, gel?" he asked, sounding more than a little annoyed. "A prince? A bloody prince?"

Elizabeth rose and dropped the elderly gentleman a curtsy. She grimaced. "No twaddle at all, my lord."

Gallantine shifted his attention to Lady Upperton so quickly that the older woman startled. "Have you been able to talk any sense into her?"

Lady Upperton shook her head. She tossed her hands in the air defeatedly. "She has convinced herself, and will not hear any argument as to the complete impossibility of the notion of a royal marriage."

A small squeal of frustration slipped out between Elizabeth's teeth. "That is because I have yet to hear an argument that proves me wrong."

"Really?" This comment seemed to intrigue Lady Upperton. "Then do allow me to oblige you by providing one."

Elizabeth nodded hesitantly. She always had to watch herself around Lady Upperton and the Old Rakes. She had been warned about them by her sister Mary shortly after their first meeting with the elderly quartet. They were all so kind, charming, and good-natured, that it was only natural that others would drop their guard when they should be on their highest alert—for there was no more cunning group in all of London than Lady Upperton and the Old Rakes of Marylebone.

"For the sake of argument, let us say that the gentleman you met was, in fact, Prince Leopold," Lady Upperton began.

"He *was*!" Elizabeth blurted.

"Now, now, do let me finish." Her sponsor raised a hand, prompting Elizabeth to close her mouth. "So we will assume that the man was

Leopold. Were you aware that the Prince Regent has ensconced his daughter in Cranbourne Lodge in Windsor . . . which is not so distant from London, as you well know." Lady Upperton crossed her arms and waited for Elizabeth's reaction.

"C-Cranbourne Lodge in Windsor?" She swallowed the lump that had risen into her throat.

"If I am not mistaken—but then, I am old and my memory sometimes fails me . . ." Lady Upperton straightened her back and her gaze became as keen as a razor fresh from the sharpening leather. ". . . that the tiara, the very one the man set upon your head, was to be delivered to Cranbourne Lodge?"

"Y-Yes, it was," Elizabeth stammered as she nervously scratched the side of her neck. This bit of news did complicate matters.

Just a little.

Gallantine, who had seated himself, adjusted his auburn wig upon his head. "Now that you understand that the prince likely intends to marry Charlotte, and not you, may we get on with the business of finding you a proper match?"

Elizabeth lowered her head and peered at the tea leaves swirling in the bottom of her cup.

Despite mounting evidence to the contrary, she knew she had dreamt the future. How could she be expected to simply ignore her prophetic dream and seek a match with another? It was an impossibility.

The timbre of Gallantine's voice changed, and belatedly Elizabeth realized that he was still addressing her.

"There is a private ball at Almack's tomorrow evening," he was saying. "The guest list is quite the talk of Mayfair, you know."

Elizabeth glanced up from her teacup and nodded. "We are attending. I remember. Lady Upperton has already selected the emerald satin gown for me to wear for the occasion. Madame Devy promised to have it delivered on the morrow."

Gallantine slapped his hands to his knobby old knees and pushed upon them while leaning forward for the momentum to stand upright. "Perfect. There is someone Lord Lotharian, Lilywhite, and I would like for you to meet."

Elizabeth glanced down again and focused on the curls of steam rising from her cup as she rolled her eyes. *Good heavens.* She had told them her course was clear. She would marry the prince. There was no doubt in her mind.

Why do they persist with this senseless

matchmaking? Have I not made my future perfectly plain?

Evidently not.

She looked at Lord Gallantine, who seemed quite pleased with himself at that moment, proud at whatever match he, Lord Lotharian, and Lilywhite had planned, no doubt with the help Lady Upperton, their female cohort in this constant matchmaking madness.

Well, they might have succeeded in orchestrating perfectly proper matches for her sisters, but Fate was on her side. And there was no possible way she was going to let the meddling quartet interfere. She would not go willingly along with it. And she would tell them so . . . in her own way.

"However," Elizabeth coughed into a balled fist, "I thought I might retire quietly at home rather than attend the ball."

"What is this nonsense, Elizabeth?" Lord Gallantine narrowed his eyes at her.

Elizabeth's gaze fell to the floor and remained there. "Well, sir, it is only that I have felt dreadfully fatigued since I was drenched in the rainstorm earlier . . . and I fear I may already have a cold upon my chest."

She lifted her head and her gaze darted to Gallantine's eyes, searching for any hint that this story might earn her leave from the event—and any matchmaking he and the rest of the Old Rakes of Marylebone had planned for her.

Gallantine lurched back away from her. "You are ill?" Worry pinched the crinkled skin around his eyes, making him look far older than his seventy-two years.

Oh, she should not have mentioned illness, since it was not true. But she knew ailments of any kind caused Gallantine as much, if not more, anxiety than books not being aligned perfectly on the shelf, a slip of thread on his lapel, or clutter on a tabletop. It was cruel of her to use his nature against him, terrible, but she could think of nothing else just then and, lud, she had her entire future to consider.

"Well, if you are ill . . ." Lady Upperton paused for a moment and peered suspiciously at Elizabeth. ". . . *truly* ill, then you should not attend the ball."

Oh, blast. Her sponsor knew, somehow, that she was only crafting the slapdash tale to excuse herself from the social obligation. She could see it in the old woman's eyes. Elizabeth felt her body contract and she cringed into the cushion of the settee.

Lord Gallantine tipped his head in agreement,

causing the wig to slip down from his hairline to the bridge of his nose. He shoved it back into place and then looked pointedly at Elizabeth. "Pity you cannot attend, dear gel. Once I heard about your premonition, I would have thought you would swim across the Thames to attend this particular ball." He turned with a loud sigh and started back toward the secret door in the wall of bookcases.

What is this? After hearing my premonition, he thinks I would wish to attend the ball at Almack's?

"Wait, Sir Gallantine. Please!" Elizabeth's hand shot for the tea table, and she abruptly dropped her dish of tea, sending it clattering down upon the polished surface.

"Oh!" Lady Upperton jumped at the sound and slapped a calming hand to her chest. "Gallantine, you have stirred her too greatly. Do come back and sit down."

Elizabeth leapt up and dashed after him. "Please, come back and explain what you mean?"

Gallantine stopped walking the moment she tapped his shoulder with her fingers. He pulled his arm away, staring at the place where she had touched him, then turned slowly to face her.

"I—I apologize, Lord Gallantine," Elizabeth

hid her hands behind her back, "I should not have laid my hand upon your arm given my possible . . . yet *unlikely* illness." She slid her foot backward a pace to calm him. "I only wished to know what you meant by your comment. Why might I wish to venture to this particular ball?"

"It took Lady Upperton quite a goodly amount of doing to see your name onto the list of very prestigious guests." Gallantine gave Lady Upperton a nod of acknowledgment, a gesture to which she responded in kind.

"I did not know." Elizabeth turned and dropped a curtsy to her sponsor. "My thanks, Lady Upperton. You are very good to me." When Lady Upperton tipped her head in reply, Elizabeth returned her attention to the gentleman and waited for him to answer the question she had posed.

It took several long moments before he deigned to oblige her. "Why, I thought you had heard." When he glanced across the library to Lady Upperton once again, Elizabeth chased his gaze with her own.

Lady Upperton shook her head dolefully. "I say, Gallantine, she mustn't know. Though I do not see what benefit there is to telling her now. She is too ill to attend, after all."

"Please. I must know." They were toying with her, and she was fully aware of this fact. Someone of great importance and standing must be attending. "Please, tell me." Elizabeth wrung her hands.

Maybe even . . . him.

Oh, God, could it be true?

Unable to restrain her burgeoning excitement, she took a hasty step toward Gallantine.

"No, no." The tall, lean viscount shook his head, sending his wig pivoting to the left, then the right, until it sat askew on his bald pate. "Lady Upperton is correct about this. If you are ill, telling you that Prince Leopold is rumored to be in attendance at the ball would only disappoint you, child."

"Oh, Gallantine," Lady Upperton snapped. "You might as well tell her everything." She waved her hand dismissively in the air. You've already slipped up and told her Prince Leopold was to be at Almack's."

"Did I?" He slipped his index finger beneath his wig and scratched, then righted the auburn monstrosity upon his head. "I don't seem to recall . . ." he muttered to himself.

"You did." She exhaled a long breath, and then shrugged her shoulders as if defeated. "Now she will sit in her bed and sulk about not being able to reacquaint herself with her supposed future husband. But that cannot be helped." She focused her gaze upon Elizabeth. "Because you are too ill. I am dreadfully sorry, sweeting."

Elizabeth's head swung back and forth between Lady Upperton and Gallantine as if it were affixed to a mesmerist's chain. "Perhaps I will feel better on the morrow. Yes, I am sure if I only had enough rest this evening, and an uneventful day tomorrow, I will be right as rain come time to leave for the ball."

Gallantine raised his eyebrows, and she knew he would protest her idea. So, clutching up a handful of her walking skirt, she started hurrying toward the door to the entry hall.

She looked back over her shoulder as she rushed from the library. "Good eve, Lady Upperton, Sir Gallantine."

Lady Upperton pulled the lever on the side of the settee and a small footstool shot out from beneath it. The diminutive older woman stepped down from the settee and started for Elizabeth. "My dear, we have not yet finished our tea. Where are you going with such urgency?"

"Home to Berkeley Square." Elizabeth's eyes were fixed on the open door. She did not look back for fear she would see Lady Upperton beckoning her back to the settee. "If I am to attend the ball tomorrow, I ought to adjourn to my bed—without delay!"

Within minutes she was out the door and inside a hackney headed for Berkeley Square.

Tomorrow. La, she felt positively giddy inside at the thought. Tomorrow she would meet her prince at the ball and prove to everyone that her dream would come true.

Berkeley Square
An hour later

"You can't do this, Lizzy." Anne nervously twisted her wedding ring around and around her finger. "Please."

Elizabeth looked at Anne as she stood in the center of their great-aunt Prudence's parlor, her sister looking back at her as though she was quite mad, or at the very least not to be trusted. "I am sure I do not know what you mean, Anne." Eager to avoid her sister's attention, she allowed her gaze to flit lightly over her white-haired great-aunt, who dozed peacefully in the hearthside chair, a droplet of drool stretching from her lip down toward her shoulder.

"I have a better idea to occupy your time."

Anne rushed to the bookcase and withdrew the document box their father had left them upon his death.

"Not *that*, Anne." Elizabeth sighed. "Please, not now."

But her sister ignored her words and set the box on the table. She reached inside and withdrew a brass key.

"Anne, please." Elizabeth rolled her eyes as her sister twisted off the key's ornate oval grip to reveal a hexagonal driver, then used it to release the false bottom of the box.

From it, Anne removed two small amber laudanum bottles and, allowing them to clink together, handed them to Elizabeth, who exhaled slowly and held the bottles before her eyes.

"Two bottles labeled 'laudanum' with a crosshatch below. No number listed after the crosshatch, no initials. We have both studied these for clues for hours—the last bits of father's so-called evidence—but we found nothing. They offer no proof about the events of our birth."

Anne sighed. It was clear to Elizabeth that her sister was not going to give in so easily. "Lotharian told us that Father said the laudanum had been used, by Lady Jersey or even the queen, to drug Mrs. Fitzherbert during our birth . . . or shortly afterward. And that the laudanum had not been supplied by our father."

Elizabeth snatched up Anne's hand and forcefully pressed the bottles back into them, not caring if the glass broke in the process. "Even if we knew who supplied the laudanum, it wouldn't prove whether we are the true daughters of the Prince of Wales and his secret wife! It would only prove, if the story is true at all, that another surgeon was involved in concealing our birth. So, this supposed proof does not matter at all." Elizabeth walked to the hearth before facing Anne again. "I have resigned myself to the fact that we may never have enough evidence to prove we are daughters of the Prince of Wales."

Anne looked up at her peevishly, and then returned the bottles to their hiding place inside the box. "I only thought that you might amuse yourself, while I am away, by trying to learn more about the bottles. You are so clever. I am sure you can find the meaning of the bottles."

"Stop, Anne. Please, stop now." She brought her fingers to her temples and rubbed them to soothe the ache there. She turned her eyes toward Anne. "You and Mary have seemingly given up proving Father's story of our birth. Why shouldn't I? Why should I not occupy myself with pursuing my own future—as you and Mary have?"

Anne stood on her toes and set the box high on the shelf. When she turned around, Elizabeth saw that her cheeks were growing red with frustration. "Laird and I are leaving on the morrow, Lizzy. It is to be our honeymoon. Please, promise me you will not approach Prince Leopold at the ball and do or say anything nonsensical. You must dismiss this notion that he is your future husband."

Elizabeth folded her arms across her chest. "I know better, Anne," she said firmly.

"Lizzy, all of London is abuzz with rumors that he means to marry Princess Charlotte the very instant he has the backing of Parliament and the Regent."

"Because he wishes it, or is *rumored* to wish it, does not mean he will marry the princess." Elizabeth unfolded her arms and set her hands on her hips.

"Perhaps not, but it does not mean he will wed *you*, either!" Anne expelled a growl of a breath. "Be realistic about this, Lizzy!"

"I know what I saw in my dream, Anne." Yes, she knew all of this must sound utterly mad to the rest of the world, but it should not to Anne. Her dreams were prophetic, and both of her sisters had personal proof of this. Not only had she dreamt that her sister Mary would fall in love and marry the Duke of Blackstone, despite her claims that she loathed him above others, but her dreams also correctly foretold that Anne would marry Lord MacLaren, even though he claimed to desire another! Why would Anne not listen to her now?

Anne moved forward and grasped Elizabeth's hands. "Have you considered that it might have been Princess Charlotte you saw marrying Leopold and not you at all? If the story of our birth is true, she may be our half sister. That would make us all daughters of the Prince Regent."

Elizabeth thought about her sister's words, but they did not sway her. In her dream she was gazing deeply into his eyes. Holding his hand as he pressed a golden ring onto her finger. She was looking through her own eyes, not watching the marriage of another. Not at all.

"No, Anne. I *am* the bride. Of that I am sure."

"But don't you understand? Your dreams are usually only half right." Anne's frustration was palpable. "Might the half you have wrong be that the bride is someone else—perhaps even your half sister?"

Elizabeth broke Anne's hold on her and

walked over to Great-aunt Prudence, whose eyelids were now wide open. By the look of intrigue in her eyes, Elizabeth would wager she'd been watching and listening to the entire exchange without letting anyone know she was eavesdropping, as she was wont to do whenever a conversation turned down an interesting path.

Cherie, the silent maid-of-all-work, quietly slipped into the parlor and passed between her and Anne with a glass of claret for Great-aunt Prudence. It was uncanny. Cherie had done it again—she'd sensed a need before it had been realized by anyone. This incredible ability of the French maid's never ceased to amaze Elizabeth, her sisters, or guests in Great-aunt Prudence's Berkeley Square home.

Great-aunt Prudence's lips lifted at the sight of the claret and she raised her hand from her lap to grasp the small crystal goblet. She took a sip and then tipped the glass back and gulped some claret down. She drew her lips into her mouth and sucked any remaining claret from them, then pinned Elizabeth with her gaze. "This Lord Whitevale may or may not be a prince, Lizzy, but whether he chooses you or Charlotte, he will be marrying a blood princess one way or the other, eh?" She chuckled merrily then.

Elizabeth smiled at the old woman and knelt

down before her to adjust the coverlet on Great-aunt Prudence's lap. "Let us hope he allows Fate to choose his mate, instead of Prinny." She winked at her great-aunt, who laughed heartily at her words, sending her whole body shaking and nearly causing her to spill what little claret she had left onto Elizabeth's arm.

Elizabeth leaned up and kissed Great-aunt Prudence's cheek. Even now her elderly aunt was a lovely woman who could easily pass for ten years younger than the seventy-five years she claimed to be.

Prudence was a dear if occasionally addled woman, and Elizabeth had thought it such a pity that they had not known of her existence until after their father passed away and the Royle sisters were sent to live with her in London. It would have been wonderful for her and her sisters to know their extended family when they were younger.

"Please, Lizzy, swear you will not pursue Prince Leopold whilst Laird and I are away in Brighton," Anne pleaded. Her brow pinched at the bridge of her nose and three rows of worry wrinkles appeared upon her forehead. "I am certain I will not be able to sleep a wink while I am away if I must constantly worry about you making a grand cake of yourself in public."

"Dear, Anne, I sincerely hope you do *not* sleep a wink while in Brighton, else I fear your honeymoon will be dreadfully disappointing for both you and Laird." Elizabeth looked from her fretful sister to her great-aunt again. "Don't you agree, Prudence?" She grinned, but the merriment dissolved from her lips. Great-aunt Prudence had already fallen asleep again. Or was pretending to be asleep.

With a sigh, Elizabeth dropped down upon the other chair beside the fire. "Fear not, sister, I will not pursue the prince at the ball. Nor will I marry him, even he if asks." A sly smile inched across her lips. "That is, until you and your dear earl have returned to witness my dream come true. For what would my wedding be without both of my sisters and their handsome husbands in attendance?"

"You are incorrigible, Lizzy," Anne all but hissed.

"I have given you my word." Elizabeth arched her ruddy-hued brows and widened her green eyes innocently.

Anne looked at her with growing suspicion, but Elizabeth maintained a serene countenance, knowing she was not lying.

She would not pursue Prince Leopold at the ball tomorrow evening. She wouldn't have to.

All she needed to do was place herself in his direct path, and she would not be pursuing him. He would be coming to her.

Just as fate had intended.

Chapter 3

The next morning

The sun had risen, changing the sky from a somber gray to cerulean blue, but the air had not yet been warmed by its glow, and the day still felt as crisp as an autumn morn.

The ashes had been raked from the hearth and the kitchen fire relit for the day's cooking, but the night's chill still hovered in the room.

Elizabeth wrapped a damask shawl tighter around her as she sat before the worktable in the kitchen, scrutinizing Mrs. Polkshank's market list, trying not to fall asleep. Closing her eyelids, she rubbed her fingertips over them, hoping to revive herself. She hadn't slept well after the worrisome dream she had last night. But how could she? Telling herself it was only a dream would have done no good. Her dreams weren't like ordinary dreams—hers oft came true, and last night's nocturnal vision promised naught but horror in her near future.

In the dream, she was wearing an emerald ball gown, the one she and Lady Upperton had fashioned, with the modiste Madame Devy, precisely to their specifications. Suddenly, something struck her, knocking the air from her lungs. Slowly she looked down and saw red liquid trickling down her bodice. And with that moment came a feeling of foreboding so heinous, she felt sickened by it.

Even now, just the thought of her dream left her body aching and chilled to the bone.

She tried to shake off the dreadful feeling by shaking her head and shoulders, as one might do to shake snow from their hat and coat before going inside, but it was no use. And so, she tried distracting herself by quizzing Mrs. Polkshank about the market list. "There aren't so many of us now, Cook, do we really require so much mutton?"

"A leg-of-mutton is a *leg*. I can't very well go in and ask for a knee, now can I?" Mrs. Polkshank crossed her arms over her large breasts and huffed her displeasure at the new mistress of the house—the third in two years.

The household cook, a former tavern wench who had been engaged by Elizabeth's tuppence-pinching sister Mary, had never been the sort to hold her opinion to herself. Yet, because she'd always managed to keep the family well fed with an amusing selection of dishes, despite the family's limited budget, they'd kept her on.

Or so Elizabeth had been led to believe by her sisters.

She'd only been managing the family's funds for a sennight, perhaps, since like Mary before her, her sister Anne had also had the good fortune to marry and move to her husband's grand residence. Now, all of the household responsibilities ultimately fell to Elizabeth.

Approving the daily market list was a tedious task, just like all of the other monotonous jobs she'd inherited from her sisters, such as paying the house staff, approving daily menus, and attending to all correspondence and requests for payment.

But this week her ledger of household expenses revealed an interesting change—instead of costs going down after the departure of both of her sisters, the weekly expenditures were actually increasing. Elizabeth peered charily at

Mrs. Polkshank. "Is there anything . . . less expensive?"

"It's mutton, not a side of beef." Mrs. Polkshank's words grew louder as her frustration seemed to grow. "What would you have us eat instead, Miss Elizabeth? Pigeons from the park? Rats from the alley?" She slapped her palm to the worktable, the air she'd displaced blowing the skin from an onion she'd been peeling earlier into Elizabeth's lap. "So, will we be needin' a rat catcher then? I can help with that. Know a fine one, I do."

Elizabeth brushed the onion skin off her skirt and looked down at the ledger once more. She wasn't going to allow herself to become distracted by Mrs. Polkshank's antics. Why, she could clearly see that the household food expenses had increased—nearly doubled.

Then it occurred to her, and she narrowed her eyes. Mrs. Polkshank was taking advantage of her inexperience with handling the family's money. She glared down at the page.

She should confront her now. Mrs. Polkshank would of course deny any wrongdoing and there was no way to prove her charge without hiking off herself to the butcher and the market to verify prices. And that was not going to happen. At least not today. She had too many preparations to make before the ball this evening. The ball she now dreaded after the dream she had last night. The horrible dream.

"Why, Miss Elizabeth, you're tremblin'." The cook's expression became one of concern. "The fire is roaring now. The kitchen is toasty warm. Have you caught a chill or somethin'?"

"No, no, I am well. Mrs. Polkshank, please pay my words no heed today." Elizabeth rested her head in her hands. "I am simply overwrought. There is a ball at Almack's tonight . . . and Prince Leopold may be in attendance."

Cook nodded her head. "Oh, he'll be there. At least, that is the word from the belowstairs set all across Town."

Elizabeth whipped her head around to look up at her. "Truly?"

"That's right. Last night I . . . talked to one of his strapping young footman, myself. His attendance is the worst kept secret in all of London. I promise you, Miss Elizabeth, the prince will be there."

Her heart double thudded in her chest and warmth permeated her chilled body. "*He* will be at Almack's. And so will I." The beginnings of a smile pulled at Elizabeth's lips.

Mrs. Polkshank settled her strong, reddened hands on Elizabeth's shoulders and began to knead her muscles like coarse bread dough. "And don't you be frettin' none about what the others say about your dreams, miss. I don't think you're mad. *I* believe you. Truth to tell, I've had dreams like that myself once in a while. I think we all do, only most are just too afraid of admitting as much."

Elizabeth wrenched her neck around and stared at Cook. "How did you know about my dream?"

The plump woman chuckled deliberately. "Nobody knows more about what goes on in this house, or with my ladies, than me, Miss Elizabeth." There was movement in the doorway just then and Mrs. Polkshank glanced up as Cherie appeared in the kitchen. "Except," she tipped her head to the maid, "maybe that tight-lipped little frog right there."

Cherie stretched out her slender hand and held out a billet of sale. Elizabeth took it from her and passed her gaze over it. She turned her eyes up to Cherie. "B-But . . . I thought Madame Devy was having the gown delivered. I require it tonight. She knew this." A tingling of dread skittered across her skin.

The mute maid-of-all-work shrugged her shoulders.

"I'd offer to fetch it for you, Miss Elizabeth,

but Cherie is worthless when it comes to toting a hefty leg-of-mutton. Look at those bony arms of hers. Pitiful. And as it is, she's got her own duties today, including going all across Town to place an order for your great-aunt Prudence's special claret." Mrs. Polkshank raised her bushy eyebrows.

Before Elizabeth was able to utter her next thought, Mrs. Polkshank had crossed that option off her list as well. "MacTavish is polishing all of the silver this morn. I shouldn't think you'd want him touchin' your gown after that. No matter how well he scrubs up after, he'll smudge the silk."

No, she was not about to risk anything happening to her emerald gown. Especially not after the nightmare she had about it last night.

Elizabeth slapped her hands to the bare wooden worktable and pushed up to stand. "There is plenty of time. I shall simply go to Madame Devy's myself. Please excuse me." With a nod to the staff, she stomped out the door and up the stairs.

At this early hour she'd expected to find a short line of hackneys waiting for passengers at the corner of Berkeley Square and Bruton, but there was none. She would have to walk to

Madame Devy's. Walking would not be so bad, in fact, the activity might even shake some of the weariness from her. After all, the shop was near enough, and as long as the rain held off, she would be fine.

As she walked, she glanced up at the clusters of clouds draped low over the buildings. The sky peeking between the gray-bottomed clouds was still a cheery blue. Her steps slowed. There was likely no need to worry about a downpour this morn. She stopped and stared upward. No, she did not wish to risk losing another gown to rain. Spinning around, she raced back down the pavers and into the house to fetch her umbrella.

Elizabeth flung open the door and nearly collided with her great-aunt, who stood, straight-backed and almost vigorous, in the center of the passage. "Prudence!"

Seeing the woman walk anywhere except to her chamber was a rare occasion, to be sure, but Elizabeth had never seen her great-aunt appear so . . . able-bodied. She smiled at the old woman. "You must have had a good night's sleep. You are so spry this morn."

Great-aunt Prudence stared back at Elizabeth, who hastened to her side, then lifted the old woman's arm over her shoulder and started her toward the parlor. "Here, do allow me to help you to your chair. I can fetch a book for you. Would you like that?"

Cherie appeared at the end of the passage, dressed for heading out to Piccadilly to place the claret order. The instant she saw the old woman standing in the middle of the passage, her eyes rounded. Rushing forward, she quickly relieved Elizabeth of Great-aunt Prudence's weight.

"Why, thank you, Cherie, but I could have managed. I should not wish you to strain yourself." Elizabeth was astonished as she watched the petite maid support Great-aunt Prudence's heft until they reached the chair beside the fire.

Elizabeth stared at the little maid with the bony arms. What could Mrs. Polkshank have been thinking? Cherie was perfectly capable of carrying a leg-of-mutton! For heaven's sake, she'd just hoisted an old woman up and nearly carried her through the parlor.

Cherie and Great-aunt Prudence exchanged a quick, meaningful glance, then the tiny maid hurried past Elizabeth, only to return a moment later with an umbrella.

How did she know that this is what I returned for? Silently, Elizabeth nodded her thanks, then walked through the front door and out to the square.

Gorblimey. As efficient and kind to Great-aunt Prudence as Cherie was, there was something about the maid that completely unnerved her.

Within the hour Elizabeth had left Madame Devy's shop with her exquisite emerald-hued ball gown. It was certainly the most beautiful gown she now owned, and she was quite pleased when Madame Devy took the care to wrap the confection of fine Chinese silk in a linen cover to protect it from the elements.

Elizabeth's gaze lifted to the sky once more. The clouds were darkening and now only an ink spot of blue poked through their girth here or there.

No, do not risk it. Spend a few shillings. Find a hackney. Protect the gown. Protect the gown.

She walked to the jutting corner of Grafton and Bond Street and stood on the edge of the pavers to scout a hackney. She looked down the length of Old Bond Street and New Bond Street, but not one hackney was to be had. The only conveyance in sight at all was a fine town carriage sitting a short distance away outside of the Clarendon Hotel. She sighed.

But as she gazed at the carriage a little longer, an idea sprang into her mind. If the owner was inside, she would make an appeal for his or her assistance in seeing her to Berkeley Square before the rain swept the street with her and her lovely gown. Simple.

There was always the possibility that the owner was not inside the cab, however. Should this be the case, Elizabeth decided she would just bribe the driver to take her the short distance to Great-aunt Prudence's town house. He could be back in front of the hotel before the owner ever realized the carriage was missing. She smiled at her own cleverness. Perhaps her association with the cunning Old Rakes of Marylebone and Lady Upperton had advantages she never imagined.

As Elizabeth walked toward the carriage, she loosened the bag's ties. It was best to be prepared. Why, she might be required to show the owner her gown to convince him of her great need for sheltered transportation. After all, once anyone saw the unmatched quality and color of the silk, who could deny her assistance? No one.

With that belief firmly affixed in her mind, she scurried down New Bond Street to the carriage and made her plea to a pleasantly featured young woman who sat inside.

Elizabeth did not wait to be asked, but dropped the umbrella she held under her arm, then released the bows at the top of the linen cover and revealed to the woman the bodice of her glorious emerald gown.

"You are quite an audacious young lady, aren't you, dear?" the woman said, her gracefully curved eyebrows lifting in amusement . . . or perhaps astonishment. Elizabeth could not discern which.

"No, my lady. I am desperate," Elizabeth replied, and glanced up at the sky again just as the first droplet splashed on her cheek. She gasped and thrust the gown forward, into the cab, to shield it. But then, to her horror, the woman took her protective gesture as an invitation to touch the silk.

"It is a grand gown, and the color matches your eyes, even in this low light."

"Yes, my lady. I cannot allow it to be ruined. There is no other like it." She looked at her umbrella lying on the pavers. "You see, my umbrella is not large enough to shelter the gown sufficiently." Cool droplets of water dotted Elizabeth's back, and she leaned farther into the cab. She looked at the interior of the grand carriage and at the woman's superior clothing. "I know you, of all people, can understand. Please, won't you help me?"

The woman laughed and slid across the

leather bench, patting it with her gloved hand as an invitation for Elizabeth to enter.

She set her foot upon the step and then bent to carefully arrange the gown on the opposite bench so it would not wrinkle. When she was satisfied, Elizabeth sat down beside the woman.

The footman closed the door to the cab, but for some moments the carriage wheels did not move. "Oh good heavens, please do forgive me, I was so concerned about my gown that my manners were left on the pavers, I fear. My name is Miss Elizabeth Royle, currently of Berkeley Square—where we are headed. Thank you so much for rescuing me, my lady."

The woman smiled broadly. "Oh . . . one of the famed Royle sisters, are you?"

"Yes, my lady. I am the youngest. By several minutes, or so my father told me."

"He was the Prince of Wales's personal physician." The woman's eyes twinkled with knowledge. She rapped on the wall of the cab and the carriage started rolling down the street.

"Yes, he was." Elizabeth's curiosity was piqued. "I beg you pardon, but I must ask. How do you know so much about me?"

It was almost as if her rescuer had heard her thoughts. "Because I am Miss Margaret Mercer

Elphinstone, one of Princess Charlotte's camarilla of ladies." She grinned a bit then. "Though most would call me one of her dearest friends and confidantes. We met once, though only briefly and not formally. You were lying on your back in front of Carlton House."

"Oh my word. You were with Princess Charlotte the day her carriage almost ran me down," Elizabeth said absently. Then something occurred to her. "This . . . this is the carriage."

Miss Elphinstone laughed. "Yes, it is. And it has brought us together yet again."

"And once more, in a manner, you are saving me."

"Well, I could not allow such a lovely gown to become ruined. You told me yourself, there is not another like it." The lady gave her a playful wink.

Elizabeth sat quietly, completely in awe of Miss Mercer Elphinstone. She was clever and amusing, and regaled her with short anecdotes of the *ton* for the few minutes it took to reach Berkeley Square.

Elizabeth was so disappointed to have to leave the lady that for a moment she thought to pretend she was disoriented and did not know where her great-aunt Prudence's town house was to be found. But that consideration was just a wishful fantasy.

When at last the footman opened the door, she paused. "I very much enjoyed meeting you," she told Miss Elphinstone. "I do hope we may speak again—at the ball at Almack's tonight, perhaps?"

"While I am certain we shall meet again, Miss Royle, we are not to attend the ball this eve. In fact, I am to return to Cranbourne Lodge at once."

Elizabeth then noticed the folded sheet of foolscap the lady held in her hand—a letter emblazoned with the unmistakable seal of Prince Leopold of Saxe-Coburg. Noticing Elizabeth's focus on the letter, Miss Elphinstone whisked it from view and surreptitiously tucked it beneath her paisley mantle.

The footman handed Elizabeth down, and the lady gently lifted the dress and had just turned to hand it to her when she stilled. "Lord above! What is *she* doing here?"

"Who?" Elizabeth whirled around, not knowing what to expect, but all she saw was Great-aunt Prudence watching them from the parlor window. She chuckled. "That is only Mrs. Winks, my great-aunt Prudence."

"No, no, I am certain it is not." The woman leaned forward and stared at Prudence.

"I fear you are mistaken, for that woman is indeed my great-aunt Prudence. Would you perhaps like to make her acquaintance?"

Miss Mercer Elphinstone paused for a moment or two before shaking her head. "Another time perhaps. I must away."

The rain was coming down harder, but Elizabeth squinted through the lines of rain over her shoulder once more to be sure they were actually speaking of the same woman. But no one else was in view. She glanced around the street. Indeed, no one else was visible in all of Berkeley Square.

"Do forgive me, Miss Royle," the lady said sheepishly. "The rain blurred my view, 'tis all. I have certainly mistaken your great-aunt for another. How silly of me." Miss Mercer Elphinstone still looked rather shaken as she handed the gown down to Elizabeth, who stood on the wet pavers outside the carriage. "Hurry inside now, protect your gown." With a parting smile, she allowed the footman to close the door, and at once the carriage began to roll forward.

"Thank you for your generosity," Elizabeth called out. She bobbed a quick curtsy, then spun around and ran for the house.

Chapter 4

The Clarendon Hotel
New Bond Street

Sumner and Prince Leopold stood before an enormous floor-to-ceiling mirror, admiring the splendor of their formal dress finery. Or rather, Sumner was admiring his appearance; Leopold was scowling at him.

Sumner turned to his left and to his right while peering critically at his reflection. "No, no. I tell you, something is not right."

" 'Tis the sash," Prince Leopold sighed as he rolled his eyes. "I would wear a red sash for the event."

Sumner turned to him and extended his hand. "Well then, where is it?"

65

Leopold begrudgingly gestured to his valet, who disappeared from the dressing chamber and returned a moment later with a crimson swath of satin.

The valet glanced up at the prince, and when His Royal Highness nodded, the slender gray-haired man stepped before Sumner. He placed the middle of the sash atop his broad shoulder, then draped one-half of the length across his back and the other across his expansive chest. The valet fastened the two ends together with an ornate military brooch of sorts, but when he could not coax the sash to drape properly, he started again. After several attempts at perfection, he removed the sash and turned to Prince Leopold. "Your Royal Highness, I am afraid I must report that the red sash is too short to be worn by . . . this man."

"Too short?" Leopold looked as though he'd eaten something very sour. "Impossible. I wear the sash regularly."

"He means it is too short for *me*." Sumner lifted his brow mockingly. "I am sure it fits your form perfectly."

Leopold snarled at the comment. "The other red sash then. Fetch it." The valet bowed and silently left the chamber. "It is for state occasions more formal than a ball, but it should have the length required to cross your ridiculously muscled girth."

Sumner chuckled. "Thank you, dear cousin."

The valet returned a moment later and quickly set the sash upon Sumner. He pinned the edges together, then adjusted it across Sumner's form. When he'd finished, the valet released a sigh of pleasure. *"Perfect."*

"Not quite. Something is still not correct." Sumner looked down at the valet. "Were the prince attending the ball at Almack's, is this how you would outfit him—down to the very last detail?"

"No, Your Royal—" The valet winced. "No, my lord."

"What else then?" Sumner extended his arms to allow the valet to complete his sartorial inventory.

"I would include . . . medals. You are a large, imposing man. I would add many more of them." He slipped a nervous peripheral gaze at the prince as if gauging the royal reaction to his statement.

"Oh, damn it, man, take what you need," the prince barked. He thumped his chest. "Take these as well. Take them all. I have no doubt it will take every one to cover *that* chest." Prince Leopold straightened his back and the valet removed the panel of medals from his coat.

Leopold sat down in gilt chair covered with white silk striped with wide bands of indigo. He crossed one leg over the other. "You are certain Charlotte will not be in attendance? Nothing has changed?"

"No, nothing has changed since Miss Elphinstone departed with your reply." Sumner raised his chin as the valet lifted his collar higher.

"Damnable Prinny. He learned that I am in Town, somehow, and has forbidden Charlotte to attend the ball at Almack's this night." Prince Leopold exhaled. "Thankfully, Mercer was able to make this known to us."

"And that we were so quickly able to create a contingency plan." The valet wrapped the neck cloth around Sumner's throat, making it difficult for him to speak. "I will attend the ball in your stead, drawing the full attention of the *ton*, and whoever has taken it into his mind to see you planted."

"Just do not gallop about as you dance. Society will believe I am the one in need of a dance master."

"I do not gallop, Leopold. Horses gallop," Sumner snapped.

"Exactly." The prince cocked his left eyebrow. "I have seen you gallop across the dance floor on several occasions. Do not deny it."

Sumner growled. "Do allow me to continue with our strategy for this evening, Leopold."

Leopold waved a hand, giving Sumner leave to begin without being interrupted by barbs.

"Whilst I am certainly-not-galloping at Almack's, Charlotte attempts to rendezvous with you at the appointed spot beside the Serpentine." Sumner stilled the valet's hands for a moment, and then looked at his cousin. "Everything has been arranged. A hackney has been hired to arrive here at half past eleven."

"I travel in a common hackney, while you enjoy the splendor of a carriage?" Leopold's elegant countenance revealed no emotions, but Sumner knew his cousin too well.

"It is the only way we can ensure your safety. A simple blue coat, gray breeches, and Hessians will prevent you from drawing undue attention." Sumner shot a glance at the valet to make sure he understood his dressing instructions.

"Oh, yes, I am sure to win over Charlotte's heart wearing such finery." Leopold let out an uncharacteristically forlorn sigh.

"She wants to see you. Progress has already been made toward a union."

"Now that she has retired her interest in Prince Augustus." Leopold uncrossed his leg and leaned back in his chair. "Interesting how that bit of information found its way to the newspapers, secreted as it was."

Sumner remained impassive. "I suppose it might have helped your petition for her favor . . . somewhat. As has her uncle, the Duke of Kent."

"Is there something you are not telling me?"

"Nothing you need to concern yourself with, Leopold. Your only task is charming the princess, and I am sure you will complete this task with great ease."

When the tall case clock in the corner tinged half past ten, the prince came to his feet. "You should be off. Draw the attention of everyone around, but do watch for your own safety, and for God's sake do not embarrass me. Remember, no galloping." He clipped Sumner's chin, then snapped his fingers for the valet to follow him. "Time to don my 'ordinary man' costume."

"Costumed or not, you will never be an ordinary man, Leopold," Sumner called over his shoulder, and then turned to take one final look at himself in the mirror. He had to admit, he did look quite regal. And far more ruggedly handsome than Leopold ever had.

Before his reflection, Sumner practiced his most gallant bow. It was important to him that it be as elegant as one of Leopold's, for tonight he planned to honor the lovely Miss Royle with such a bow before their very first dance.

"Miss Elizabeth, Lady Upperton and the gents will be comin' around verra soon," Mac-Tavish, the family's Scottish butler, warned. "Should Cherie not be dressin' ye already?"

"In a moment." Elizabeth straightened the woolen coverlet draped over Great-aunt Prudence's knees. "I decided I should dress at the very last moment, so there will be no opportunity for the gown to be marred."

"That's my clever gel," the old woman replied, spreading her lips into a proud smile.

Cherie appeared in the doorway, and once she had claimed Elizabeth's attention, turned her head to peer up at the clock in the passage just as it sounded the half hour.

"I am ready, Cherie." Elizabeth rose to start for the passage.

"Time for claret," Great-aunt Prudence chirped excitedly as the bell ping faded from hearing at last.

"So it is," Elizabeth replied. "MacTavish, will

you please do my aunt the honor of filling a glass of claret for her?"

"Aye, Miss Elizabeth." Belatedly, the ancient butler decided to bow, but since his long legs were already moving across the parlor, his sincere attempt at courtesy instead appeared a clumsy trip.

Elizabeth smiled and nodded her appreciation of the gesture.

When Elizabeth entered her bedchamber a minute later, she nearly gasped at the beauty of the emerald gown Cherie had carefully laid out upon her bed. She hurried toward it when out of the corner of her eye she saw Mrs. Polkshank's champion mouser slip into the room.

Within an instant the cat leapt into the air for the bed. Elizabeth threw her body between the cat's claws and her emerald gown at once, willing to sacrifice her skin to protect it.

Four paws hit her back solidly, and claws sank into tender skin and held, as the marmalade feline frantically tried to keep from falling back onto the floor.

But like an angel, Cherie appeared at the bedside. She scooped her arms under the cat's belly to support it while she removed each individual claw from Elizabeth's stinging back.

Elizabeth could feel the threads of her walking frock pulling away as Cherie worked, but it was worth the loss of her day dress if the green silk gown would be preserved.

The instant she was free of Mrs. Polkshank's wicked cat, Elizabeth rolled from the bed. Her heart pounded inside her ribs as she hurriedly ran her hands over the gown, smoothing it as she surveyed it for any possible damage.

But there was none. None at all.

She exhaled a breath of pure relief. "Please, Cherie, take that cat to the kitchen and close the door. I cannot risk anything happening to this gown."

Cherie dropped a quick curtsy, then disappeared from the room with the cat.

Sitting down on the bench before her dressing table, Elizabeth pressed her hands to her heart and took several deep breaths. *Lord help her.*

She only had to make it to the ball. Fate would take care of the rest.

At fifteen minutes before the hour, she descended the staircase. Her long copper hair was swept up at the sides and pinned with dozens of sparkling brilliants, while the rest of her locks tumbled down her back. Somehow, against the vibrant color of the emerald gown, her hair did not appear as garishly red as it normally did. Tonight she actually felt . . . beautiful.

The emerald silk gown was like air on her body, and even when coupled with her dew-thin chemise, she felt almost as if she wore nothing at all. The thought brought a flush of color into her cheeks as she entered the parlor, where Lady Upperton, Great-aunt Prudence, and the Old Rakes of Marylebone waited for her.

There was a communal intake of breath as the group beheld her for the first time in her gown. A jolt of pure happiness whisked through her, because their reaction gave her hope that the prince would exhibit a similar response when she entered the ballroom at Almack's an hour hence.

A barely stifled sob slipped from Great-aunt Prudence's mouth. "So, so beautiful," she whispered, as a tear rolled down her cheek. She raised her wrinkled hands to Elizabeth, beckoning her to her chair.

Elizabeth lifted the short train of her ball gown over her wrist and rushed to her great-aunt's side. "Dear Prudence, do not cry. Tonight promises to be one of the happiest occasions of my life. I am certain of this. I only wish you could be with me to share it and make my happiness complete." She leaned close and Great-aunt Prudence kissed her cheek.

"The claret!" Lady Upperton squealed. "Mrs. Winks, your claret!"

Elizabeth looked down and saw to her horror that Great-aunt Prudence had dropped her crystal of claret on the floor.

Oh, lud, not the gown! She lurched backward, arms spread wide. She could not seem to catch her breath.

"Missed." Great-aunt Prudence was smiling. "It missed."

Elizabeth looked down and saw that the wine had indeed splattered on the carpet and the momentum had sent a flourished spray of red wine along the left leg of the mantel.

But somehow, by the saints, Great-aunt Prudence was correct. Not a single drop had touched her emerald gown.

Elizabeth released her pent breath, and then smiled at Prudence. Her great-aunt laughed with delight, a deep throaty laugh that in a moment had everyone in the parlor holding their sides as they laughed along with her.

Lord Lotharian took Elizabeth's hand and placed it on his arm. "I have never beheld a more beautiful woman in all my years, Miss Elizabeth."

Elizabeth's cheeks filled with warmth. "Tonight I will take you at your word, my lord." She tipped her head and looked up at him through her thick lashes. "Though I have my suspicions that you have shared the very same sentiment with half the ladies in London."

"Touché, my dear." Lotharian grinned. "But I do not exaggerate. I swear to you, no one will be able to overlook your beauty this night."

"I agree," echoed Lilywhite. "Perhaps a certain young man might swell with emotion at the sight of our girl and make an offer this very night."

Elizabeth flushed. "I only hope the prince remembers me."

"Oh, I was not referring to the prince, Elizabeth," Lilywhite said, "I meant—"

"Let us not delay any longer," Lotharian interjected, cutting off Lilywhite's next words. "The carriages await. Shall we?" He raised a large hand and gestured toward the passage. Everyone in the party bade Great-aunt Prudence good night and one by one they headed for the front door.

They had all reached the passage when Elizabeth noticed that Lord Gallantine was not among them. She turned and peered back into the parlor.

Cherie brushed past her as she hurried into the parlor, knelt beside the burst of wetness on the carpet and began to dab at the stain.

There, the overtall viscount with the auburn wig stood fixed in his spot. His gaunt face twisted into an expression of horror as he stared at the stain on the carpet and the bloodlike trails of red dripping down the mantelpiece. "We cannot leave with claret on the floor. It won't do. It won't!" he sputtered.

"Missed," Aunt Prudence repeated to Lord Gallantine, and then again to Cherie. "It missed."

Cherie looked up at the old woman, then nodded her head and smiled.

"Lord Gallantine, Cherie will see to the spill," Elizabeth said. "She is very skilled, and when we return, I am sure there will be no sign of the claret having ever been on the carpet or on the mantel." She raised a hand and gestured to him. "Come now, we do not wish to arrive late. The doors will be closed promptly at eleven." She rose up on her toes and whispered in his ear. "And I do believe you promised to introduce me to someone *special*."

"What?" Lord Gallantine lifted the edge of his wig with his little finger and scratched his bald pate. "Oh, yes. I did indeed." Now that he was distracted from the wet mess, his mood seemed almost buoyant. "And wait until you meet him. You and he are meant for each other. In fact, though I know it is a mite early to predict, I think a Michaelmas wedding may be in order."

From the corner of her vision, Elizabeth thought she saw Great-aunt Prudence narrow her eyes at Gallantine at the very moment he mentioned a wedding.

She turned her gaze back upon Gallantine. "Well, my lord, if we tarry much longer I shall not have the opportunity to meet anyone this night." She took his arm and tugged him along with her to the passage. "Come, let us away."

The ladies collected their wraps, fans, and reticules from the entryway table, and the cadre was about to depart the house when Mrs. Polkshank called out. "Miss Elizabeth! Might I have a moment before you leave, if you please?"

Elizabeth turned her head and glanced over her shoulder at Cook, feeling very confused "Certainly."

"Hold still just a tick, miss. There is a dark spot on your gown." Mrs. Polkshank rushed forward. "Oh, I would not intrude on your party, but I know how important this gown is to you. Everything must be perfect."

Elizabeth froze, not daring to move. "Are you sure there is a spot? I saw nothing."

"I do not see anything marring the gown at all. Elizabeth looks perfect to me." Lady Upperton lifted a quizzing glass from her reticule and peered through it. "What are you going on about, Cook?"

Mrs. Polkshank pulled a rag from the waistband of her apron and touched it to her tongue, then dabbed a tiny area on Elizabeth's back just below her shoulder blade. "Looks like a speck of blood. Got it, though. The trick to getting a bloodstain out is never letting the blood dry."

Elizabeth gasped and spun around to look in the mirror. The cat had scratched her back. Had she bled onto the gown? She squinted her eyes, but like Mrs. Polkshank had said, there was no indication of blood on the gown.

Elizabeth's stomach tightened then and she thought she might become ill. For though there was no blood on the gown, there was now a saliva stain the size and shape of a guinea.

"'Ere now, just keep your wrap over your shoulders until you arrive. It'll all be dry by then, and no one will be the wiser." Mrs. Polkshank eased Elizabeth's shawl around her. "Good luck, Miss Elizabeth." She winked.

"Though you won't need it, will you? I believe in your dream. Tonight your prince will come."

Lady Upperton turned Elizabeth around and marched her through the door and into a carriage waiting before the house on Berkeley Square.

Everything was supposed to be perfect. But suddenly it wasn't.

Something wasn't right.

Elizabeth could feel a sense of foreboding vibrating through her body, like a plucked too-tight violin string the moment before it breaks . . . and the music dies.

Chapter 5

Almack's Assembly Rooms

For an exclusive gathering, Elizabeth was quite astounded by the sheer magnitude of the number of guests present. Truth to tell, within thirty minutes she was utterly convinced that every citizen of even the slightest social prominence was present in Almack's this night.

Everyone, that is, except the one person she longed to behold: her prince.

She snatched a glass of carrack punch from the passing silver salver of a footman who seemed wholly focused on finding a trail along the perimeter of the overcrowded assembly room. The shifting pathway practically assured eventual collision with a guest, most of whom were too preoccupied with seeing and being seen to notice a dozen glasses of sloshing liquid headed directly for them.

Glancing anxiously down at her precious gown, she recalled the moment of horror in her dream—when a stream of red trickled over her bodice—and a bone-chilling sense of doom fell over her like a death shroud. Shuddering, Elizabeth turned away from the footman, not wishing to view the inevitable sartorial disaster.

"There you are, my dear." Lord Gallantine clamped his hand around Elizabeth's wrist, making her glass of punch tilt precariously in her gloved fingers. Her hand began to twitch nervously as she tightened her grip to force the crystal level again. "These are the gentlemen I was so desirous that you meet," Gallantine told her, gesturing before him.

She looked up from her glass and manufactured a pleasant smile as he commenced introductions to Sir Henry Halford and his young protégé, the Honorable William Manton. She dropped a careful curtsy to the gentlemen, though could not help but peer around them hopefully for a glimpse of her prince beyond.

"Sir Henry was an esteemed colleague of

your father's, dear," Lord Gallantine told her. "Years ago, of course. Today, Sir Henry is physician in ordinary to the king."

Sir Henry Halford was a distinguished-looking baronet, but Elizabeth did not care for the manner in which he seemed to study her with those dangerously intelligent eyes. Nor for the pleased flick of his heavy dark eyebrows, which stood out in marked contrast to his pale skin and smattering of gray hair, as his gaze fixed on a particular part of her that seemed to catch his interest most.

By contrast, the Honorable William Manton was entirely well-mannered. He was broad shouldered with fair hair and vivid blue eyes, bringing the image of a Viking of days of old to her mind.

"Miss Royle, your father was an eminent physician, with excellent perception and sound judgment," the baronet told her. One dark eyebrow lifted, and Elizabeth somehow knew that Sir Henry was about to request something of her. "I will be in Bath for several days, but when I return I am hosting a dinner for a number of my colleagues from the Royal College of Physicians. I wonder if you, Miss Royle, and Lord Gallantine, of course, might condescend to join us. I would consider it an honor to hear about

Dr. Royle's mysterious years in Cornwall. Does Thursday two weeks from now suit?"

Elizabeth did not wish to be anywhere near the smarmy Sir Henry, even after knowing him for a mere two minutes. But how could she refuse him? "Thursday?" she stammered, sifting furiously through her mind for any excuse to beg off of the dinner.

Mr. Manton stepped closer and leaned his head lower so she might better hear his words. "I know I should greet the chance to become better acquainted with Dr. Royle's lovely daughter with even *more* anticipation than Sir Henry." He met Elizabeth's gaze and held it firm until, flustered and somewhat flattered by his attention, she surrendered her agreement to attend the dinner.

"Very well, Thursday two weeks hence." Elizabeth looked to Lord Gallantine. "*We* graciously accept the invitation, do we not?"

Lord Gallantine smiled at her, obviously quite pleased, and nodded. "Curzon Street, is it, Sir Henry?"

"Indeed it is, at ten of the clock. Do be prompt, for I have a unique surprise to show you both." Sir Henry swept Elizabeth one final time with his oily gaze, making her desire nothing more than to hurry off to the ladies' withdrawing room to wash the film of his disconcerting attention from her skin. "I look forward to seeing you both again, then."

Elizabeth's skin was positively crawling. She turned her gaze around the room. "I had heard rumor that Prince Leopold would be in attendance tonight. Is it true? Is he present?" she asked Lord Gallantine.

Sir Henry interrupted. "I had heard the rumor as well, but I believe that it is all it is. The word at court, always a better source for the truth of a matter, is that the prince is secretly in London to woo Princess Charlotte—and she is in Windsor. Were I the prince, I would not venture to Almack's if the princess was out of the Town, even if I were the unnamed guest of honor."

Elizabeth suppressed a scowl. *He will come. He will. It is fate.*

She had just pinned her gaze on a lady and gentleman, completely unknown to her, deciding she would pretend they were friends, when the young medical protégé of Sir Henry disposed of her glass of punch, then offered her his arm.

"Miss Royle," William said softly to her, "might I have this dance?" To offer his arm before she replied was a mite presumptuous, to Elizabeth's way of thinking, but she was genuinely thankful, for at last she had a proper means of escaping Sir Henry.

She lifted the edges of her lips and took Manton's arm, offering a demure gaze to Lord Gallantine and Sir Henry. "Please excuse us, gentlemen. The dance floor calls." She giggled like a miss, to give Gallantine the impression that the Old Rakes' matchmaking scheme was working, then allowed herself to be led to the dance floor.

They took their places at the lower corner of the square and waited for the French quadrille to commence. The selection of this particular dance as her escape from Sir Henry was most unfortunate. The dance had only just been introduced to Almack's by Lady Jersey, which meant Elizabeth had to focus her attention entirely on each step so as not to accidentally back into another during the *chaise anglaise*. And so, for several wretched minutes, she found herself unable to survey the assembly room for her prince.

She was not entirely sure if it was the unnatural degree of concentration the dance required or the great number of guests in the assembly room, but by time the French quadrille concluded, she felt her cheeks glowing and damp with perspiration.

"Thank you, Mr. Manton, for the dance. I greatly enjoyed it," Elizabeth said, and curtsied politely, "but I see my sponsor, Lady Upperton, near the door, and I require a brief interview with her before I lose sight of her again."

Mr. Manton, his fine features looking uncharacteristically perturbed, bowed gracefully before her. "I do hope we may dance again before the event adjourns, Miss Royle."

"As do I, dear sir." With a quick nod and a fleeting smile, Elizabeth spun around and made her way from the dance floor and through the crowded assembly room in the direction of Lady Upperton, who was now speaking with Lord Gallantine and Lilywhite.

She glanced back at Mr. Manton to ensure he had rejoined Sir Henry and not decided upon pursuit of her. When she looked before her, another footman, holding a grand tray of goblets filled with wine punch, was only two strides away and headed straight for her. *Blast!* She'd had naught but ill luck this evening and was not about to chance being doused with wine. She would not tempt fate in summoning her own doom. Or her gown's, either.

Sucking in a great mouthful of air, she carefully pinched the emerald silk skirt and lifted her hem from the floor. Spinning around to the left, she charged into the clustering throng, but the footman skillfully turned into her wake and remained behind her.

Gorblimey! Did she have an archery target pinned to her back?

Suddenly, she slammed into someone. Cool trickles of what smelled like wine ran between her breasts and down her gown.

She gasped and looked low, fearful of what she would certainly see. A burst of wetness saturated the elegant bodice, changing it from brilliant emerald to the darkest of forest greens. The backs of her eyes began to sting.

No, not my gown. My beautiful gown.

But oddly, though she felt greatly saddened that her gown was ruined, the overwhelming feelings of fear and dread she had felt so strongly in her dream were absent. How could this be?

"I do beg your forgiveness," came a deep, resonant voice. Elizabeth lifted her head and through her tear-blurred eyes perceived what, at first, she took to be a dark blue wall. She took a step backward as she renewed her breath in preparation to chide some idiotic man for ruining her gown.

Until she noticed the medals.

Oh, God. And the red sash.

"Miss Royle! I—I did not realize—" came the voice again.

Slowly, she turned to look upward, and forced down the huge stone that seemed to have risen in her throat. "Y-Your Royal Highness."

There was a hand suddenly pressing down upon her shoulder. She glanced sidelong to see that Lord Lotharian was now standing slightly behind her. "Curtsy, Elizabeth," he whispered in an overloud tone so she might hear him over the din of the crowd.

And so she did, wishing with all her heart that she could leave her gaze puddled on the floor so she would not have to look up again and allow Prince Leopold to see her cheeks, which were certainly glowing like red hot embers.

Damn it all. Sumner had intended to seek out Miss Royle this evening, to dance with her, to begin his courtship of her. But not like this. Not by emptying his champagne down between her—he could not help but look down at her—full, white breasts.

He wrenched his improper gaze from her décolletage to her vibrant eyes, which appeared as green as her emerald gown—before he had ruined it.

"I beg your pardon, Miss Royle, I—I did not

see your approach." Sumner bent, took her slender arm and released her from her too long, too gracious curtsy.

When she faced him, he saw that her eyes were filled with tears and her cheeks flushed with embarrassed color. Damn him twice over. Out of the hundreds of others in the assembly room, he had somehow drenched and humiliated the only woman who had filled his every thought since their first meeting a day ago.

She was more beautiful than any woman he had ever beheld, even wearing a champagne-splattered gown. Even with her eyes reddened from her tears.

She was perfect in every way. *For him.*

From what he had been able to learn about her during the short time since they met, Miss Royle had not been born a society miss. But if the *ton*'s chatter was to be believed, she was like him. Of the bluest of blood, but not of the name.

He realized then that he was staring down at her like an ill-mannered oaf. "Miss Royle, if you will permit me, I should like to contact your modiste to fashion another gown for you."

Miss Royle smiled and then forced a small laugh. "My gown matters not, Your Royal Highness." She tilted her head then, and he saw that the tears seemed to have already drained from her eyes.

Though he could not comprehend how, it seemed, she had decided to forgive his clumsy offense. She leaned close to him and he felt her breath on his cheek.

A hint of a grin touched her full, pink lips. "Though I had thought," she whispered, "when we last met, that you said you were . . . *Lord Whitevale*."

A surge of alarm shot through Sumner momentarily. *Bloody hell*. When they had met, he was not yet posing as Leopold! Instinctively, he glanced about to be sure that no one was close enough to have heard her identify him. But it seemed no one had. He exhaled in relief. Miss Royle's statement posed no risk to Leopold's security. Still, he knew he had to ensure her silence. And so, he put his mouth to her ear.

Despite the champagne with which he had showered her, she smelled like orange blossoms in the spring. He drew in the scent of her, closing his eyes for a blink of time, before replying. "I was incognito at the jeweler's shop. May I trust you not to reveal my alter ego?"

He grinned playfully as he straightened his back and looked down at her. Her eyes were no

longer glistening at all and her cheeks had
calmed to reveal their true rose-colored hue, the
way he remembered them when he'd placed a
tiara upon her head in Hamilton and Company.

"Incognito?" Her reply was held to a whisper. "Oh, now I understand. It all makes sense."
Then her lips twitched and her shoulders began to shake with amusement. Quickly, she
clamped her gloved hand over her mouth.
When she lowered it some seconds later, her
lovely countenance was impassive. "Of course,
Your Royal Highness. You may trust in my
complete discretion."

It was then that he belatedly became aware of
the tall, elderly gentleman standing a pace behind her. "Forgive my tardiness in addressing
you. I do not believe I have had the honor, sir."

Miss Royle broke in. "Your Royal Highness,
allow me the honor of making known to you
Earl Lotharian. He is one of my guardians."

Lord Lotharian bent into a gallant bow, which
took several seconds of grunts and gasps to
disengage. "Your Royal Highness."

"I am honored to meet you, Lord Lotharian."
Sumner swallowed hard. The man, though late
in years and certainly no physical threat, was
looking at him quite menacingly.

The old man did not return the pleasantry,

but took a step closer and another, until the space between felt too confined. "Rumor has it that you are in London to request the hand of Princess Charlotte," the old man brashly stated. "True?"

"Lord Lotharian!" Miss Royle gasped. For an instant Sumner thought he detected something more in Miss Royle's shocked response to her guardian's words. Anger, was it? Certainly not embarrassment, which was what he might have expected her reaction to be.

Lord Lotharian did not abandon his stubborn gaze. It remained fixed on Sumner as he awaited a reply.

And so, he decided to tell the truth. "This night my only thought was to beseech Miss Royle for a dance. Nothing more." Lord Lotharian was tall, nearly as large as himself, and so when Sumner addressed the gray-haired gentleman, he looked him directly in the eye.

Lord Lotharian did not say a word, but for some moments Sumner had the distinct impression that he was studying him. But a time came when he could no longer endure the earl's earnestness. He turned back to Miss Royle, who now appeared somewhat shaken at the intense exchange of attention between him and Lord Lotharian.

Sumner smiled agreeably, hoping to calm her. "I would have wished to request a dance . . ." He glanced down at her bodice, then returned his gaze to her stunningly beautiful green eyes. ". . . but since I have soaked your gown, Miss Royle, I wonder if you would do me the honor of leaving Almack's for a short while for a stroll in the night air. Your gown will dry and the relative quiet of the street at night is far more conducive to conversation than this crowd of merrymakers." He looked to Lord Lotharian momentarily. "That is, if you will permit it, my lord." His gaze fell upon Miss Royle again.

She was blinking up at him as if she could not quite believe what he was asking of her. She turned, appearing wrapped in her nerves, looked to Lord Lotharian and waited silently for him to give her permission to leave the ball for a short while.

The old man glanced once more at Sumner, and then at Miss Royle. "Very well, my dear. But do not tarry overlong. Lady Upperton will wish to speak with you."

"Thank you, my lord." Miss Royle excitedly bounced on her toes for an instant, but quickly renewed her ladylike composure.

Sumner lifted his arm to her, and as she took

it, a great smile brightened her face. Together, as they strolled arm in arm through the crowd, she seemed no longer aware of the wine blooming across her bodice. Instead, she appeared extraordinarily happy. And this pleased Sumner immensely. Somehow, he had been redeemed.

They had just descended the stairs and a liveried footman had opened the doors for them to depart the assembly rooms when it occurred to Elizabeth to look over her shoulder. "There are no guards?"

The prince shook his head. "No need this evening. Besides, I am a trained soldier. I know precisely what to do in the event of an attack. So I warn you, do not try *anything*. I have been schooled in the defensive arts."

She laughed and, quite unexpectedly, he felt her tighten her hold around his biceps. "I do not doubt that you have been," she said, looking up through her lush lashes at him.

"Thankfully, unless you are secretly planning an attack, I do not believe there will be any need to call my military training into use this fine evening." He felt the softness of her breast pressing against his arm, and even in the relative coolness of the evening became aware of the heat growing below.

She cocked her head and glanced up at him as they walked. "Why did you introduce yourself as Lord Whitevale when we first met?"

"I told you I was incognito." He turned his head and smiled back at her, before looking ahead again. "I did not wish to draw unwanted attention."

"Of course not," she conceded. "As I told you, you can rest your faith in me."

His legs were long, and for the first time in her life she had to double step to keep up during a stroll. After a few minutes of this trotting, they turned onto the familiar grand stretch of Pall Mall. A stitch of exertion pained Elizabeth's left side, and to her embarrassment she was compelled to stop walking until it passed.

"I apologize," he told her. "I have been in the primary company of soldiers for so long that I—"

Elizabeth waved off his comment. "No need to apologize. Truly." It was then that she noted the long row of carriages lining Pall Mall. Only three back was a carriage emblazoned with the Upperton coat of arms. *Oh, thank heaven.* "Would you like . . . to rest for a moment or two? My sponsor's carriage is just there." She looked up without bothering to conceal the pleading in her eyes. She could not race along the street just now.

He chuckled at that. "Very well. It will allow you some time to catch the wind in your sails again. But I warn you again, no attacks." With utmost grace, almost as though it were a dance step, he drew her close and turned her in the direction of the carriage.

He did not free her immediately. Instead, they stood clinging together. She did not wish for him to release her and so she held onto him and looked up into his eyes.

She felt the heaviness of his breathing as his lungs expanded and contracted, pressing his hard, muscled chest against her. Her breathing quickened, too. She lowered her gaze to his mouth, and without thinking of it, ran the tip of her tongue over her lips. It was too late when she realized how obvious her romantic wishes had become to him.

His expression suddenly became very serious. She heard his breath hitch a scant second before he cupped his hand behind her head and drew her mouth to his.

His warm lips tasted of champagne as they moved gently over hers. Her arms lifted up and, of their own volition, slid up under his arms to his back and pulled him tighter into her embrace.

His mouth teased her, his tongue, hot and

slick, prodded her lips apart and then slid inside, where it mingled in an ancient dance with her own.

As he groaned with pleasure, a sound of longing welled up from deep within him. She felt that flutter in her middle . . . but this time lower as well.

Just then there was the sound of gunfire, followed by a hiss beside her head. Abruptly, her back slammed down upon the pavers. The prince's heavy form fell atop of her.

He's been shot. Her head was pounding as she struggled to wriggle out from beneath him. *Oh my God. Oh my God. He can't be dead, he can't.* She slapped her hand to the cool pavers and tried to push up, but his weight made it impossible for her to move.

Another shot rang out, puncturing the carriage beside them. She whimpered with fear.

"Don't move. Stay where you are, Miss Royle. I will protect you." His breath was hot in her ear.

"Are you hurt?" she whispered.

"No. Remain still." He rose up from her, then bent into a crouch. Warily, he surveyed the street, then came to his feet.

Elizabeth remained on her back, as he had ordered, until she saw movement in an upper window of a shop twenty paces down Pall Mall.

"In the window! He's there!" She rolled to her feet and flung open Lady Upperton's carriage door.

She caught the prince's wrist and yanked, miraculously knocking him from his footing and into the open cab. She pushed him down onto the floor of the cab just as a third shot rent the still night air. This time her prince didn't move.

The thud of footfalls on the pavers drew Elizabeth's attention, and when she glanced up, she saw a dark figure running toward her. Her heart was pounding in time with the throbbing in her head. *Oh, God!*

Without delay, she heaved the prince farther inside, and was at work bending his long legs to force them into the cab when Lady Upperton's longtime driver, Edmund, raced up to the carriage and appeared next to her. "Oh, thank goodness it is you," she gasped.

"Bloody hell, Miss Elizabeth! What is happening?"

"Don't just stand there gawking. He's been shot. Please help me!" she pleaded. "We must away. Now!"

Edmund climbed into the cab and pulled the

prince completely inside, positioning him on the forward bench. He reached out a hand and pulled Elizabeth inside. "He's bleeding fierce, miss."

"I know. I know." Her nerves were screaming, her mind a complete jumble. "Can you take us from here, at once? I know it is dangerous to help us now, Edmund, but I need you to climb atop the carriage and take us from here. Someone is trying to kill the prince."

"Aye, miss. I am your servant." Edmund gave a parting look at the prince, then scrambled from the cab and latched the door behind him. "Where to?" he called back.

"Hyde Park. The Serpentine," came the prince's low voice. "Hurry."

"Hyde Park, Edmund. At once!" Elizabeth knelt down on the floor beside the prince as the carriage lurched forward and departed the carriage queue.

He opened his eyes as she smoothed back his hair from his face, then peeled open his coat and then his lawn shirt. She slid her right hand under him and felt a round hole in the back of his coat. She exhaled.

The prince winced as she slipped her finger around the opening of the hole, and then he tried to sit up.

"Do not attempt to rise," she said as she tore a swath of silk from her skirt and balled it up. "You've been hit just below the shoulder. It seems to have gone through cleanly, but you are bleeding quite a lot."

Through his pain, he managed a weak smile. "How do you come by your medical expertise, Miss Royle?" He bit into his lower lip as the carriage tilted, rounding a corner.

She forced a practiced nurse's smile at her patient and began to chatter as calm gave way to great concern. "Did I tell you that my father was a physician? My sisters and I all worked by his side as we were growing up. I tell you this because I can help you. You will be feeling much better very soon." She peered into his half-open eyes. "Only what I must do now will hurt. Please, remain as still as you can. I am going to bandage you to slow the bleeding."

She ripped a second piece from her skirt and positioned one of the silk pads she'd fashioned atop the entry wound and the other atop the place on his back where it exited. She removed the dark blue ribbon that encircled her ribs and tied it around both pads. It barely reached.

The prince blinked up at her and sighed. "I apologize for marring your gown—for a second time." He tried to laugh, she knew, but his effort sounded like a groan the moment it left his mouth. "I've bled all over your gown. This time I fear a little air will not suffice as a remedy."

Elizabeth looked down and saw a rivulet of blood trickling down her bodice. She touched the wetness and traced it upward along her neck, to her ear, and to a place throbbing just above her temple. Warily, she settled her finger atop it. Pain seared through her skull, making her dizzy and nauseous. The blood on her gown was not his. It was her own.

"I fear . . . this time," she muttered, "you were not at fault."

"Dear God." His eyes went wide with concern. "You've been shot?"

"It is nothing," she replied, not wishing for him to worry since his injury was far more severe. "It is only a scratch. Minor cuts to the head are notorious for bleeding." But then she felt it—overwhelming fear. Doom.

Her nightmare had come true.

Chapter 6

Elizabeth heard the driver's leather whip crack in the night air as he urged his team onward, faster. It took only a clutch of minutes to reach the gates of Hyde Park, and by then the prince had managed to sit propped upright on the bench.

His strength and fortitude, after being literally shot through, astounded Elizabeth. Why, she almost believed he had commanded by sheer will the color to begin to return to his lips and cheeks.

He hadn't been so successful, however, in concealing his emotions after the attack. The prince's brow was drawn down in concern and he was biting into his lower lip; in pain or anxiousness, she did not know. He was peering fretfully out of the window as the carriage sped toward the Serpentine.

"We have escaped." Elizabeth winced as the first word jettisoned from her mouth. Even the slightest movement of her jaw sent a stab of pain through her head. "You needn't worry any longer."

He slowly turned to look back at her, then without a word silently returned to his vigil at the window. When finally he spoke a moment later, it surprised her. "How much longer before we reach the Serpentine—where it meets the Long Water?" His words were clipped, and he inhaled a deep, bracing breath after he finished his question.

"Only a few minutes more, I should think." She reached across and gently laid her hand on his knee. "Why must we hasten to the Serpentine, Your Royal Highness? You need to be examined by a doctor."

Again he turned from the window to look at her. Even in the wide ribbon of moonlight shining into the cab's interior, she could see her question alarmed him in some way. He paused for some moments, as if to gather strength, before replying. "I worry for the safety of my cousin. He is here."

"Your cousin? But why would your cousin be in any danger? The bullets were clearly intended for you. I saw the shooter in the window. His gun was trained on you."

The prince's gaze became darkly somber. "You saw the gunman?"

Elizabeth nodded. "I did." The notion struck her coldly. She did see him, not that she could attribute any detail to his appearance due to the darkness. But if she saw him, that meant the gunman likely saw her as well—especially if he had been following them. "Your Royal Highness, how did he know you would be walking along Pall Mall?"

The prince shook his head slowly. "I do not know. Until I spilled the champagne on your gown, my only thought was to spend the evening at Almack's and possibly to dance—with you."

At his encouraging words, a little thrill jolted through Elizabeth.

He wished to dance with her. He had intended to seek her out at the ball. He'd admitted it.

She leaned back out of the glowing reach of the moonlight so he would not observe the smile spreading across her lips, despite the pain in her head.

"Which means," he managed to say, "we were followed."

"Followed?" Elizabeth crinkled her brow. "But he was in a first floor window above a shop."

"I think it likely that he trailed us from Almack's, and possibly decided he needed height to affect a proper shot." He sucked in a deep breath before continuing. "So, he either found an open door, or broke into a darkened shop and made his way to a first floor window facing Pall Mall." The prince fell silent. His breath came in pants and gasps now.

"Either way, he was probably at the ball this evening. Which means, perhaps . . . he was of the *ton*." As Elizabeth looked to the prince for any reaction to this revelation, one of the carriage wheels bumped through a hole in the moist earth of Rotten Row, causing her to grimace.

Instinctively she raised a hand to her aching head. She no longer felt a stream emanating from the area just beyond her temple. Now there was only a slow, steady drip falling from the edge of her jaw and splashing onto her bodice from time to time. But that was a favorable development. The blood was clotting now.

Hopefully, the prince's much more severe wound was doing the same.

A few short minutes later the carriage rolled to a halt. The conveyance bounced, earning pained groans from both occupants, as Edmund leapt from the vehicle and opened the door. "We're here, Miss Elizabeth." He handed her down and then crawled inside the cab to assist the prince to his feet.

As the prince stepped down and gained his footing on the damp earth of Rotten Row, he straightened to his full height. Just then Elizabeth caught sight of two men racing forward from the bridge over the Serpentine. The prince grabbed her and pulled her against him, wrapping his strong arm around to protect her.

The moonlight caught the gleam of swords at their sides, and as they neared, Elizabeth saw that each man brandished a pistol. "They're armed," she gasped, and threw her slight weight against the prince, urgently hoping to shove him inside the carriage once more. But he did not move.

He tightened his hold on her, then raised his right arm and called out to the men. "No need for panic. It is I." The men appeared to recognize the prince and slowed to a jog before ultimately stopping altogether. When they did, they each bowed deeply before him.

Then a gentleman in a dark frock coat, and what Elizabeth took to be a cloaked woman, emerged from the shadows and started toward them.

"What is it, cousin?" the man called out. "Should I be alarmed?"

The prince peered across the sparkling dark waters of the Serpentine, not deigning to speak until the gentleman and his lady were standing directly before him. Only then did he release his hold on Elizabeth to clasp his cousin's arm for support. He held his voice low, and his tone was deathly serious. "There *is* need for alarm. We must return at once."

So, this was the prince's cousin, Elizabeth thought as she studied the smaller man. Yes, quite so. Even in the darkness she could see the familial resemblance between the two. But the woman. Who was she?

Elizabeth bent at her knees and tried in vain to discern the woman's identity. Her face was partially obscured by the hood of her cloak. What she could see of her countenance was awash in a blue blur of moonlight, the definition of her features all but lost.

The woman was looking at her as well, and judging by the way she suddenly stiffened, Elizabeth was almost sure she recognized her.

"You are injured," the cousin exclaimed, gesturing to the prince's open coat and the dark black bloodstain gleaming in the moonlight on his crisp white shirt.

"So is she," the woman added, nodding to Elizabeth. She reached out and lifted the blood-damped lock of Elizabeth's hair to trace the origin of the bleeding. "We must take them both to a physician." She looked at the prince and then at his cousin, waiting for agreement.

"We'll be well," the prince replied. "It is more important that we return to the hotel."

"You are not well, and you will both see a physician," the woman practically commanded.

Elizabeth tried again to see her face. Judging from her imperative tone, she was a lady of some prominence, used to having her own way, her orders followed.

"My own surgeon lives nearby, and he can be trusted. He tends to all of my family. Even my father trusts him, and he trusts no one." The woman looked at the two armed men nearby and raised her arm. One of the men whistled, and from behind a blind of twiggy maples rolled a gleaming, black carriage.

Elizabeth looked at Edmund and was about to direct him when the mysterious woman spoke again.

"You may dismiss your driver. My carriage

will serve us all," she said haughtily. "Do it now."

Elizabeth scurried over to Edmund. "Thank you, dear man. You should return for Lady Upperton now. We have alternative transportation."

He tipped his head, and Elizabeth turned on her heel to return to the others when a thought entered her mind. She whirled back around. "Do wipe down the benches—and please, please, do not mention anything to Lady Upperton. I will speak with her on the morrow and explain everything."

"Yes, miss." Edmund climbed atop the carriage, cracked his whip in the air, and the horses turned a half circle and retreated down Rotten Row in the direction they had come.

Had she known that the woman intended to bring them to Curzon Street, bleeding from her head or not, she would have walked back to Berkeley Square.

But had she known, too, that she was being brought to the residence of Sir Henry Halford, physician ordinary to the king—and by some set of extraordinary circumstances to this woman as well—she would have leapt from the carriage as it raced through London's streets.

Elizabeth was now sitting before a low coal fire, and the handsome protégé of Sir Henry, Mr. Manton, was dabbing a salve on the wound near her temple.

His touch was gentle, and the way he occasionally turned to look into her eyes to be sure he was not causing her pain was rather . . . well, endearing.

"Fate was with you, Miss Royle," he told her. "The bullet only grazed your head. You might have been killed."

Elizabeth smiled. "Fate is always on my side, dear sir."

He looked puzzled by her reply, she could see, but he did not quiz her about it further.

"Did you see the maniac who fired upon you?" He leaned back from his tending and waited for her reply.

"No . . . I mean, *yes*. I did see him."

His blue eyes rounded. "Then we must summon an investigator—at once."

"I daresay, I do not think the prince would agree with you," Elizabeth replied softly. "And while I did see the man, I could not tell you a single thing about him. It was far too dark and he was too far away. I saw little more than a silhouette of a man with the pistol in his hand."

The woman descended the stairs and headed directly for the front door so quickly that Elizabeth barely registered that it was she passing by.

Pushing herself up from the chair in which she was seated, she edged her away around Mr. Manton to reach the woman. "Will he recover? Do you know?" she called out desperately before the woman could leave.

The woman pulled her cloak up over her head and drew it low over her eyes before slowly turning around. Only her nose and lips were visible to Elizabeth. "Yes. The ball went through cleanly."

Elizabeth's muscles relaxed at the news. "May I see him? Do you know, will Sir Henry allow it?" she asked, trying not to convey her desperation.

The woman ignored her comment entirely, though upon hearing the footman open the door for her, she added a departing comment. "A hackney will be waiting on the street for you once Mr. Manton has finished tending your wound, Miss Royle. The prince requests this, not I. He said he shouldn't wish for your family to worry. You should feel honored that he is showing you such consideration."

"I do. And I thank you for informing me as to the prince's condition," Elizabeth managed, but before she could ask to know who she was, the woman disappeared through the doorway.

"Thank heavens she knew to bring you both here," Mr. Manton said from somewhere behind her.

Elizabeth spun around. A wave of dizziness assailed her and she staggered, catching herself against the ornately carved doorjamb.

"I will accompany you to your home, Miss Royle." Mr. Manton rushed to lend her his arm for support. "The prince is well. There is no need for concern. You stopped the bleeding early. You might have even saved his life."

Elizabeth breathed a sigh of relief. "Thank you for tending to me, dear sir, but . . ." She looked at Mr. Manton with all earnestness. ". . . might I ask . . . just who was that woman?"

"You really do not know?" Sir Henry's deep, almost mocking voice emerged from the darkness of the staircase.

Startled, Elizabeth grasped the doorjamb and turned to see him. "I do not, Sir Henry. Please, won't you tell me?"

"I shall, indeed." The baronet laughed quietly, then gestured to himself proudly. "After all, *I* know her well. I have tended to her and members of her family for several years." He paused for what seemed to be the simple purpose of making Elizabeth anticipate his disclosure of the woman's identity even more. "That, my dear, was none other than Princess Charlotte."

"The princess?" Wooziness clouded Elizabeth's head, and she felt her knees give out beneath her.

Chapter 7

Berkeley Square

The next morning, Elizabeth opened her eyes to find herself tucked into her own tester bed. At least, she assumed it was morning. The room was awash in smoky blue light. She could just make out a tray bearing a steaming cup of tea and a plate of sliced green apples sitting on the table beside her.

But then the curtains were suddenly thrown open and there, standing before the window in the bright sunlight, was Cherie.

"How did I get home?" A painful throb pulsated in Elizabeth's temple. "I c-can't remember."

Cherie raised her gracefully curved eyebrows,

as if coaxing her to try harder to recall the events of the night before. While the tiny maid waited, she poured Elizabeth a dish of tea and guided it into her hands.

Raising the teacup to her lips, Elizabeth let the steam waft over her face. She breathed in the welcoming scent of the tea and immediately recognized it.

Hyson! What was Mrs. Polkshank thinking? Hyson was far too dear for a mere family member's breakfast. The expensive leaves were meant to be reserved for taking tea with prominent guests. No wonder the household expenses were increasing. Such wastefulness! Well, she would have to speak with Mrs. Polkshank about it this very day.

Then it happened. Brief flashes of images unexpectedly appeared in her mind's eye. A small crowd of gentlemen huddled around her, lifting her. Opening her eyes in a dark rocking carriage. The thudding of a heart. Rubbing her nose because a jingling red swath of fabric was tickling it. Strong, capable arms carrying her. Being laid upon her bed by . . . by—

"Good heavens!" Elizabeth jolted upright, sending the tea in her cup sloshing over the side. Cherie stretched out her hands and rescued the dish. "The prince brought me here?

He laid me in my bed?" She stared incredulously at the maid.

Cherie smiled, then shrugged her shoulders.

"No, he was injured. Impossible. Impossible!" Elizabeth thrummed her fingers on her lower lip. But the images were so clear. She reached out and wrapped her fingers around the maid's tiny wrist. "Did it happen, Cherie? Did it? Or was I dreaming?"

The maid shook her head. The edges of her lips pulled downward. It was clear she didn't know.

But someone in this household must.

Someone had let her, and whoever brought her home to Berkeley Square, into the house. She would have her explanation within the hour. From someone.

"Cherie, please, help me dress." Elizabeth threw her legs over the edge of the bed and started to stand when a wave of dizziness forced her to immediately sit down upon the mattress again. She raised her eyes to the startled-looking maid. "I am well, Cherie. No cause for worry. I just need to move a little slower until I am fully awake."

Cherie offered her the dish of tea again, which she took without hesitation. Maybe Mrs. Polkshank was right in brewing the full-bodied, pungent hyson tea this morn. Yes, it was probably just the thing for her weakened constitution. How wise Cook was.

Cherie watched her drink the hyson with an expression of mixed worry and surprise, until the only thing left in Elizabeth's teacup was a few twisted tea leaves.

She needed to know how she arrived here, and that the prince, indeed, was well. And she would have her answer. Only this time she decided not to be so hasty. She handed the maid her teacup, then slowly stood, crossed the bedchamber, and eased down before her dressing table.

When she peered into the mirror, she understood Cherie's aghast expression. Dried blood matted the hair on the entire right side of her head.

Good heavens! She must have been far more seriously injured than she'd imagined. So much blood. Her hand trembled as she raised it and pulled back several thick strands of copper hair so she might observe the wound.

Leaning forward toward the silver of the mirror, she peered closely at it. No plaster had been applied, which surprised her for there was such a large amount blood. Mr. Manton, however, had administered some sort of foul-smelling ointment to the crusting dark red scrape, about the length and width of her pinkie finger.

Her stomach turned a bit, which unnerved her.

When assisting her father over the years, she'd never had an aversion to the sight of blood. She even stopped a spurting wound by turning a tourniquet tightly whilst the doctor stitched a farmer's leg gash closed. In all her life she had never even blinked at the sight or smell of blood . . . well, perhaps once when a spray fanned across her face, but she would have done the same had the liquid been water, so that incident foretold nothing.

But this time it was different. This time it was her own blood.

"Cherie, I should like to wash my hair." With a disgusted sigh at her own appearance, she dropped the matted locks she held back into place.

The maid shook her head vehemently and her dark eyes peered pleadingly at Elizabeth's reflection in the mirror.

"Lud, Cherie, please, see to heating the water. Please." She exhaled a hard breath. "You know very well that I can't leave the house looking like I just escaped a mad assassin's knife. I must bathe and don my finest morning dress if I am to inquire about the prince's health this day."

Cherie nodded, bobbed a quick curtsy, and then hurried from the bedchamber.

Elizabeth turned her head and gazed at the position of the grazing. Hmm. Her wide-brimmed straw bonnet, the one embellished with pale roses and a stunning green satin ribbon, would cover it perfectly.

She smiled at herself in the mirror and pinched her cheeks to liven her pallor. How lucky she was to have such a keen sense of style.

Two hours later

Descending two flights of stairs proved more difficult than Elizabeth had anticipated; it made her head bobble, and each minuscule movement hurt as surely as if someone had thumped her skull. No matter. She would simply ask Mrs. Polkshank to locate the willow powder for the pain in her head, after she thanked her for the invigorating yet-too-costly-to-use-for-such-purposes hyson tea. Then she would be out the door and headed for the Clarendon Hotel, where she had heard whispers that the prince, and likely his cousin, were lodging.

She had just settled her hand on the newel post and stepped to the floor in the entry passage when she heard Lord Gallantine's voice call out from the parlor.

"Do not think it, my dear," he said in what, surprisingly enough, sounded like quite a stern voice.

Elizabeth grimaced. That he would be angry with her, especially after her ordeal last evening, made no sense. So she pushed Gallantine's nonsensical warning from her head. He was likely speaking to Cherie anyway ... or someone else. Certainly not her. He probably had been informed that she was dressing and did not even know she was present on the first floor yet. And so she decided to hurry to continue her quest for the willow powder before making her way into the parlor to see to her caller.

"Elizabeth, dove," came Lady Upperton's sweet voice. "We heard your footfalls on the stair treads. Do come into the parlor."

Blast. Elizabeth froze in her steps and squeezed her eyes closed. She would have come, right after partaking of the willow powder. Slowly, she opened her eyes and sighed heavily. After checking her appearance in the mirror—the wound was perfectly concealed beneath a double twist of hair, pulled up and then pinned at the back of her head—she hoisted a pretty smile and, holding her head as level and steady as possible, glided into the parlor.

Her head jerked painfully the moment she saw that not only were Gallantine and Lady Upperton present, but so were Lord Lotharian, Lilywhite . . . and, of course, her dozing great-aunt Prudence. "I do apologize. I had not realized anyone had called and wished an interview with me."

"Is that so, Elizabeth?" Lord Lotharian peered at her through narrowed eyes. "After our charge is chased by a gunman through the streets of London—with Prince Leopold of Saxe-Coburg, no less—and then shot, why, pray, might we come to speak with you?"

A flush heated Elizabeth's cheeks. "It's only a flesh wound. As you can see, I am well enough." She swallowed. "Has . . . anyone heard about the prince's condition this day?"

"Only that he survived. But then you know that, don't you, gel?" Lotharian said, still observing her in that unsettling way of his.

"Yes." She lowered her gaze, hoping to disengage Lotharian's overly focused attention. "I only wondered—"

"You might have been killed, Elizabeth!"

Lilywhite snapped, drowning out her words. He hastened over to the tantalus, and though it was still quite early in the day to be drinking, by the *ton*'s or anyone else's standards, he poured himself a glass of brandy. "Anyone else like a calming bit of liquid sustenance?"

Her great-aunt's eyes opened immediately. "I would." She raised her hand and beckoned for a glass. Lilywhite obliged her almost instantly, and she took the brandy and began sipping happily.

Elizabeth settled herself in an empty slipper chair near the doorway. "H-How ... did you hear about last night's incident?" *Oh. Right. Edmund.* Forgetting herself, she slapped her palm to her head. "Damn!" She looked up and was immediately met with shocked looks from the elderly group. "Please forgive my outburst. 'Tis my head ... very, very sore."

Cherie flitted into the passage with a tray holding a glass of cloudy water. Before she could enter the parlor, she was immediately halted by the butler MacTavish, who had only just taken up a sentry stance outside the door. He looked quizzically at the little maid until she gestured to her head and then to the glass.

Elizabeth, who, from the periphery of her vision, had been observing the whole delay in receiving her much-needed willow powder, was about to spring from her chair and snatch up the glass when the butler entered the parlor and at last offered it to her.

She drank down the bitter powder, but knowing it would take some time to ease her pain, she began to consider joining Lilywhite and Prudence in a noon-time libation.

"Actually, 'twas Miss Margaret Mercer Elphinstone who communicated the astounding news of your adventures with the prince last night," Lady Upperton revealed. "You remember her, do you not? Princess Charlotte's lady's companion?"

Elizabeth sat silently, trying to piece together the events that might bring Miss Mercer Elphinstone to Lady Upperton's door.

"You have made her acquaintance. Yesterday, in fact," Lady Upperton added. She lifted her fluffy white brows excitedly. "And you must have made quite an impression."

"More, please." Great-aunt Prudence raised her empty glass in Elizabeth's direction. "Chop, chop, Lilywhite."

Elizabeth, dumbfounded by Lady Upperton's assertion, started to rise to refill her great-aunt's glass herself when she felt Lilywhite's heavy hand on her shoulder.

"I'll it fetch for her, gel," he said. "Fancy a refresher for myself, anyway."

Elizabeth looked directly at Lady Upperton. "On my word, I do not know how I could have made an impression at all on Miss Elphinstone. Our time together was so short." Nothing this day seemed to make sense to Elizabeth, and she began to wonder, fleetingly, if her injury had somehow rattled her brain. "Why did *she* contact you?"

Lord Gallantine rose from his place on the settee beside Lady Upperton and came to stand before Elizabeth. "You must have done something extraordinary, dear. Something *very* extraordinary."

Elizabeth tilted her head back and peered up at him. "Why do you say that, Gallantine? You seem so confident in your charge."

"Because, Elizabeth, she called at first light with a letter—from Princess Charlotte." He paused then, as if Elizabeth might already know the contents of said missive. But she didn't, and, lud, she wished they all would stop dancing the quadrille around the facts and tell her everything!

"The princess has requested that you join her at Cranbourne Lodge, temporarily . . . just until Michaelmas," Lord Gallantine added.

"Join her—the princess?" Elizabeth shifted her head this way and that to peer around Gallantine, hoping, praying, someone could enlighten her as to this extraordinarily strange turn of events. "But why?"

"To act as one of her lady's companions—like Miss Elphinstone, herself," Lady Upperton offered.

"But why . . . *me*?"

"Well, we do not know, dear," Lady Upperton admitted. "We had hoped that you could provide us with that vital information. Of course, we agreed to her request and sent Miss Elphinstone back to the princess with the happy news."

That bit of news propelled Elizabeth straight to her feet. "Y-You agreed?"

"You leave the first of next week, if you are well enough. And it seems by your appearance this day that you already are fit. So, it is all arranged." Lady Upperton was smiling proudly. "We knew it would be what you wanted. We knew you would be most delighted to get to know the princess. After all, you said it yourself—she is likely your half sister."

Elizabeth sat down again, her strength drained from her limbs at this revelation. This was utter madness!

Yes, in recent months she had wondered

about Princess Charlotte, her likely half sibling. Had fantasized about what it would be like to live like a princess—had the circumstances of her birth been different.

But now . . . now destiny had become revealed to her. She was to marry the prince. She could not leave London and her future husband behind. Not now.

It seemed, however, that her guardians had already sealed her fate by agreeing that she would serve Princess Charlotte.

Lilywhite held a glass of brandy in the air. "Bet you'd like one of these now, Elizabeth, eh?"

Elizabeth raised her hand to take it.

God above, please let this all be a dream.

Within seven days she knew for certain that she was not dreaming. Her course was now very clear. During this week, she had received no word as to the prince's condition. And when she slipped out of the house to inquire about him at the Clarendon Hotel, where he was reportedly lodging, she was politely told that the prince was not in residence at this time.

Elizabeth was left wondering if he had returned to Paris, or even Coburg, depending on the severity of his wound.

Either way, her dream, her vivid vision of

their eventual marriage, was rapidly becoming naught but a wishful fantasy fading into the wind with each passing hour.

When the day of her dreaded departure for Cranbourne Lodge arrived, her hopes for a reunion with her prince had all but vanished.

Cherie had packed a portmanteau with necessities, and saw that her trunks were strapped atop the carriage. To Elizabeth's embarrassment, two hefty trunks had been required, for Lady Upperton had taken it upon herself to see that that the gowns Mrs. Devy had been engaged earlier to create would be delivered before her departure—even though seven additional seamstresses had to be employed to complete the sewing.

Elizabeth's only task had been to rest so she would be invigorated when called upon to serve the princess. Even now, she had still no clue as to what her service would entail, which was more than a little disconcerting.

After a bumpy three hour journey from London, the carriage bearing her and all of her worldly belongings rounded the last curve in the road, and Cranbourne Lodge came into view at last.

Elizabeth gasped to think she was actually to reside in such an imposing structure.

The grand, pale-hued house seemed to absorb the golden afternoon sun, transforming the lodge's massive tower into a column of gold. She strained her neck in her attempt to see the top of the tower from the window, and when she did see it at last, imagined that were she to stand atop of it, she would be able to view London, some twenty miles distant.

It didn't appear to be such a bad place to spend one's day, if that was what you wished— though she did not—for Cranbourne Lodge was pleasantly situated, not far from Windsor Castle, at the edge of an overgrown ancient garden flanked by the lushness of Windsor Forest. Its beauty and history was unquestionable.

Being afforded the opportunity to come to know Princess Charlotte was an unimaginable gift . . . had she still wanted it.

To live like a princess, to be free of dreary household responsibilities and the task of caring for her family, had been her grandest dream since the moment she and her sisters arrived in London. And now that dream was coming true.

Elizabeth could only discern one problem with being at here at Cranbourne Lodge, and that was that her prince was not.

Nor was the princess, it seemed. Princess

Charlotte had gone to Windsor to visit her aunts and the queen, and was not expected to return to Cranbourne Lodge until late that evening.

Elizabeth wondered if the queen knew she was here. Princess Charlotte, Elizabeth assumed, must have heard the rumors swirling the *ton* about the Royle sisters' lineage—and then realized, if she believed the story, that she and the Royles were half sisters. The princess knowing of her possible blood connection would at least explain her interest in a commoner from Cornwall. And what better poker to torture her powerful father with than his bastard?

Elizabeth grimaced. Even if Princess Charlotte knew who she was, or could be, the queen must not—assuming her father's story was authentic. If it was true, the queen was oblivious to the fact that the sisters had survived despite her and Lady Jersey's best efforts. Or the queen simply did not know that she was at Cranbourne. There was far too much at risk for her granddaughter, Princess Charlotte, to spend time with one of the babes the queen tried to kill to protect her son's future claim on the Crown.

Elizabeth considered what her stay at Cranbourne Lodge might bring. A sighting of the queen herself? A meeting? She lingered on the thought.

Just one formal introduction to the queen, one moment for the queen to truly realize who she was, and Elizabeth was convinced she would know the truth of the matter instantly by the look in the woman's eyes.

Only, were such a collection of moments possible, she did not know if she could endure meeting the gaze of the woman who would have seen her dead.

Elizabeth shook off the chilling thought. No matter the reason she had been summoned to Cranbourne Lodge, good or bad, she had been properly looked after. She had been situated in a small but comfortable room with an arched window and sweeping views of a verdant meadow, currently dotted with small rabbits munching on the new grass.

Already it had occurred to her that time moved at a dreadfully slow pace here.

To occupy herself, she worked alongside a lady's maid to unpack her trunks and shake her new gowns from their travel folds. She fidgeted with the coiled locks of hair concealing her scabbed-over wound, and then laid out her powders, perfume, pins, and brushes on the dressing table.

Then, with nothing else to do, Elizabeth decided to venture down to the stables and borrow a horse from one of the grooms. It would be most diverting to take a short ride around the grounds before the sun set.

Deer lifted their heads from the soft grass and flicked their tails nervously as Elizabeth's bay trotted down the packed earthen road leading away from Cranbourne Lodge.

For several minutes the thought of riding all the way back to London nagged at her brain. But she knew that doing such an irresponsible thing would fling her into the role of social outcast, and then, were she ever to meet her prince again, a future between them would be impossible. And so she bucked herself up and resigned herself to her temporary duties for the Crown.

The air was warmer than she had expected it would be at this hour of the afternoon. She reined in her horse for a moment to untie her fichu. Whisking it off, she waved it before her face. But the circulation of warm air provided no respite from the close heat.

The pounding of hooves on the road drew her attention, and she yanked the reins and guided her horse under the cover of trees. There, in the distance, advanced a young man atop a huge black gelding.

As he neared, she saw that he wore no neck

cloth. His lawn shirt billowed open, revealing the muscled mounds of his firm chest.

Beads of nervous perspiration erupted at Elizabeth's hairline as his horse galloped closer, and she dabbed her forehead with her lace fichu as she studied the gentleman's form. His very familiar form.

He did not wear a coat in the warmth of the summer evening, nor did gold epaulets flutter in the air with each rise and fall of his gelding's hoofs. No scarlet sash draped over his shoulder to reach down and across to his lean hip.

But still, though he was garbed like the veriest country farmer, she knew him.

He was her prince.

What trick of light is this?

Sumner reined his massive horse to a halt. He raised his hand against the glare of the low hanging sun and squinted his eyes at the figure nearly hidden in the dappled sunlight beneath a mature oak tree.

A tremor pulsed through his muscles. He'd felt the sensation many times before. The excitement when the first cannon fired. When the first rifle sounded, sending his body into motion. When the drums of a grand military procession pounded.

But never at the sight of a woman.

"Miss Royle?" His voice shook, though he thought he had controlled his entirely too visceral reaction to her. "Can it be?"

She nudged her bay forward, leaning over the pommel as she passed beneath a cluster of leafy branches. As her mount fully emerged into the sunlight, Miss Royle straightened her back and smiled. Her cheeks were flushed with rosiness and were glowing, from the heat of the day or perhaps from a vigorous ride, he did not know, but the sight of her stirred something deep within him.

"Are you well?" She looked concerned at first, but then raised her hand and covered her mouth as she laughed softly. "What a daft question. Look at you. You are glorious." Her horse stepped forward and she lowered her hand and clutched the reins tightly. The smile evaporated from her lips all at once. "Do forgive me, Your Royal Highness. I did not mean . . . that is to say . . . you appear to be in glorious health."

"As do you, Miss Royle." That was an understatement. She looked beautiful. Even in the heat of the summer, after a ride, she was ravishing. Perfect.

She looked away and muttered something that sounded a lot like "glorious" under her breath. When she met his gaze again, the curve to her lips was manufactured, clearly born of embarrassment. "Thank you, Your Royal Highness."

There it was again—*Your Royal Highness*. A twinge of guilt stabbed deeply at his conscience. He wanted to go to her, to confess and explain his reasons behind the charade. But he couldn't now. He and Leopold had agreed on this point. It had to be this way. For the time being, anyway, for Leopold's safety as well as Miss Royle's.

Instinctively, Sumner tightened his legs' grip on his horse, and it moved forward until their horses' heads where parallel. "What force from the heavens could have brought forth such a joyful happenstance as meeting you on the road?"

A quick breeze stirred up dry clouds of earthen dust around them, but rather than close her lids against the burst, she met his gaze, her eyes sparkling like glittering emeralds in the afternoon sun. "I do not know whether the heavens had anything to do with this happy turn of events," she said, a hint of mirth lifting her voice, "though I believe we can perhaps thank Miss Elphinstone for the fortuitous co-incidence of our presence at Windsor."

Sumner's eyebrows drew close. "What do you mean, Miss Royle?"

She conveniently sidestepped his question momentarily and instead posed her own. "Have you taken lodging at the castle?" She seemed oddly discomfited by the very question she posed, but was evidently somehow compelled to ask it.

"No, of course not. Our presence here . . ." He lowered his head, and focused ridiculously on a stone near his mount's right hoof, wishing he could simply tell her. ". . . is a closely guarded secret."

"Not so close," she interjected, "for I stumbled across you, did I not? Is your cousin about?"

Leopold? Why would she ask about him? His chest tightened. "Why are you here, Miss Royle?" He leaned up in his saddle and glanced around her. "I see no others, no hamper of food to indicate an afternoon sojourn to the country."

His gelding's bit and bridle jingled, and he looked down to see his horse nuzzling the neck of Miss Royle's bay. He felt strangely embarrassed by this. Or perhaps he only wished the riders were doing the same down by the Thames on a blanket, without a care between them. But propriety and his need to focus on Leopold's safety prevented it.

"There is no basket; no others." She turned and glanced up the road. "I am in residence at Cranbourne Lodge. As of today, I am one of Princess Charlotte's lady's companions."

"You are at Cranbourne?" Sumner felt that odd jolt of excitement again.

"Yes, Your Royal Highness, I am."

Sumner felt a grin of anticipation on his lips. "Then I shall see you this very night."

Miss Royle lifted her eyebrows in apparent surprise. "My, my, you are a very confident man, aren't you?"

"Do forgive me, Miss Royle. I meant I would see you . . . at dinner." That beguiling blush filled her cheeks again, and for an instant he wished he had been rakish enough, just then, to mean what she had supposed.

So she looked up at him with false coyness. "So may I assume you are lodging . . . secretly . . . nearby?"

"You may indeed, secretly, of course, Miss Royle."

Miss Royle tipped her head in *adieu*. "Good afternoon, Your Royal Highness. I hope we shall speak again very soon."

Sumner nodded his head to her, and watched

Miss Royle tug at the reins and turn her bay in the direction of Cranbourne Lodge. "We shall, Miss Royle. Of that, I am certain."

When she disappeared around the bend in the road, he jerked his reins and galloped into the forest.

He had to speak with Leopold.

At once.

Chapter 8

Cranbourne Cottage

When Sumner approached the thatch-roofed gamekeeper's cottage at the edge of Windsor Forest, Leopold was sitting on the window ledge of the upper level to take in the air. Despite the heat, he was wearing a crisp white lawn shirt and a loosely tied cerulean neck cloth, though he'd at least had the good sense to dispense with his coat.

"Bit warm for a neck cloth, Leopold, eh?"

Prince Leopold, who was always as formal in his public attire as with his manner, waved off Sumner's comment. "Princess Charlotte is near," his cousin called down from the window.

"I intend to be presentable should she honor me with her company."

A young groomsman came running toward the cottage, shoving his unruly, sweat-dampened, butter-colored hair from his eyes. Sumner swung his leg over the horse and dismounted, then handed off the gelding to the young man. The groomsman bowed silently, never raising his eyes to Sumner—the prince—or so the lad obviously believed.

Just as it must be.

Just as it had always been—posing as another for the protection of others. It was a sad truth that only two others in this world ever knew Sumner's true identity . . . and neither one was Leopold. Even to this day. Leopold believed him to be his cousin, and that was the truth Sumner lived by.

In their youth, they were trained as soldiers together. Leopold studied strategy and history, while pain, brutality, and trials of wit tested Sumner's body and mind for his eventual position as a warrior in the military. But their paths always ran parallel, and they were at each other's sides through campaigns and battles.

As they were today.

Sumner waited until the groomsman had trotted the horse clear of the yard before he responded to Leopold. "She shan't ever come to the cottage, despite her penchant for disobedience. Too risky for her." He ducked through the entrance and before he closed the plank door behind him, Leopold had appeared at the bottom of the staircase. "Do not look so grief stricken. I met Miss Elphinstone in the glen and all is well. We are to dine with the princess and her companions this very eve—in secret."

"Her companions? What is this nonsense?" Leopold practically snarled. He walked across the room and sat upon an oak bench beside a front window, thrown wide to catch any small breeze that might bless the cottage on this stifling day. "No one is supposed to know we are here. It could be a matter of life or death— *mine!*"

"I did say that the dinner will be conducted *in secret*. Only a few trusted members of princess's staff, Miss Elphinstone, and Princess Charlotte know we were provided with refuge here at Cranbourne Lodge." He paused then. "Oh, and there is one other." He lifted his eyes to peer at Leopold.

The true prince came to his feet. "Why do you delay? Who is it? Should we be concerned?"

Sumner shook his head. "I think not. It is Miss Elizabeth Royle."

The surprise was plainly visible in Leopold's eyes. He said nothing for some moments before speaking again. "Was it . . . wise to inform her of our presence, Sumner?"

Sumner shrugged his shoulders. "For her sake, I do not know. For your sake, I would venture to say the miss poses no threat."

Leopold bent at the knees and sat down again.

"But you may decide that for yourself tonight, cousin."

"She is here?" Leopold sat very still for several seconds, then shook his head slowly. "Why did you ask her here? You know how perilous it is. She has already been shot in the head— simply because of her association with you!"

Sumner raised his hand to halt the prince's tirade. "I did not ask her to Windsor, and yet she is here. I met her on the road to Cranbourne Lodge only twenty minutes past."

"How then?" Leopold stretched out his arm and rested in on the windowsill.

"From what I gather, she was engaged by your dear friend, Mercer, as a lady's companion for Princess Charlotte."

"Miss Royle—a lady's companion? Odd choice." Leopold lowered his arm and rested his elbows on his knees. "The direction surely came from Princess Charlotte. No one would be asked to join the princess, and most not especially now while we are here, without it being her expressed royal order."

"Or the Prince Regent's." Sumner raised his eyebrows. "Though I think we are in agreement that if the Prince Regent knew anything about Miss Royle, or her sisters, he would not allow her anywhere near his headstrong Charlotte."

Leopold nodded, then looked quizzically up at Sumner. "Do you think Princess Charlotte knows about her possible kinship with Miss Royle? Or is it that she may have simply detected a fondness on your part for Miss Royle and wished to play matchmaker?"

"I do not doubt that she or Mercer might be driven by a measure of boredom and a wish to play at matchmaking." Sumner rubbed his chin as he thought about it. "I think it more likely that Princess Charlotte knows exactly who Miss Royle may be, and that, moreover, is why a mere commoner was engaged as companion to the princess."

Leopold rested his head in his hands momentarily and appeared to consider what Sumner had theorized. He nodded, slowly at first, then faster as he grasped the notion more tightly. "I believe you have the right of it, Sumner. But my question to you is this—since I am not known but by a very few souls in London, other than by name, very few people in Town know me by sight."

Sumner agreed and sank into a chair beside the cold hearth. "Everyone at Almack's seemed to believe I was Prince Leopold. Even Miss Royle, whom I originally introduced myself to as Sumner Lansdowne, Lord Whitevale, believes I am . . . well, *you*."

"Exactly."

"So what is your question, Leopold?"

Raising his index finger, he tapped it in the air several times in Sumner's direction before continuing. "Why is that?"

"Why is what?" Sumner was becoming increasingly exasperated by Leopold's round-the-track way of asking a question.

"Why, after hearing from your own lips that you are *not* Prince Leopold, does she still believe that you are?"

Sumner let his gaze fall to the clean stone floor. "I do not know for certain." He lifted his eyes to Leopold. "At Almack's, she asked me why I pretended to be Whitevale when we first met at the jewelers. At the ball, it was evident that she believed I was Prince Leopold. So, I toyed with her, telling her I had been 'incognito.'"

"And you were incognito—at the ball." Leopold grinned a bit. "Not when you first met."

"I had to tell her something to quell her curiosity and thankfully my claim served. What she saw at the ball was stronger than what she heard at the jewelers." Sumner's jaw tightened. "What is your point in this discussion?"

Leopold sat quietly.

"Do you suspect Miss Royle of something?" Sumner's mind was swirling. Had he missed something? Had his attraction to her, his emotions, clouded his critical thinking and put Prince Leopold in danger? *No. No.* He had always had a keen sense about people's natures. And he was sure of one thing—that he could trust Miss Royle with his life. She saved it once already, after all. "You are wrong about her, Leopold."

"I said nothing." Leopold rose slowly and turned to peer out of the window.

"She believes I am the prince, and I will maintain this ruse until we return to Paris or I am convinced your life is no longer in danger." Sumner realized at that moment that his breath was coming fast. His words were clipped. His temper had flared.

He drew in several deep gulps of air into his lungs. His cool detachment, his control—which had always allowed him to make crucial decisions, whether in battle or in ensuring the safety of Prince Leopold—had already been compromised by his emotions.

That wouldn't do. Wouldn't do at all.

"You needn't fret, Leopold." He took another deep breath. "I will not allow my feelings to have a place in your protection. I swear it."

Leopold turned and headed for the front door. As he passed Sumner, he clapped him on the shoulder. "I never had any doubt."

One hour until midnight
Cranbourne Lodge

A loud growl emanated from Elizabeth's stomach. "Oh, dear. Are there wild cats in Windsor Forest?" She looked over her shoulder in the direction of the window, and then turned to the three others who sat before the expansive table in the low, insufficient glow of only two flickering candles.

Princess Charlotte cast a barely concealed grin in her confidante Mercer's direction. She had only just returned from visiting her grandmother and aunts at the castle, which necessitated the lateness of the meal. "Yes, Miss Royle, I do believe there are. Hares and badger, too, though I daresay I have not heard a peep from them this evening."

Mercer's shoulders shook slightly, and Elizabeth realized she had fooled no one. Her cheeks heated with color.

"I heard a wild cat just as we drew up before the lodge," the prince's cousin said. "Didn't you, Leopold?"

The prince showed no emotion, and yet he agreed. "I did indeed, cousin. There must be a goodly number of them in the forest."

Elizabeth nervously dabbed her serviette to her lips. She peered at the prince's cousin. "Do forgive me, but with all of the goings-on the night of the ball, I did not register your name, sir."

The prince's gaze flew to his cousin. The cousin's gaze shot to Princess Charlotte, who turned, wide-eyed, to Mercer.

"I do apologize," Elizabeth said with no little degree of suspicion that something unknown to her was afoot. "Have I asked something I should not?" The three of them continued silently casting gazes askance to one another.

The princess finally met Elizabeth's eyes. She reached out and took her hand. "Dear Miss

Royle, the prince's cousin is . . . the Marquess of Whitevale." She raised her surprised eyes to the prince and then to the cousin in way of introduction.

"L-Lord Whitevale?" Elizabeth muttered. She turned in her chair to face the prince. "But, Your Royal Highness, you introduced yourself as Whitevale when we met in Hamilton and Company."

High color skimmed the prince's cheeks. "As I told you at the assembly rooms, Miss Royle—"

"Ah, yes," she interrupted, " 'incognito.' I understand."

"Miss Royle," Miss Margaret Mercer Elphinstone broke in, "—and do please call me Mercer, everyone does, and now that you are one of us, so shall you, I hope. How do you find Cranbourne Lodge?" She smiled prettily at Elizabeth as she posed her question.

Miss Margaret Mercer Elphinstone was a stunningly beautiful woman, with smooth pale skin, wide eyes, and glossy sable hair. She presented herself, in both manner and appearance, as being several years older than both the princess and Elizabeth. Or perhaps her poise, polish, and sophistication only made her seem more mature. From what Elizabeth had been told by Lady Upperton, Miss Mercer Elphinstone was quite well respected in London society and a favorite at routs and fetes, known for her charm, wide and varied connections, and quick wit.

"I find it quite . . ." *Oh, lud, how does one put this nicely?* ". . . conducive to thought." Elizabeth smiled at the completion of her statement, quite pleased she had managed to express herself and her meaning so gracefully.

That is, until Princess Charlotte and Mercer began laughing merrily at her reply, making Elizabeth wonder if she'd stepped in something she oughtn't again.

"Dear Miss Royle, how refreshing you are. But we knew you would be," Princess Charlotte told her, her words punctuated with missish giggles. "I am so glad you have come. You are so different from my dreadfully dull governesses."

"Darling Charlotte, where are the old jail keepers? Have you packed them away somewhere—for what a chance you are taking in bringing our esteemed guests to the lodge this night," Mercer said in all seriousness. "If your father was to hear of this, he'd pop you back off to Warwick and I would have such a time of trying to see you."

The prince and Lord Whitevale pushed up

from the table and made to leave, but before either could utter a word, Princess Charlotte had leapt to her feet and was overtly gesturing for the gentlemen to be seated again.

"No need to concern yourselves. Though I know circumstances require that the Leo and Whitevale must reside in the protection of the forest for a time for their own safety, I will not have my future . . . my . . . the Leo taking his evening meal in a gamekeeper's nook every night." Charlotte looked to Mercer, set her hands proudly upon her hips and spread her feet, making her appear very much like a strong-willed boy. "Besides, no one will be the wiser. My governesses were encouraged to remain at the castle, after they enjoyed goblet after goblet of prime Madeira gifted to my family by Wellington himself. Now, I ask you all, how could they refuse?" Princess Charlotte leaned back her head and laughed heartily. "I, myself, actually made a game of playing mother—but with Madeira rather than tea." Charlotte snorted a most unprincesslike laugh.

"You are wicked, Charlotte. Positively wicked," Mercer said, with no pretense of formality with the princess at all. "Which is why you and I get on so famously." She turned her clever gaze on Elizabeth. "And why I have a suspicion Miss

Royle will be such an interesting addition to our number."

Uncomfortable did not quite describe the way she felt at the realization she had been shoe-horned into their intimate group as a court jester meant for their entertainment.

Still, Elizabeth turned her head to levee a cheerful smile in Princess Charlotte's direction. But when she did, she saw that the princess's gaze was already well fixed on her. It was an appraising, almost wary gaze. One that she next directed upon "the Leo," the silly, too familiar way she had addressed the prince this evening.

The princess realized Elizabeth's awareness of her observation almost at once. "Miss Royle—"

"Oh, do please call me Elizabeth," she begged them all. "After all, we are to be friends." *Oh, la, that sounded truly nauseating. What an inane thing to say! I do not meld well with royalty. What had I been thinking when I boarded the carriage this morn? The blow to my head has made me entirely mad.*

"Very well, Elizabeth," Princess Charlotte began again. "What do you think of the Leo, here?" She inclined her head toward the prince, almost as though nudging Elizabeth's attention to him.

Mercer leaned forward in her chair, licking her lower lip in anticipation of the answer.

Elizabeth glanced at the prince. He did not meet her gaze. In fact he seemed immediately ill at ease and pushed back in his chair.

"I—I think the prince is very kind, very brave . . . and strong," Elizabeth stammered. *Lud, would this night never end?*

"He is very handsome, too," Mercer added, "just like his cousin." Mercer flashed a sly, covert grin in Princess Charlotte's direction before looking back to Elizabeth. "Do you not agree, Elizabeth?"

Elizabeth felt her eyes widen. "I . . . I . . . well, yes. He does cut a fine form." *Where is that gunman? Here I am. Come, come shoot me now.* Anything was preferable to this torture!

The prince set his hands on the table and stood. "Will you please excuse me? I believe I must take some air." He glanced sidelong at Elizabeth, then tipped a bow to each of the ladies before walking from the dining room.

Whitevale shot a quick, almost imperceptible scowl in Mercer's direction. Of course, he would not deign to cast such an expression to the princess, who after all was the true cause of the prince's uneasiness. Not Mercer at all. "Elizabeth . . ." He gestured in the direction of the doorway. "I should not wish him to be alone. Would you join him, please?"

Elizabeth shook her head. "I beg you, please, do not ask me to do such a thing. It is evident the prince wishes to be alone."

Whitevale looked up at Princess Charlotte. "He may, but he was injured so recently, I shouldn't wish to leave him to himself—and if I were to go, he would accuse me of coddling him."

Princess Charlotte grimaced and stood. "*I* will go, then."

Whitevale, his cousin, shook his head. "Please, allow Elizabeth, Your Royal Highness." He grinned at her, and she giggled. "I would like to discuss the hunting in the forest with you."

Charlotte draped her arm over the back of the chair. "Well, sir, you already know there are plenty of wild cats about." She mouthed a silent growl and pawed the air, then giggled uproariously.

Elizabeth lifted her brow at the display. That was it. The princess had obviously partaken of the Madeira herself. La, she might as well follow the prince out into the night. Tonight's conversation was too convoluted for such a simple miss as she to comprehend.

"Do excuse, me," she said, rising from her chair and pushing it back beneath the table. "I believe I shall see to the prince after all. You are quite correct, Lord Whitevale, he should not be alone."

Mercer waggled her gracefully arched eyebrows at Princess Charlotte. "And I believe I shall retire for the evening. Such a long day." She rose, and as she passed Charlotte, squeezed the princess's hand. "Good night."

Mercer looped her arm around Elizabeth's. Oddly enough, the intimate gesture felt quite natural, for Mercer had an easy way about her that made everyone feel comfortable—even, it seemed, when she was being mischievous. Together they walked toward the entry hall.

"Dear, Elizabeth," she said as they strolled. "You are at Cranbourne Lodge for a reason, and that reason has nothing to do with me."

Elizabeth's eyebrows drew close. "What reason might that be then, Mercer? Please, share it with me."

"That is for you to learn," Mercer replied as she disengaged her hold, "but the discovery of that reason will be half the fun." As Elizabeth stood near the front door, Mercer headed for the grand staircase. "Miss Royle, do not waste this gift. Your time is short here. Do make good use of what you have."

"I—I . . ." Elizabeth struggled for the right words, but before she could seize them, Mercer had disappeared up the dark staircase.

An ancient, liveried footman opened the door for Elizabeth. She breathed in a deep, cleansing breath, then stepped into the night.

About twenty paces from the door, the prince stood in a column of blue moonlight. His back was to her and he did not seem aware anyone had come from the lodge.

Mercer was right. This was a gift. She thought she had lost him once, but Fate had gifted her with another chance.

She would not chance losing him again.

To missed opportunities. Or even to Princess Charlotte.

Confidently, Elizabeth lifted the hem of her gown from the ground and silently walked up behind him.

She gently laid her hand upon his shoulder.

He turned with a bit of a start and stared into her eyes, as if he could not believe she was there. "Elizabeth," he breathed.

Chapter 9

Cranbourne Lodge
Norman garden

Elizabeth.

A rumbling like the thunder of a distant storm shook through Sumner as his gaze met Elizabeth's glittering eyes. His hands jerked, needing to reach out, to draw her to him. His lips quivered with want of feeling the warmth of her mouth on his.

But as had always been his way, his mind tamped down his physical needs and wants. His duty steeled his body against her.

If only it could do the same with his heart.

"I wished to be alone." Sumner took her shoulders in his hands, and though he felt her soften and lean into him, he straightened his arms, forcing her to step back. "Please, go back inside and rejoin the others. You may tell my cousin, if it was he who sent you, that I am well and that . . . that I do not need a pointed reminder that my desires come second. I know my duty." He let his hands fall away and settle at his sides.

"Know your . . . duty?" Elizabeth, not conceding, stepped toward him again. "I do not know what that means. Your cousin did ask me to stand with you. I came because I wished to be with you. I . . . I needed to be here. With you. Can't you understand this?"

The rumbling inside of Sumner transformed from a steady tattoo to a thunderous pounding inside his chest. "Now is not the time. Please, leave me, Elizabeth."

"Now *is* the time." She took yet another step closer. He could feel the heat of her body as she neared. He had not the time to retreat to her movement, or maybe it was his will that was lacking.

She reached one small hand up and slowly caressed his cheek. Her right hand settled atop his heart.

Something inside of Sumner broke at that moment. He had not been prepared for her tenderness—for her touch of true affection, that sort that fills the heart's dark, hollow spaces like a healing salve.

Heat pricked in the backs of his eyes, surprising and shaming him at once. His duty was to Leopold. She, and what she made him feel, was a liability. One he could not afford when Leopold's life was at stake.

He tried to tell her again, to explain, but his words burst forth harshly instead. "I have my duty. *Go!*"

She trembled against him and lurched backward a pace. He hadn't meant to frighten her, to hurt her. His hand rose up from his side, reaching for her, but he forced it down.

Elizabeth didn't know . . . she had come too close. He needed her too much.

But . . . his duty was to Leopold. He could not let his weakness for Elizabeth jeopardize the prince's safety or his strategic union with Princess Charlotte.

Her eyes became glossy and wet, shining in the moonlight. Her chin quivered, but she stood strong, facing him, holding her position firm. "Do you think I have not heard that the handsome Prince Leopold is in London to secretly court Princess Charlotte? That he means to marry her?"

Sumner opened his mouth to reply, but no words came. How could he respond to this truth?

She raised a finger to him. "You call it your duty—your duty to what, Saxe-Coburg?"

He was stunned, and turned his head away from her. He couldn't look at her. Not now, when he knew anything he would say to aid in his cause would hurt her. He looked out at the carpet of white flowers illuminated by the bright moonlight.

"Why cannot your first duty be to yourself?" she asked. There was desperateness in her voice. "I know our kiss meant something to you. And I can see by your reactions that Princess Charlotte does not."

Sumner heard the soles of her slippers on the gravel before she reached him. Whirling around, he grabbed her and pulled her against him. He tilted her head toward his and claimed her mouth hungrily with his own.

The soft fingers of both her hands moved across his cheeks then eased back over his temples and wriggled through his thick hair.

He felt his body harden to her, felt his want of her.

Your duty.

This singular thought revived his senses.

He caught her hands and pulled them from his hair. "Don't you understand, Elizabeth? I have my duty. *This* cannot be." He shook her hands in his, and then released them. "*We* cannot be!"

What he had expected her reaction to be, he did not know, but it wasn't the smile on her face. It was not an expression of false courage. It wasn't a plaster to prevent a gush of strangled emotions. It was a smile.

"That is where you are wrong. We can be," she told him. "And no matter what you do, or your duty demands, we will be together." She brought her hands to her heart and pressed them there. "I feel it—*here* . . . and so do you. I know you do."

He was on vulnerable ground just now. Any word he spoke, any forward move he made, would be wrong. And so he did what he had been trained never to do. He turned and started for the stables in retreat.

"Fate has decided," she called after him. "You and I are meant to be together. And so it shall be."

Sumner lengthened his strides, but he could not outpace her words.

Fate has decided.

How he wished he could believe it. How he

longed for a future with this beautiful, compassionate woman.

If only it were possible.

But he knew it was not.

He owed his very existence to Leopold's father. He would not let the prince or his family down.

Ever.

Instead of returning directly to the lodge, Elizabeth walked deeper into the wildly overgrown Norman garden, where she found a small marble bench to sit upon. Settling her hands behind her, she leaned back and stared up at the huge, brilliant moon in the sky.

She was still smiling . . . for Fate had indeed decided. She and that man—that stubborn, beautiful man—were to be together. Forever.

If there had been any doubt, it disappeared the moment he grabbed her and kissed her with a passion that even now made her knees feel weak and limp, like a candle left too long in a sunny window.

Elizabeth raised a hand and touched her lips with her fingertips. Her mouth was still tender, and slightly swollen perhaps from the fervor with which he had claimed it with his own. She ran her tongue across her full lower lip.

She could still taste him a bit. She sucked her lips slightly into her mouth. Salty with just a hint of wine.

She lowered her hand and flashed a full grin at the moon. And he wanted her. That was quite evident, too.

His hardness, pressed so intimately against her, had startled her at first—until she realized just exactly what it meant he was feeling for her. Then her own body responded, heat pooling below, making her wish for things maidens should not even consider . . . even in the moonlight with a prince.

Leaning forward, Elizabeth rested her elbows on her knees and her chin in her hands. It would all be so easy for them both, she thought, if it wasn't for his ardent belief in his so-called duty.

She sighed. Though she knew that their feelings of attraction would grow into love and in the end their love would blossom and prevail, she also knew that, drat it all, he truly believed he had a duty—to marry Princess Charlotte for the benefit of Saxe-Coburg and England.

Elizabeth straightened her legs and stood. She had quite a Herculean task before her.

What could she possibly propose to a prince that would convince him to marry her, a commoner from the wilds of Cornwall . . . instead of a woman who would one day be Queen of England?

She wandered through the garden pondering this very question until she climbed a slight rise and came upon a labyrinth paved with crushed white oyster shells.

Elizabeth glanced up at the moon, and then at the circular labyrinth before her. It was as if the moon and ringed web of paths were mirror images of each other—with one notable difference: while she could simply stare up at the glowing celestial body and weigh different options for winning the prince in her mind, the labyrinth was meant to be walked while meditating.

And so she set one foot before the other as she pondered the question of what she could possibly do to win the prince. Around and around the turns of the huge labyrinth she paced, moving ever closer to the center and sure illumination.

At last she finally reached the core of the labyrinth. She raised her hands out to her sides and tilted her head back to catch the moonlight, patiently waiting for enlightenment— which was sure to come after walking in circles so many times that her head spun.

She drew in a hearty breath and closed her

eyes. And waited a while longer. And then a few minutes more. "Show me the way," she whispered into the night. "Please."

After standing there at least a quarter of an hour, her arms were aching and her muscles quivered as violently as if she'd been practicing archery all day. She let her arms fall limply to her sides.

Their destiny was fated. She'd seen it in her dreams. Felt it in his kiss. Why wouldn't the answer come to her? She should know this. She should!

She peered up at the moon and focused on the dark marring on its glowing surface.

Suddenly, Elizabeth realized that she already knew the answer—*fate*.

Of course. It was so clear to her now!

Anything she did from this moment forward was meant to happen—because they would be married before the summer ended. She had seen it.

She whisked her hands to her mouth to squelch the laugh of realization welling up in her throat.

There was no need to worry at all.

No need to doubt that any course of action she chose would not be the right one—because it would be. It had to be.

Her every action, every word, was already fated to bring the prince to her.

Elizabeth bounced on her toes with excitement, then raced from the labyrinth and dashed toward the lodge. She had to get some sleep, after all.

She had a prince to woo in the morning.

Chapter 10

O n her first morning at Cranbourne Lodge, Elizabeth awoke before the sun had fully risen. Though she tried to stay in her bed, she could not. She was far too excited to learn what her duties as a lady's companion would be, and how they would differ from that of the princess's governesses.

The moment she stirred from her tester bed, the chamber door swung open and a pretty golden-haired lady's maid hurried in with a ewer of steaming water, cloths, and towels, and set about preparing to assist Elizabeth with her morning ministrations.

"Has the princess arisen?" she asked the maid as she toweled her face dry.

"Oh no, miss. She'll not rise for several hours

more." Her gaze flitted over Elizabeth, but her eyes quickly shifted to the wardrobe situated across the chamber, and she scurried to it.

"Oh, quite right." Elizabeth felt like such a goose. Certainly no one would be awake at this early hour but the house staff who were compelled to do so—and, of course, one overeager lady's companion.

When the young woman turned around again to face Elizabeth, she was blushing fiercely.

"Is something amiss?" Elizabeth asked, wondering if, even though she had only been out of bed for two minutes, she had already done something wrong.

"Oh no, miss." The maid's gaze dropped low.

Though her coloring appeared pronounced, Elizabeth decided that to avoid a bout of unnecessary worry she would assume that the flush was just the reflection of the newly pink morning sky on the maid's cheeks and nothing more.

"The rose morning dress, miss?" the maid asked, holding out one of Madame Devy's new confections.

"Are you quite serious—*that* gown?" Elizabeth thought the red gown more suited for a musicale or soiree. La, the sleeves did not even extend to the elbow, and the neckline was . . . well, not the least bit demure.

She sighed inwardly, supposing that here, in the company of the Princess of Wales, the rules of proper dress were on an entirely different plane. She gave an enthusiastic nod, sure that the maid certainly knew better than she what would be appropriate for the morning of . . . well, some sort of companion duties . . . at Cranbourne Lodge.

Since no one else was about after her hair and form were dressed, Elizabeth took a light breakfast of fruit and tea in her bedchamber, and then decided to take a walk to view the garden in the daylight.

Though she questioned the wisdom of wearing such a daring gown for walking in the cool morning air, she knew that her mantle would cover what her frock did not and she would be quite comfortable, even if she did feel a mite overdressed for a stroll.

As she walked through the opening in the ruin of what had obviously once been a high stone wall and into the garden, she could not help but gasp at its simple beauty. The morning dew still sparkled in the grass and on the fading purple, white, and pink blossoms of foxglove that stood as natural gatekeepers just inside the Norman garden. At first she almost thought she could hear the bell-shaped flowers ringing in the day, but then, as she moved through the garden, the faint jingling of bells mutated into clinking.

She clutched her gown in her fist, to protect her hem from the wet grass, and hastened toward the labyrinth, where the sounds seemed to emanate.

In the distance ahead, she heard the shuffling of boots, low groans and grunts mingled with the high-pitched reverberations of metal violently crossing metal.

"Damn you to hell, Sumner! You're far too quick for man your size," came a man's laughing voice just as Elizabeth broached the rise and came upon the labyrinth.

There, before her, two shirtless men, their bodies gleaming with sweat, swung swords at each other.

Leopold and Lord Whitevale.

The assault halted the moment the noblemen beheld her. Then they lowered their broadswords.

She blinked in astonishment. *Sumner must be Whitevale's given name. Certainly this is so.* How odd that she hadn't recognized the voice she had heard. But then, they were in the midst of swordplay. Strain and exertion was likely the cause for his altered tone. Certainly, that was the reason.

"I—I apologize for disturbing your bout," she stammered, trying hard not to stare at the definition of the prince's hard, muscular form. "I awoke early and decided to take a stroll."

The prince did not seem to care whether staring was polite or not. With his gaze pinned on her, he immediately stalked straight toward her.

Good heavens, what have I done now? Elizabeth instinctively scuffled backward.

When he reached her, there was no way possible she could avert her gaze from his broad chest. He was simply breathing too hard, and the movement was far too distracting for her to maintain a ladylike disinterest.

He reached out his hand, then stooped and retrieved her mantle from the ground.

Lud, she hadn't even realized it had slipped from her shoulders. She smiled as he handed it to her.

Heat seemed to well up from her beneath her chemise, shoot up over her bosom and settle in her cheeks. Horrified, she glanced to the sky, and saw that its earlier pinkish hue had transmogrified to a glorious vibrant blue.

"Good morning, Your Royal Highness." Why had her courage, which she had possessed in such great abundance only last eve, suddenly evaporated more quickly than the morning dew? "Such fine form you display."

He raised an amused eyebrow.

Dash it all. "I—I mean . . . your advance, of course. Delightful."

"You had lost your wrap, Miss Royle. I only sought to retrieve it for you."

"What? Oh, no, no." *Gads.* Elizabeth stopped speaking long enough to gather her wits about her, along with her mantle. "I was referring to your forward movement—your balestra. But, yes, thank you so much for returning my mantle to me." She dropped an unsteady curtsy.

"It was my pleasure, Miss Royle." He bent toward her. Instinctively, Elizabeth chased him with her mouth before realizing, too late, he was only bowing to her, not angling for a kiss.

She was mortified, but would not just walk away. Anything she did, she reminded herself, whether meaning to or not, was fated to happen. *Fated.* "W-Would you like to join me for a walk, Your Royal Highness?" she asked, pleased with her sudden surge of bravery.

"I do regret that I cannot, Miss Royle."

"Elizabeth. Please call me Elizabeth."

His eyes rounded momentarily. "Yes, Elizabeth. I am in the middle of a bout just now with . . ." He turned to gesture to his cousin. But he was gone. The labyrinth was deserted. His hand fell to his side. "With no one, it appears."

"So, shall we?" Elizabeth did not wait for an answer but brushed past him and headed for the center of the labyrinth. She scooped up his discarded shirt and brought it back to him. "It is such a fine day, is it not?" She raised her eyebrows with expectation. "But a little cool at this early hour."

The prince took his shirt from her, chuckling softly as he eased it over his head, then he fastened the sword at the sash at his hip. "It would be my honor to walk with you back to Cranbourne Lodge, Miss—*Elizabeth.*"

Damn you, Leopold. Sumner clenched his fist as his eyes scanned the treeline for his wretched cousin. The prince knew he had no desire to be left alone with Miss Royle . . . or rather, *Elizabeth.*

Actually, he had desire, that was the problem. He had too much of that, which was why it would serve him, and Leopold, best if he simply stayed as far from Elizabeth as possible.

He wanted her too much. Needed her even more. And she was bloody well too much of a distraction—one that could very easily become a deadly diversion if he was unable to carry out his duty and protect the prince.

Sumner glanced at Elizabeth, who strolled too slowly beside him. At this rate it would take ten minutes at least to return her to the lodge.

Her copper hair was gilded with sun, making it gleam in the morning light. His gaze followed a coiled lock from her temple to where its end puddled in the crease of her décolletage. What had she been thinking when she donned a French-inspired gown for a morning walk?

He swallowed hard and forced his gaze to the path before them. He could not allow himself to dwell on her beauty, her allure. Or how he wanted to hold her against him. To feel her full breasts pressed, warm and soft, against his chest.

Bloody hell. He felt himself stiffen, and was immediately grateful that he had not taken the time to tuck his lawn shirt into his breeches.

Sumner raised his head and looked straight forward, not daring to look down. He was sure his lawn shirt would cover any evidence of his interest in her, but if he looked down to be sure, her gaze might follow, and he did not wish to risk that embarrassment.

When his attention alighted on the path once more, he realized that his inattention had lead to a fatal mistake. They were not headed in the direction of Cranbourne Lodge at all. There were turning onto the river trail along the Thames—in the opposite direction. This wasn't wise.

"Should you not return to Cranbourne Lodge, Elizabeth?" He stopped and turned away from her, pretending to look at the Thames in the near distance. "Will not the princess be rising soon and wish for your assistance?"

She came and stood next to him, so close that he could feel the warmth of her body. "The lady's maid informed me that the princess will not rise for a couple hours or more." She laid her hand on his arm and turned him to face her.

Her innocent touch seared him like a brand, and he felt his penis twitch with anticipation inside his breeches.

"It seems she and your cousin were rapt in conversation until early into the morning hours." Her eyelids were held low over her brilliant emerald eyes against the sun, and even when she stopped speaking, her mouth remained slightly parted, as if in want of a kiss.

A kiss like the one he barely, perhaps stupidly, avoided at the edge of the labyrinth minutes ago.

He turned his head from the seductive sight of her and started down the river trail again. He had to clear his mind. Had to focus on his duty. Nothing more.

His strides were long and quick, each step sending bits of gravel popping from beneath the force of his boots on the path.

Blast him. Why is he making this so difficult? Elizabeth hiked up her skirts and trotted after him. She caught up with him where the trail rounded a bend and the river rushed by several feet below the lip of the footpath. "I cannot keep up with you, Your Royal Highness. Please, won't you slow your pace just a mite?"

He whirled around unexpectedly. "Will you please stop referring to me as Your Royal Highness?" he snapped.

Elizabeth's mouth fell open. "How then . . . I mean, I thought . . . how shall I refer to you? Prince Leopold? Or simply . . . Leopold?"

"No!" His eyes widened and his outburst seemed to even startle himself. "Please . . . just . . . do not refer to me at all." He spun around and charged up the trail again.

"Well, I can't very well do that, now can I? We are both here at Windsor and our paths will certainly cross." Elizabeth scooped up her skirts again and raced after him.

He stilled his step, then stopped in the middle of the trail and raised his hands to his temples.

"Sir . . . I should not wish to present myself as indecorous in your presence," she added, aware that she was frustrating him but unable to stop her own chatter.

He lowered his hands and stood silently for several moments before slowly turning around to face her.

"*Sumner.*" His eyes were flashing, but with anger, frustration, or something else; she could not tell. "If you must address me privately, *Sumner.* Just please cease calling me Your Royal Highness while here at Windsor. I haven't got a crown upon my head, do I?" He looked away from her.

Elizabeth blinked several times. "Sumner," she repeated to him. She watched his shoulders ease as she spoke the name. "*Sumner.*"

He stared at her silently for a long moment before speaking again. "It . . . is a family name—one that only those closest to me use." He paused again. "Only those who do not truly know me would ever think of me as 'Leopold.' "

This made no sense to her at all, but she was honored that he considered her close enough to use a private family name rather than his title. As a commoner, she could not understand why being referred to as "Your Royal Highness" was so irksome to this man.

The only conclusion she could possibly give any credence was that Leopold was a minor prince as far as the world was concerned. While Princess Charlotte . . . well, she was the true daughter of the Prince of Wales—his *legitimate* daughter—unlike herself and her sisters. Whether the Royle sisters' noble lineage was ever proven or not, England would never see them as anything but . . . royal by-blows.

She only hoped that no one here at Windsor would reduce her complicated circumstance of birth to that horrid descriptor. At least not in Sumner's presence.

Blast. Sumner was off down the trail again. "Wait for me!"

Not far ahead an adjunct path that looped back in the direction of Cranbourne Lodge would adjoin the trail along the Thames. It was where he headed.

"Wait, Sumner."

Damn it all. Why the hell had he given her his Christian name? Because she had asked? Now that was showing mastery of counterinterrogation skills, wasn't it?

"Sumner. Slower, *please.*"

God, why must she keep saying his name? To remind him that he had completely forgotten his military schooling—forgotten his duty to the prince?

"Please, do not leave me alone out here in the forest," she called out. "I do not know the way back to the lodge."

He was acting quite the fool, wasn't he? His mind was muddled with so much emotion that not only had he forgotten his training as a soldier, but as gentleman as well. Sumner stilled abruptly. "I will not leave you, Elizabeth." He whirled around.

He had not realized that she had come up so fast upon him.

Surprise filled her eyes and she stumbled backward until she teetered on the lip of the trail. Her arms swung around in wild circles as she tried to retain her footing.

He lunged forward to grab her, but his sudden movement seemed to steal the last shreds of her concentration and she disappeared, feet over head over the side.

"Elizabeth!" Sumner yanked his sword from his waist and dove off the trail edge after her.

When Elizabeth opened her eyelids, she was peering up into Sumner's concerned gray eyes. It took her a moment more to realize that he cradled her in his strong, able arms . . . and a few breaths more for it to dawn upon her that both he and she were soaked to the skin.

What exactly had happened? She remembered falling, the river water rushing over her . . . then nothing. Until now.

"Thank God, you are breathing." He tipped his head back and gazed through the tree canopy to the blue sky above. Water rolled down his face and dripped from his angular jaw, to splash on her neck and trickle down between her breasts.

"What do you mean? Why wouldn't I be?" Elizabeth said, but her words met the cool air in a raspy grate. Her throat burned as surely as if she'd swallowed an entire goblet of brandy. She brought her hand to her throat. Her eyebrows inched toward the bridge of her nose in confusion. What had happened?

He looked down at her, and she saw that his eyes glistened with feeling. Before she could say another word, he lifted her head and nuzzled her wet cheek, then without warning moved his lips over hers tenderly, passionately.

She groaned at the sensation of his hot mouth, of his tongue slipping between her lips and writhing against her own.

This was not a kiss of relief. It was one of need.

He cupped her head in his large hand and turned her deeper into his kiss, claiming every part of her mouth, plunging and retreating in his conquest of her.

Elizabeth slid her hand around his neck and held him tightly, not wishing this moment to ever end.

Her eyes remained closed, but she felt herself being lowered. She opened her lids when her back settled on a blanket of soft moss and their mouths reluctantly parted.

Sumner tried to lean back from her then, but she would not release her hold around the back of his neck. She pulled him to her again, and to her amazement, he did not resist.

Instead, he rested his weight beside her and kissed her softly, pressing her deeper into the bed of spongy moss.

His left hand brushed a few damp strands of her hair from where they clung to her face. "Elizabeth . . . I . . . I am sorry."

"I slipped. That is all." She smiled. "You bear no fault for my . . . soggy gown this time." Her voice was barely a whisper, but words were not truly necessary just then. Their bodies did not seem to feel the need for them.

Elizabeth reached up, peeled back the soaked lawn shirt from Sumner's skin, then eased her palm inside to his warm muscled chest. Rolling toward him, she draped her arm around his waist and pulled her body firmly against his.

He was as hard as stone where his body abutted hers at the apex of her thighs. Heat ripped through her at the realization. Instead of shying, her body drove her on and she pushed against him, wanting more.

Wanting him closer. Wanting to touch him. Wanting him to touch her.

Sumner swore under his breath. Desire fired within him and he could not restrain himself any longer. His hands slid up over her hip and cupped a heavy breast, easing his thumb over her pert nipple, driving it to a hard peak.

She groaned huskily and his erection jerked.

Sumner's breathing sounded labored even to his own ears as he pressed her uppermost shoulder back to the ground. He did not waste an instant in coaxing her smooth breasts from the dampness of the low-cut French bodice and opening his mouth to draw in the pink-tipped cabochon. His teeth pulled gently at it as his slippery tongue flicked the peak of her breast in quick, darting licks.

Elizabeth arched her back and threaded her fingers through his hair, boldly moving him to her other breast as she gasped with pleasure.

He leaned up and kissed her, harder this time, dipping his tongue deep into her mouth, then sucking gently before sliding it out, and doing it all again and again.

She twisted at her hips and tried, without success, to press against his throbbing erection. He was nearly mindless with need of her, and his hand instinctually slid up beneath her sodden skirts.

Elizabeth gasped in a ragged breath as his fingers grazed her thigh, and then again as he raised his knee and nudged it between hers, lifting her chemise.

He gazed into her jewel green eyes as he parted her thighs to his touch. His palm pressed against the red curls between her legs and he eased one finger between her swollen female lips and into the heat of her wetness.

He was touching her most sensitive of places, his tongue lashing at hers, thrilling her—all at once. Elizabeth could feel his hardness flinching and throbbing against her hip in a motion that made her urgently want to pull him against her, inside of her.

His finger, wet with her slick essence, slid up and caressed the rose pearl between her lips in slow, rhythmic circles. She bucked against his hand as her excitement grew.

Her fingers dug into his shoulders. "I want to feel you inside of me, Sumner. *Please*."

"I—can't." His voice was deep. His muscles were tight and hard, and she knew his claim was naught but a lie. He wanted her as much as she wanted him. She knew this.

"Yes, you can. I—want—you." Elizabeth tried to pull back from his teasing finger, wanting him inside of her. *Him*. Now.

But he did not oblige her. Not exactly.

He kissed her again, and without removing his lips from her, pressed her legs wider still. She braced herself, holding her breath as she anticipated his hardened length entering her and piercing her as he breached her maidenhead.

Instead, she felt what seemed like two or three fingers sliding into her, plunging into her before slipping out of her heat, while his thumb maddeningly encircled her core.

The feeling of fullness, brought on by his teasing touch, was dizzying. She gasped against his mouth, arching her back, pressing her breasts against him.

A moan rode from her mouth into his as a pounding tide of ecstasy washed through her body. She clenched her thighs closed, trembling with pleasure, holding his hand still until she could think clearly again.

He kissed her gently, and after a few moments slid his fingers from her. She felt wetness on her thighs as a breeze stirred the hem of the skirts still bunched around her hips.

Sumner sat up and then pulled her skirts down to cover her thighs. He looked down at his fingers for a long moment, then at Elizabeth. She glanced down, too, and saw blood on his fingers.

"Elizabeth—" The expression in his eyes was nothing less than horror. "I didn't mean—"

She knew what he meant, and drew a shading hand to her head, closing her eyes. "I—I didn't feel any pain. I had always heard that it would hurt."

Sumner caught her wrist and drew it from her eyes. "I am sorry, Elizabeth. I thought if I was careful, gentle . . . if I didn't—" It seemed that his eyes were searching hers for the right words.

"It doesn't matter." Elizabeth leaned up and rested her weight behind her on her elbows. "You did nothing wrong, Sumner."

"Yes, I did, Elizabeth." It seemed as if the shame he evidently felt prevented him from looking at her.

"No, you didn't." She sat upright and laid her hand on his cheek. "You did nothing I did not want—that I did not ask for."

"But I ruined you."

"Ruined? Hardly." She huffed a small laugh. "Do you mean by touching me? What an over-noble goose you are being. And even if you had ruined me, it matters not at all. We will marry soon enough."

"No, Elizabeth. Why do you believe this?" Sumner came to his knees, then jerked to a stand. "Don't you understand? We cannot be together. I have my duty."

Elizabeth stared blankly at Sumner, unable to comprehend what he meant. Surely, he did not mean . . . after this morning . . . that he still sought Princess Charlotte's hand?

Surely not.

He reached down, took her arm and pulled her to her feet. Still he did not look at her. "Come along, Elizabeth. It is late. You must return to the lodge and dress. The princess will be rising soon."

A lump climbed up into her throat and threatened to choke her.

Why was this happening? Why?

Silently, blinded by burgeoning tears, she followed him down the trail.

He can't mean this.

He simply cannot.

In her heart and in her mind they were already wed. She would not give up now. She was a Royle, after all. And Royles did not give in. She would do as both of her sisters had done—when circumstances became difficult, they became creative. And so would she.

No matter what it took, she would simply have to change his mind, and she could do it. After all, Fate was on her side, she reminded herself. Fate was on her side.

Chapter 11

Cranbourne Lodge

Miss Margaret Mercer Elphinstone stood aghast. After hearing Elizabeth's story of her eventful morning, she clapped her hands over her mouth, stifling a gasp, as she peered down at Elizabeth, who sat before her dressing down as the lady's maid ordered a hot bath to be drawn for her. "Good heavens, dear, you might have drowned had he not saved you!"

Elizabeth plucked a telltale dead piece of brown moss from her hair and surreptitiously dropped it to the floor, then settled her soaked slipper down atop of it. "I really do not remember much at all about what happened. One moment I was walking on the river trail, and the next I was peering up into Sumner's gray eyes."

"Sumner?" Mercer's brow furrowed. "I thought you said—did you say . . . Sumner?"

Elizabeth nodded, then turned around to look up at Mercer. "The prince. He asked me to refrain from referring to him as Your Royal Highness while at Windsor, but 'twas in deference to Princess Charlotte's greater standing, I assume."

Mercer looked most pensive for some moments, and then her happy self seemed to emerge again. "Yes, I am sure you are completely right on the matter. I have heard his cousin call him Sumner once or twice. He must feel very at ease with you. Though, were I you, Elizabeth, I would not deign to be so familiar as to use the name in the presence of anyone other than we four."

"Yes, he said exactly the same thing. And I shall abide by his wishes, of course." When Elizabeth looked into the dressing mirror again, Mercer came and stood behind her, settling her hand on the rumpled sleeve of the red crimson gown.

She pushed back an errant sable lock behind her ear and looked down at Elizabeth's sodden gown. "Pity it is ruined. It must have looked stunning on you." She pinched a bit of the once lovely fabric between her fingers, then leaned around and peered at the neckline. "Elizabeth, you did say that this accident occurred . . . this *morning*, did you not?"

Elizabeth nodded as she passed a boar's bristle brush through her thick, tangled red hair. "I could not sleep, and arose early. I decided to take a short walk to pass the time until the princess awoke."

"And you chose this . . . this *gown* as your morning frock for your walk? Interesting selection, my friend."

"Oh, no. I did not choose it." A tiny broken twig caught at the end of her hair, and then unexpectedly shot like an arrow to the floor under the downward force of her brush. Elizabeth followed its trajectory with her gaze and tapped her slipper around the area, hoping to find it and nudge it beneath the hem of her gown. "I am but a miss from Cornwall with no knowledge of what might be considered *à la mode* for morning in the presence of a princess."

Mercer turned her head as the lady's maid entered the room with two other maids who toted great buckets of hot water for the hip bath. "Did you choose Miss Royle's *morning* gown this day, Aida?"

The lady's maid's cheeks flushed brightly and she cast her eyes to the floor. "No, miss. I—I just offered it as a choice. Miss Royle chose the gown herself."

Mercer let out a great sigh. "And who bade you to misdirect Miss Royle's choices in her dress? The gown is French and not suitable for morning at all—as you well know."

The lady's maid did not say a word, but shook her head slowly, adding a small shrug.

Mercer swiped a finger at her. "Never mind, Aida, I know the culprit and I shall speak with her directly. You cannot argue your orders, but nor will I rely on you to assist Miss Royle again. Be gone; send my Georgiana to tend to Miss Royle. At least I know *she* can be trusted."

With a sniffle, Aida slinked from Elizabeth's bedchamber.

Stunned at what she had just heard, Elizabeth was still staring at Mercer's reflection in the mirror when Aida closed the door. "Someone asked Aida to dress me inappropriately? Who would do such a thing, and why?" She turned on the bench to look directly at Mercer.

Mercer laughed resignedly. "Well, our dear Charlotte, of course."

"B-But, why would the princess wish to embarrass me so?" Elizabeth suddenly felt her household position was as precarious as her footing had been on the river trail.

"Oh, my innocent, Elizabeth." Mercer knelt before her and took her shoulders in her hands. "Charlotte is my dearest friend, but she can also be childish, ill-mannered, and mischievous at times. You would do well to be on your guard during your stay at Cranbourne Lodge."

"I don't understand, Mercer. Why would she wish for me to attend her as a lady's companion if she only wishes me ill fate?"

Mercer came to her feet quickly. "I did not say she wishes you ill. Only that she is mischievous and entirely too bored, being restricted to the confines of Windsor." She walked across the bedchamber, dunked her index finger into the bathwater and yanked it out. "Too hot. Best wait a few minutes." She looked back at Elizabeth. "At least it is better here than at Warwick House. There, I was fortunate to see a letter or two to Charlotte. But Leopold was sly enough to call upon her for tea there, though Prinny was in residence at Carlton House, only a stone's throw away. Courage or insanity—or could it truly be love?"

Love? Elizabeth's breath seemed to freeze in her lungs. "Prince Leopold called upon Princess Charlotte in London?" She was feeling increasingly uneasy, realizing that she had not considered that Leopold had a past with the princess.

"Oh, yes. He managed to slip out before Prinny heard the news, which was most fortunate, because Charlotte's father was roiling mad when he heard that a prince had taken tea with his daughter *alone*."

Elizabeth did not care for the way Mercer selectively intoned *alone*. Her scabbed temple began to throb and she rubbed all around the wound, trying to soothe her head as she struggled to find a way to discount Sumner's relationship with the princess.

"If the Prince of Wales knew that Prince Leopold called about his unwed daughter without his knowledge," she said, "which I would assume would be taken as a showing of disrespect, how can Sumner . . . er, Prince Leopold hope to win approval to marry the princess?"

Mercer laughed and fairly ran to Elizabeth. She snatched up her hand and squeezed it in her excitement. "Because Charlotte lied—she told her father that she was not alone and, furthermore, that the prince who called was Prince Augustus—not Leopold, as he had assumed." Mercer laughed. "And he believed her! Charlotte is a gifted storyteller when she chooses."

"Oh." Elizabeth's spirits sank. Only this morning she believed she and the prince were fated to be husband and wife. Now, she just felt like a fool.

Anne had been right. She should just give up this silly idea that she had dreamed the future, and learn to live the truth—that Prince Leopold of Saxe-Coburg would marry Princess Charlotte.

And there was nothing she could do to make her happily ever after with the prince of her dreams come true.

". . . but now that her father has given up his ridiculous notion of marrying the princess off to the Dutchman, he considers Cranbourne Lodge a secure enough prison for the time being. What a lark, eh? The one fortress he believes to be secure, and Prince Leopold walks right in."

Elizabeth felt a hard tug at her arm and realized she had been staring blindly into the mirror, feeling sorry for herself, and hadn't caught all of what Mercer had told her.

"Are you listening to me, Elizabeth?" Mercer asked, sounding most annoyed.

"Uh, yes." Elizabeth turned fully on her bench and leaned close to Mercer. "I was only wondering what Prinny would do if he caught

Prince Leopold and his cousin here at Cranbourne Lodge."

"Oh, he would be furious, certainly. Which is why they cannot stay any longer. It has been more than a week now. I tried to warn Charlotte about giving the prince refuge here at all, but she would not hear of it. Someone meant to kill the prince, and Charlotte was adamant that she offer him safety until other arrangements could be made. And, thankfully, they have been safe."

Elizabeth straightened her back. "Are you telling me that they . . . are leaving?"

"Yes." Mercer was immediately distracted, and said no more about the prince leaving Cranbourne, when her own lady's maid entered the room. "Georgiana, please assist Miss Royle. She is ready for her bath."

Georgiana displayed the beautiful dark hair, pale skin, and blue eyes of the Welsh. She also had very strong arms. Without asking Elizabeth to stand, she wrenched her from the bench. Turning her around, Georgiana began to strip Elizabeth of her hopelessly ruined gown.

Elizabeth was about to question Mercer further regarding the departure of the prince and his cousin when she heard Mercer giggle.

"I will leave you to your bath now." She

started for the door, but turned her head and peered over her shoulder before reaching it. "Charlotte will expect to see you in the morning room after she breaks her fast. Listen for the clock to sound the noon hour. Come then."

Mercer opened the door then turned yet again. "Georgiana, you will be sure to remove all of the moss from Miss Royle's hair, won't you?"

"Yes, miss."

"Good morning, Elizabeth . . ." she called out as she closed the door behind her.

"Good morn—" *Oh botheration. Why even say the words?* What had begun as the most brilliant of mornings was now the worst day of her life.

When Elizabeth entered the morning room, Princess Charlotte was draped across a settee with a damp folded flannel upon her forehead. One leg dangled from the seat, her blue satin slipper hanging precariously from her big toe. "Do close the door quickly, whoever you are," she moaned. "My head pains me."

"It is I, Miss Royle," Elizabeth whispered softly as she began to close the door, only to have an elderly liveried footman seize the handle from her and shut the door himself.

"Elizabeth!" Princess Charlotte yanked the

cloth from her head and dropped it on the floor.

A young maid scurried to the settee to scoop the cloth up in her hands, then returned to the corner of the room, where a footman poured water into a basin to begin soaking a fresh cloth for the princess.

"Mercer told me of your ordeal this morning. How dreadfully exciting it must have been for you!" the princess practically squealed.

"Actually, I could have made do without the excitement of this morning quite easily." Elizabeth smiled, then when she saw the princess didn't respond, she laughed.

Princess Charlotte seemed confused for a moment, until Mercer, who sat at a writing desk nearby, began to laugh uproariously. "Oh, you had us there, Elizabeth," Mercer said. "'Tis every woman's dream to be rescued by a tall, handsome nobleman."

Princess Charlotte laughed, too. "To think I thought you were serious. But I see now you were just having us on. Oh, you are most diverting, Elizabeth. But I beg you—tell us about the moment you awoke in his arms. Please, Elizabeth. My life is so horribly boring. Nothing so brilliant ever happens to me."

"Oh, pish posh, Charlotte," Mercer said. "You

rushed into the street and escaped a very angry Prince of Wales in a hackney—*a hackney!* Did you ever hear of anything so daring, Elizabeth?"

"Never!" Elizabeth exclaimed. When the princess looked to Mercer, Elizabeth crinkled her brow. *Riding in a hackney? That is Princess Charlotte's definition of exciting? What about meeting crowned royalty from every part of the world? Dancing at glittering balls?*

Having the most handsome prince in the world wishing to marry you?

"Still," Princess Charlotte amended, "last week Elizabeth was shot in the head—"

Elizabeth raised her chin. "Well, it only grazed my temple."

"—then, this morn, she falls off an embankment and is whisked away by the chilled water of the Thames. I ask you, who lives the more exciting life—this young woman from Cornwall or I?"

"W-Well, you do, by far," Elizabeth muttered.

The edges of Princess Charlotte's lips lifted. "Oh, you jest. You would never wish to trade your life for mine for even one day."

"Most certainly, I would!" Elizabeth exclaimed, knowing that for some reason, the princess needed to be assured that her life was one to be envied.

"You are just having me on, Elizabeth." Princess Charlotte glanced at Mercer, and for the first time since she entered the room, Elizabeth realized that another game was afoot. One she had until now been completely blind to.

"No, no." She wondered if even saying that was too much, for Princess Charlotte leapt to her feet, nearly tripping over her discarded slipper.

"Do you hear that, Mercer? She wishes to do it. She said so, just now." Princess Charlotte set her hand on her hips and gave her head a good firm nod.

"She hasn't agreed to anything, Charlotte, except that she would trade lives with you if given the opportunity." Mercer gave Elizabeth a glance loaded with wariness.

Charlotte walked over to Elizabeth, so close that the princess, being a shorter woman, stood nose-to-chin with her. "What if I gave you that opportunity, Elizabeth—for just one day?"

"Gave me the opportunity . . . to live your life for one day?" Elizabeth knew she stammered and sounded like a lingering echo off the cliffs of Cornwall, but she could not help herself.

"Yes." Princess Charlotte cast a sidelong glance at Mercer, before looking at Elizabeth with a dead serious expression. "Today, in fact."

"T-Today?" Elizabeth knew she could not deny the princess, but whatever Princess Charlotte had planned was making her feel very, very uneasy.

Elizabeth stood very still as Mercer fitted a turban to her head, taking care to stuff any exposed red tendril of hair under the matronly headdress. "This will never fool anyone. I am at least a head taller than the princess and our countenances are not remotely similar."

"Oh, they are more similar than you perhaps realize," Mercer responded. "And it shall work." She stood back and surveyed her work. "What think you, Charlotte?"

Princess Charlotte flung her upper body over the arm of the settee and let her arms dangle from it. "It will work perfectly," she whined. "Is it not time we go?"

"Almost." Mercer looked at Charlotte. "You are wrinkling your gown. You do wish to appear mature and in complete command of your life. A wrinkled gown will not communicate that to the Prime Minister."

Charlotte is meeting with the Prime Minister? Oh, dear. Elizabeth thought. *What was this ruse about and why had she agreed to it?*

Princess Charlotte slid back to her seat, and then stood to straighten her gown, before plopping back onto the settee.

Mercer looked critically at Elizabeth. "Now then, the modistes are French and have never met the princess. They have been instructed not to speak or look you directly in the face. They will only pin-fit the gowns, so there is no reason for you to speak at all, either."

Elizabeth felt as twisted with nerves as the coils of fabric around her head. "Wouldn't it be easier to simply schedule the modistes' work for another day?"

Princess Charlotte huffed. "No. You are missing the point, Elizabeth. I have informed my governesses that I will be engaged in fitting until sunset at least, and then I will retire early, for I am always thoroughly exhausted after having so many gowns fitted to my form."

"Your posing as Charlotte with the modistes, then retiring for the night, will give Charlotte the time she needs to travel to London to meet privately with Lord Liverpool and to return again," Mercer explained.

Elizabeth was thoroughly confused. "Why

must your meeting remain a secret? I do not understand. You are the Princess of Wales, after all."

Princess Charlotte huffed out her frustration with Elizabeth and shot a glance at Mercer, as if ordering her to deal with the dull miss from Cornwall on her behalf.

Mercer interceded. "Charlotte plans to inform the Prime Minister that she wishes to marry Prince Leopold."

"Oh, oh—allow me to show you both the oration I have planned." The princess folded her hands primly in her lap. "Lord Liverpool, my time at Cranbourne Lodge has been conducive to thought . . ." She glanced proudly at Elizabeth. "You gave me that bit." Princess Charlotte straightened her back and instantly wiped all emotion from her face. "I know it is my duty and in the best interest of my country, as the daughter of the Prince of Wales, to make an advantageous marriage. I, therefore, decided I should choose from those I consider to be the most appropriate candidates for a husband— and from these, I have selected. And I only wish to confirm that you—being far wiser than I in judging how such a match would affect the country politically—support my decision. Putting my own personal criteria aside, and those of my country first, I have chosen Prince Leopold of Saxe-Coburg."

Elizabeth stared at the princess, dumbfounded by what she was hearing. If Parliament supported a match between Charlotte and the prince, her own last threads of hope would snap.

Dark specks began to dance before her eyes. She dropped down upon a slipper chair and stared dully at Princess Charlotte, who was grinning from ear to ear.

"Oh, I know, Elizabeth," the princess said, addressing her bout of faintness. "My oration was powerful, indeed. I was most convincing, was I not?" She looked to Mercer for her reaction. "I thought the bit about seeking his wise counsel was a perfectly manipulative touch, do you not agree, Mercer?"

"I do indeed." Mercer looked down at Elizabeth, who was still sitting stupidly in the center of the room. "Oh, good heavens, Elizabeth. Did you not just hear my warning to Charlotte? Stand up, before you've wrinkled that gown."

Elizabeth rose, but immediately felt herself teeter and fall.

When she opened her eyes, after losing consciousness for the second time that day, Mercer was standing over her looking most concerned.

"Are you well? Perhaps you ought to lie on the settee and rest for a time before the modistes arrive. Your body has surely been taxed from your accident today."

"I am well. I believe I just need to sit for a moment," Elizabeth replied softly, for she could not admit that hearing Princess Charlotte's plan to address Lord Liverpool was far more of a blow to her body than plunging into the waters of the Thames.

"Do not worry overmuch, Mercer. This turn actually enhances our most excellent plan for the ruse," Charlotte was saying. "For it gave me another idea. I will be sure to have Aida report to the governesses that I was so horribly fatigued, yet did not seem the least ill, that I collapsed and require rest. Perfect! Oh, you are a wonder, Elizabeth."

Mercer helped Elizabeth into her chair. "Shall I remain here with you?"

Elizabeth's mind was beginning to clear and an excuse for fainting in the presence of the princess somehow made its way through the fog in her brain. "No, no, I was simply unaccustomed to wearing long stays. They are much more restrictive to breathing than the short, aren't they?"

At the sound of the carriage wheeling its way

to the front of the house, Princess Charlotte rushed to the window. "Quick, Mercer, give me your maid's cloak and gypsy bonnet. It is time."

"Yes, it is." Mercer lifted the bundle sitting on the edge of a glossy table near the door and handed it to the princess, who excitedly settled the bonnet upon her head and swirled the cloak around her shoulders, obscuring from view the vibrant blue satin gown edged with layers of frothy ivory lace. "Now take a deep breath, my dear Charlotte. For today may well be the single most significant day of your young life."

The princess grinned excitedly and drew a lung-filling breath, then, with a twinkle in her eye, turned and dashed for the door with Mercer at her heels.

At the door, Mercer turned to Elizabeth one last time. "I am to understand that you have agreed to loyally assume your role as the princess on this important day?"

"You may count on me," Elizabeth said confidently, though she felt anything but confident. "I am the princess's most loyal servant."

She knew there was no possible way she could carry off this ill-thought-out ruse.

Chapter 12

The Gamekeeper's cottage
Cranbourne Lodge

Leopold crossed one leg over the other. "The princess is like a golden filly, full of spirit and energy, but sadly, completely without discipline, control, and restraint." He rested his elbow on the arm of the chair and gestured, palm up, to Sumner, who sat in the companion chair a stride away. "The only way to bring out my dear Charlotte's full potential, her grace and elegance, is by breaking her."

"I have not heard one word from you about your attraction to her, or of love," Sumner said. The acrid scent of the cold hearth beside him irritated his nose, but he did not move away. He needed an answer. "How can you wish, so keenly, to marry her? I do not understand."

Leopold shook his head, as if he were about to needlessly explain his obvious reasoning in this matter to a child. "Cousin, I am the first to admit that after meeting Princess Charlotte in London last year, I had no reason to believe I stood a chance to win her hand. She was in love with another, and her father still had aspirations, and still might, that she marry the Dutchman, William of Orange." He lifted a bruised hothouse orange from the small bowl of fruit on the side table, gave it a little squeeze, then returned it to its place. By the slightly damaged look of it, it was not the first time Leopold handled the orange in that manner.

Sumner rose and refilled Leopold's glass, then returned the decanter to the table, earning a pleased sigh from his cousin.

"Everything changed the moment I received a letter from Mercer advising me that if I still had aspirations regarding Charlotte I should return to London directly. The princess would very likely respond favorably to my attentions."

"But you did not return then?"

"Certainly not, our regiment was on active service at the time and Napoleon was on the march with an army a quarter million strong,"

Leopold said, making Sumner feel that his question had been taken as a personal affront to the prince's character. He lifted a sharp gaze to Sumner. "I do have my duty, after all."

Sumner narrowed his eyes, wondering if Leopold's comment was a not so subtle reminder meant for him. But he would put the interests of Saxe-Coburg first. He would sacrifice his happiness, perhaps even his life, to help Leopold claim Princess Charlotte's hand in marriage. "Why did you not inform me of this letter?" He leaned forward and awaited his cousin's reply. There had never been any secrets between them since they were children.

Except one—one very large secret.

"Because Charlotte was rumored to be extremely fickle. I knew that to come rushing to her was the surest way to see her shy from my advance." Leopold smiled to himself. "And it seems as though my delay was the right decision. After Waterloo and my subsequent installation in Paris, I received another letter from Mercer, informing me that Charlotte had set her heart on marrying me. My delay in contacting her and crossing the Channel made me far more desirable. Why, I do not know. The princess is a romantic, it seems." He drank deeply from the crystal.

Sumner gazed down into his untouched glass of brandy. "You knew, however, that now was the time to slip away from Paris to solidify your claim for her hand."

"I did." Leopold uncrossed his legs and leaned toward Sumner, pinging the side of his glass agitatedly with his index finger. "I beg you, do not judge me for what you do not understand as clearly as I. My family lost vast holdings to Napoleon, and we are only now able to reclaim what was taken. But I learned a valuable lesson from this. A minor prince, of good manner and quite handsome features"—he grinned over his glass at Sumner—"has the ability to make an advantageous marriage and never risk his family's ancestral holdings again."

"I see." Sumner lifted his gaze and peered directly at Leopold. The next question was very important. "So despite appearances to contrary, there is no love between the two of you."

"Oh, no." Leopold chuckled confidently. "She loves me quite dearly, or has convinced herself that she does. And why shouldn't she?"

"But *you* do not love her."

Leopold dropped his head back against the rest. "Once she is brought into line, I am sure I will one day come to love her immensely. But my feelings have no place in this matter. My duty to my family, and the principality, must come first." He paused for several moments, adding weight to his next words. "I know you, of all men, can understand that, Sumner."

Sumner remained silent and nodded solemnly.

Indeed he did. All too well.

Cranbourne Lodge
Princess Charlotte's bedchamber

No less than nine French drapers and modistes crowded about Elizabeth, pinching fabric around her waist. Twisting and tugging her arms this way and that, pinning and poking, and accidentally stabbing her thrice with their stitching needles, they worked to ensure that each gown, riding habit, walking dress, and morning frock fit . . . perfectly.

Elizabeth's own slim frame.

Not Princess Charlotte's shorter, more curved, royal figure.

They were only meant to pin the gowns, not complete the fitting with needles and thread. Charlotte had explained this quite clearly to her. Worried over this problem, Elizabeth tried to complain that she required more room for movement, and that they should only pin the fabric, but her French was limited to a few fashionable phrases, courtesy of Lady Upperton, and those were sadly insufficient to communicate her needs. She snatched up a cushion of pins and held it out to them, but the modistes only took the pins from her and set them out of her reach. Waving her arms and patting her waist, she attempted to gesticulate to help them understand her words, but this attempt, too, was to no avail. They would not look directly at her, for they had been instructed to avoid doing so.

After enduring seven hours of their torture without making herself understood even once, Elizabeth ultimately decided that the princess had to have anticipated that using a taller, thinner woman as a dressmaker's form for pin-fitting would result in longer, more slender-cut gowns and ensembles. And la, she could not stop them from their final fittings. They were simply too quick and efficient.

There was simply no way to stop the busy modistes without abruptly marching from the bedchamber and destroying the illusion that she was Princess Charlotte. And she was not so daring as to draw the moody princess's wrath by doing that.

No, she would adhere herself to the princess's plan and simply hope for the best.

When the crickets began to chirp as night fell, and the modistes had departed, Elizabeth sat gazing out of the princess's bedchamber window as the last glimmers of orange light sunk down beneath the line of trees at the horizon.

There was knocking at the bedchamber door. Elizabeth looked up and waited. Three more raps. It was the signal from Aida, who had been ordered to undertake sentry duty, to warn Elizabeth that she should turn away from the door so her evening meal might be brought in without the bearer realizing she was not the true princess.

Elizabeth remained motionless and continued to stare out into the cloudless night sky. She sniffed as the aroma of beef drifted past her nose, making her empty stomach growl. It was sad that eating her beef would be her greatest diversion all afternoon and evening.

After just one day of pretending to be the princess, Elizabeth already pitied Princess Charlotte. Even she could hardly believe it.

She, the commoner from Cornwall, pitied the grand princess. The same woman who would put a quick end to her dream. The young royal who, even now, was working to garner support of Parliament for her own marriage to Prince Leopold.

But pity her, Elizabeth did.

Cranbourne Lodge, so large and beautiful, was naught but a gilded cage imprisoning the young royal. Freedoms were few, and only, from what Elizabeth had witnessed herself, claimed by the princess more often through deceit and trickery of others. From all accounts from house staff and even her closest confidante, Mercer, it was a sad, tiresome life the princess led most of her days.

Princess Charlotte's own mother, unable to endure it, had fled the court and her marriage to the Prince of Wales, for a life of freedom on the continent. No wonder the princess was so ill-mannered, Elizabeth concluded. She would be, too, if she had to endure life as a prisoner— even if she could wear a glittering tiara atop her head.

Suddenly, she realized that not once had she seen the tiara that the prince had sent Princess Charlotte from Hamilton and Company. She leapt to her feet and quietly began searching the princess's bedchamber, until she came upon a box marked with the company's name tucked beneath the princess's dressing table.

She lifted the lid of the box, holding her breath, hoping upon hope the tiara was inside. Her tiara. The one Sumner had placed on her head. Her heart thudded hard as she untied the lacings of the linen bag inside the box and reached inside. Her fingers alighted at once upon cool stone and metal and snatched it up.

Carefully, she lifted the tiara from its hiding place and stared at it admiringly for several minutes, before sitting down at the dressing table, intent on doing the unthinkable.

She peered into the mirror and imagined Sumner was holding the tiara in his hands as she lowered it down atop her head. She exhaled softly as she beheld her image.

Quietly, she studied her reflection, wanting to hold onto the memory of the day she first met her prince. Wanting to preserve it, before the princess returned this night and the moment was twisted from the grasp of Fate and placed into Parliament's hands.

A tear budded in the innermost corner of one of her eyes, for she knew it was already too late. By now Princess Charlotte had obtained Lord Liverpool's promise of support. It was only a matter of time before Prinny would be convinced to do the same—and Prince Leopold would marry Princess Charlotte.

Elizabeth gulped back a sob as she whisked the tiara from her head and replaced it in the box beneath the dressing table. She propped her elbows on the table's surface then rested her face in her hands and let the tears she had fought off come at last.

Shortly after midnight, Elizabeth decided it would be permissible to return to her own bedchamber. Princess Charlotte and Mercer would no doubt be returning from London very soon, after all. Quietly, she eased open the door, to find Aida slumped against the doorjamb. The maid's mouth was agape and a slight snore met the air with her every exhalation.

Elizabeth squeezed her shoulder, calming the startled maid as she awoke with a gentle "Hush." Elizabeth settled a quieting finger over her lips, then waved good night and headed up another flight of stairs to her own bedchamber.

She changed from the princess's dressing gown and into her own, then sat at the edge of her tester bed. She was too restless to sleep, however. She could not rid her mind of upsetting thoughts of a future without Sumner. Rising from the tester bed, she paced the bedchamber before finally realizing that, lud, if she remained inside the life-stifling lodge a moment longer, she would surely scream.

Stepping into her slippers, Elizabeth hurried

from her bedchamber, down the dark staircase, through the doorway, and then raced out into the night.

A light breeze parted the opening of her dressing gown and blew the sides behind her like great gleaming banners of blue. She didn't bother to conceal her silk chemise, for no one but a distraught lady's companion would be about at this hour.

For the second night, the moon, set on a bejeweled black velvet blanket, was bright and nearly perfectly round. She sighed, remembering standing at the edge of the garden with Sumner just one night before and seeing the same image above.

She had been so full of hope. So filled with excitement for the growing possibility of a life together with Sumner.

But everything had changed now.

It was a fool's decision she made then, Elizabeth knew, but with the moon as her guide, she walked from the lodge until she met the river trail. Why she walked such a dangerous trail now, she didn't know. It was as if she wanted to go to the last place she and Sumner were together . . . alone.

It seemed something beckoned her, called her there.

The nearer she came to the bend in the trail, the deeper she fell into mourning what might have been. Her ribs felt contracted, the backs of her eyes stung with heat.

Her sense of eminent loss grew with every step, until she could smell the Thames, hear its rush just below the trail. Tears slipped down her cheek as she rounded the path's curve and was about to come upon the very place where she and Sumner had lain. Together.

She held her breath until she could see around the trees to the stretch of soft moss. Their bed.

Then she stopped.

She squinted against the moonlight, but there was no question. There, in a bath of silver moonlight, was her prince.

"Sumner."

Sumner was sitting on the soft bed of moss, one arm wrapped around a raised knee, when he heard his name upon the breeze over the roar of the river.

At first he thought it a game of the night and the rushing, gurgling Thames, but then he saw her, his Elizabeth, standing in a blue finger of moonlight.

He blinked, unable to truly believe what his eyes beheld. It was if his earnest wish to say good-bye had somehow conjured her from her bed to this moonlit spot.

"Elizabeth?" he murmured.

"Sumner!" She ran to him, arms outstretched.

Pushing up to his feet, he stepped forward and met her warm embrace. Without conscious thought, his arms came up and wrapped around her. She trembled against him, and he bundled her even more tightly.

He didn't ask her why she was on the river trail just now. It didn't matter. What did was that she was here, in his arms, where he wanted her to be. Needed her to be.

So that, God help him, he could tell her good-bye. A stab of pained reluctance cut into his heart. "Elizabeth, I—"

She leaned back a bit, so she could look up at him. Tears wet her cheeks and sparkled in her eyes. "Do not say it. I already know," she said, her voice full with emotion. "Princess Charlotte has gone to see the Prime Minister." A sob broke from her lips and punctured her next words.

Sumner pulled her toward him again. "Shh, Elizabeth, do not cry, please," he whispered into her hair, which in the bright moonlight resembled a bloodred cloak over her shoulders.

"I—I can't stop. I know she is there to gain Parliament's support—and what that means to us." She drew in a jagged breath.

"Hush now, my sweet one." He cupped her chin in one hand and gently kissed her forehead.

She raised her chin higher, and he kissed away a teardrop that had begun to roll down her cheek. And then, placing her fingertips on the edge of his jaw and tilting his mouth to hers . . . she pressed her tender mouth to his lips.

"I thought you'd gone. That I would never see you again . . . that I would soon become naught but a forgotten moment to you." Her words felt like a warm breath against his parted lips.

"I could never forget you, Elizabeth. Never." He felt an ache in his chest. He wished with all his heart he could spare this pain by telling her the truth—that he was not Leopold. That it was his sworn duty to protect the prince, his cousin, no matter the cost.

"And I couldn't bear the thought of never seeing you again. I love you, Sumner." She turned and looked up and into his eyes. "I love you."

His breath caught in his throat and searing heat surged into his eyes. Sumner pushed back from her and turned away. He couldn't let her see him like this. So vulnerable.

Her hand touched his side, and he lurched forward until he came to an ancient oak tree. He leaned his head and a hand against the tree for support.

No one had ever said that to him before.

Ever.

He had not been prepared for the overwhelming effect of those simple words. For the way it shook both his mind and his body so disablingly.

"Please, don't leave me." Her voice came from only a short distance behind him, but she might have been a league away just then. "Sumner, please."

"I have to go." His voice broke and so he hardened his next words. "It is my sworn duty."

The thrash of dried leaves beneath her feet heralded her arrival behind him. Soft hands eased around his waist and she laid her head against his back. He did not turn around. Could not, just now.

"If you must go, remember that I love you." Her voice was soft, but even now he could hear the rawness in her tone. "And if you can, some-day, please, come back for me."

Sumner's body stiffened at her words.

Come back for her.

His fingers dug into the bark of the oak. Once the agreement for marriage was secured and Leopold safely back in Paris—he could come back for Elizabeth. Yes, he owed the family much and was prepared to sacrifice his life for Leopold, to protect him as the prince carried out his own duty. But once Leopold was safe, he could resign his commission and, though until now he'd never considered a life apart from the military, he could leave it.

He could come back for her.

He could begin life anew.

Sumner turned around so quickly that her arms remained around him. He clutched her to him and held her tightly.

"I will come back for you," he said, louder than he had intended. "I will."

Elizabeth turned her glistening eyes up at him. Tears rushed anew down her smooth cheeks, but this time the tears were of happiness.

He bent and kissed her deeply, feeling more joy than he had ever known.

Chapter 13

Elizabeth was reluctant to return to Cranbourne Lodge, even though she knew she must. Her heart felt weighted with worry, now that she and her prince had left the sanctuary of the forest, that the thorns of reality would puncture her dream of the future they would share and shred his promise to come back for her.

Sumner brushed a lock of hair from her face and kissed her gently at the door of the lodge just as the sky began to change from darkest ebony to a cool gray. "Trust me, Elizabeth. I will come back for you. Believe in me. We will be together. Somehow. Someday. Soon."

Elizabeth nodded, already feeling the smile she'd affixed to her lips for Sumner begin to dissolve. She peered up into his gray eyes, but fixed her attention on the vibrant blue ring surrounding them. She had to believe in her dream. Had to believe in Sumner and in their growing love. She had to have faith. "I trust you, Sumner. Come back for me . . . soon."

She tilted her head back and their lips met again in a kiss full of promise. Wishing never to let him go, her arms had wrapped around him, when she heard the bolts being released on the door. Her eyes widened. The doors had been locked sometime after she left. "Sumner. I love you," she whispered. "But you must go. Hurry."

He leaned in and pressed his lips to hers in a heady kiss just one last time, then turned and disappeared into the morning fog hovering over the lawn.

The old footman opened the door just then, sleepily adjusting the white wig atop his head. He nodded to her. He stepped back, and without a word allowed her to enter the lodge.

As Elizabeth slowly ascended the stairs to her bedchamber and slipped beneath her coverlet, a blissful smile mellowed upon her lips. She would believe in Sumner.

Yes, he would leave for London this day for Sir Henry's Curzon Street home, where he and his cousin had been invited to stay in seclusion, if they wanted, for a fortnight.

But she no longer fretted over Sumner's leaving.

She closed her eyes with the taste of Sumner's kiss still sweet on her lips. Sleep would come easily to her now—for she knew her dream would come true.

Sumner had promised they would be together somehow, and no matter what happened, he would come back for her.

When the clock in the passage tinged ten of the clock, Elizabeth opened her eyes to find Princess Charlotte sitting at her bedside, her arms tightly folded and her mouth set in a hard grimace.

"You have returned." Elizabeth lurched upright. "Were you successful?"

The princess glared. "None of my gowns will fit me now. Aida suspected as much, but of course I was not convinced. But then she attempted to dress me in two, one after the other, and neither could be laced closed. The dresses were only meant to be pin-fitted—not finished!"

"Oh . . ." Elizabeth sighed. "I do apologize, but the French modistes insisted upon fitting the gowns and ensembles perfectly. I have no French, and was quite unable to convince them to stop once the pinning had been completed or even to leave more room for freedom of movement."

Princess Charlotte did not speak, but her eyes grew darker with anger.

"I was quite concerned, Your Royal Highness, until I realized, in your wisdom in concocting the plan, you must have considered the differences in our shapes and decided that the gowns were the price of your escape to London." Worry began to snake up Elizabeth's spine. The princess was not softening.

"You decided that, did you?" Princess Charlotte leapt up from the slipper chair. She widened her stance and set her fists on her hips. "Despite the queen's intervention on my behalf, and Henry Brougham's less than persuasive oration on the need to increase my portion, my income has not been increased. It already is not adequate to support my mode of living—let alone my staff."

"I—I was not aware." Elizabeth swallowed hard.

"I am afraid you are too great an expense, Miss Royle." Princess Charlotte whirled and stalked heavily toward the door.

"I do apologize most humbly—" Elizabeth began, but Princess Charlotte was not listening.

Before leaving the bedchamber, the princess jerked around. Her cheeks were glowing like a setting sun and she fairly spat as she delivered her next message. "*We* shall return to Warwick House within the week. *You* will return to Berkeley Square, where you will not have the opportunity to make any other costly decisions on my behalf."

Seizing the door, without the aid of the footman reaching for the handle, the princess slammed the bedchamber door closed behind her.

Elizabeth sat, startled, for several moments.

Then she leaned back against the pillow and smiled.

What did this matter? Like her prince, she was going back to London.

Her happily ever after was close at hand. She could feel it.

Cavendish Square
Lady Upperton's library

"Well, dove, I am happy to have you back with us all once more, but I daresay, do you think angering the princess was the best way to achieve your homecoming?" Lady Upperton glanced sidelong at each of the Old Rakes, who sat upon the settee in a perfect row like dark-plumed ravens.

"Angering the princess was bound to happen. Making her furious was inevitable. She is highly volatile and most childish." Elizabeth shook her hands before her, hoping they would understand. "It was only a matter of time."

"I daresay, her good opinion of you is likely gone forever. She is well known within Society for holding a grudge." Lady Upperton chewed her lower lip with worry. "I pray she does not seek to soil your name."

Elizabeth did not care in the least what the princess thought of her, though she knew she ought to. Princess Charlotte could easily make her a pariah in Society—if she was able to escape her cage long enough to do so. "I vow, I am not the only miss who irks her. In fact, the only woman she seems able to tolerate is Mercer—I mean, Miss Elphinstone—and why she tolerates the princess is beyond my comprehension."

"Is it possible, Elizabeth, that your feelings toward Princess Charlotte could be colored red by your own jealousy?" Gallantine asked as he rubbed the stubbled gray growth on his chin.

"M-My jealousy?" Elizabeth was astounded that he could suggest such a thing. "If anything, it was she who harbored feelings of jealousy for me. After all, I hold the prince's heart."

Lord Lotharian met Lady Upperton's concerned gaze. After a moment of silent utterances between the two, he addressed Elizabeth. "Parliament supports a marriage between Princess Charlotte and Prince Leopold. The only hindrance is Prinny's blessing, which he will surely grant in time."

"He will not marry her." Elizabeth smiled smugly. "He loves me."

"Dear gel," Lilywhite said, absently rubbing his round belly, "even in this day, love and marriage are not mutually exclusive."

"But I told you about my dream." Elizabeth exhaled a frustrated breath. "Please, believe me. We will marry."

Gallantine shrugged. "There is the possibility that the gel could be right. Her dreams have come . . . close to coming to fruition. And the prince has yet to receive Prinny's blessing, and there are those who maintain that he still desires a marriage between his daughter and William of Orange." He gave an inappropriate chuckle.

"What amuses you so, Gallantine?" Lotharian's hawkish eyebrows inched toward his nose.

"Only that if the Regent manages such a

union, he can pack the gel off to the Netherlands and be done with her and her antics. The people love her better than him, and he is no doubt well aware of this."

Lady Upperton scowled and shook a tiny finger most impolitely at him. "Do not encourage Elizabeth's ideas, Gallantine. What are you thinking?"

"I am only saying it is possible the young prince does have a fondness for our gel, here. And it might be remiss of us not to explore this possibility." Gallantine rose stiffly from the settee and circled the group as he considered his own statement. "After all, we did swear to Royle we'd see to his daughters' happiness and welfare—which we all agree includes marriage. What better match could we possibly achieve for Elizabeth than to a prince, eh?"

Elizabeth realized she had found an ally in her quest for the prince. "The prince and his cousin were invited to stay at Sir Henry Halford's house on Curzon Street. Mercer had let it slip that Princess Charlotte orchestrated several interviews for him with the Duke of Kent and several ministers in Parliament to help build support for a union." Elizabeth suddenly felt it difficult to draw breath. "While I believe that the prince will choose me, I believe, too, that I must do my part. If I can find a way to meet with the prince, even once more before he returns to Paris for a time—"

Gallantine began to nod. "Yes, yes. There is the dinner party at Sir Henry's house Thursday evening." A sly expression lifted his sagging features. "Miss Elizabeth and I have been invited to attend."

"Yes, yes, you're right, my lord." Elizabeth shot up from her chair. "Surely the prince and his cousin will be in attendance."

"I have an uneasy feeling about this, I must admit." Lotharian thrummed his fingers on his knee, but glanced once or twice up at Elizabeth, who did her best to plead her case with her eyes. "Will his protégé, Manton, attend as well?"

Gallantine nodded. "He did mention that he would also attend. I have a notion he fancies our Elizabeth."

Elizabeth colored. "Mr. Manton is handsome and good, and true, he is heir to a viscountcy— but . . . I love Sumner."

Lotharian's attention pricked up the moment she uttered the name. "Who have you fallen in love with?"

"*Sumner*," Elizabeth said very slowly, wondering if the old man's hearing was not quite as keen as it once was.

"Oh, you are referring to the prince's cousin, young Lord Whitevale." Lotharian's gaze seemed to bore into her. "His father was once a fellow member at White's. Can't say that I knew him well though. Don't know that anyone did."

"No, no. Not his cousin . . . *the prince*. Sumner, he told me, is the name only those who know him intimately call him," Elizabeth replied. "It is some sort of family name, I believe."

"And he allows you to address him as Sumner?" Lady Upperton asked, with a most curious expression upon her round face.

"Yes. He requested it." Elizabeth felt her cheeks heat. "We . . . we have become very close, Sumner and I."

"Sumner, eh?" Lotharian leaned his elbow on his knee and bent slightly, to twirl a few strands of one of his thick gray eyebrows. He glanced up at Lady Upperton, who was nodding her head madly.

"I say, I think she must attend the dinner party." She glanced around at the others for agreement. "After all, the prince will likely be in attendance."

Lotharian skewered Gallantine with his gaze. "My good man, do you think you can secure an additional invitation for Elizabeth's sponsor? I think it appropriate that Lady Upperton be there since, from what I have heard, the other guests will be gentlemen."

"I am sure I can manage something, Lotharian," Gallantine said.

"Good, good. I agree that Elizabeth should at least have her chance with . . . Sumner." Lotharian shifted his intense gaze to Elizabeth. "Isn't that what you called him, dear?"

"Yes." Elizabeth surveyed Lord Lotharian and then Lady Upperton through narrowed eyes.

Something was not as it seemed, she just did not know what it was. But never mind. She was going to see her prince on Thursday.

Berkeley Square

Elizabeth sat at the scrubbed pine kitchen table reviewing the household budget and Mrs. Polkshank's market list. She was quick to note that during the short time she'd been at Cranbourne Lodge, expenses were even higher than before she left. But today she wouldn't let it worry her overmuch.

She was just so happy to be home, with her own responsibilities and tasks to undertake, instead of sitting idly in royal splendor.

Handing the market list along with a small clinking pouch of coins to Mrs. Polkshank, she started from the kitchen to see to Great-aunt Prudence.

Mrs. Polkshank accepted the list and the pouch, but appeared utterly confused. "What, you ain't wishin' to argue the cost of bread and beef?"

Elizabeth stopped and turned. "Not today, Mrs. Polkshank." She cast her a brilliant smile and then started up the stairs for the parlor.

She found Great-aunt Prudence in her favorite chair, positioned between the hearth and the window looking out upon Berkeley Square. She was wide-awake.

A small book lay upon the old woman's lap, which she tried to hide between her leg and the arm of the chair when Elizabeth entered the room. She gave Elizabeth a toothy grin, while her palsied hand fumbled to conceal the book more fully.

"Chatter in the house says you will be attending dinner with Sir Henry Halford," the old woman said.

Elizabeth pulled another chair close and sat down near her great-aunt. "Yes, among others—including my prince." She lifted her lips demurely.

"How do you find that eel-backed baronet, Sir Henry?"

Elizabeth chuckled at that. "Good heavens, where did you hear that description of him?"

"From a colleague of your father's, another surgeon to the king, Wardrop was his name," Prudence said. "Granted, this was years ago. Still, he didn't trust him, and I only mentioned it because perhaps you shouldn't either, gel."

"I have had no occasion to trust or mistrust Sir Henry, I assure you." What a thing for her great-aunt to say. "How are you feeling today, dear? You seem exceedingly well."

"As well as a woman of my years can feel, I suspect."

Elizabeth reached down between the old woman and the armrest and withdrew the book she had placed there. "I see you have been reading." She started to open the tome when her great-aunt caught her hand.

"Cherie brought me the *Times* this morning. I have been reading that, too. The newspaper reports that Liverpool and Parliament support a marriage between the princess and *your* prince."

Elizabeth set the book down in her own lap and shot a glance out the window. "It is nothing."

"No, it is a *great* something. He and the princess only need that gargoyle Prinny's consent." She poked a bony finger into Elizabeth's knee to make her point.

"He won't marry her," Elizabeth insisted.

"He will. It is his duty to his country."

Elizabeth was stunned. "Why did you mention . . . 'his duty'?"

"Because that is the way of it with men, especially those trained in the military. It is always the way." Great-aunt Prudence leaned forward and tapped her finger on the small book upon Elizabeth's lap. "Open it. There is a card inside."

Elizabeth wasn't sure what Prudence was about, but she did as directed and opened the book. In the center she found an invitation and a dried, faded rose bloom. She looked up at Prudence's all too serious face. "I don't understand."

Turning her eyes downward to the yellowed card in her hand, she began to read. It was an invitation to a wedding breakfast, to celebrate the union of Miss Prudence Smythe and the Honorable Mr. Clarence Winks. She raised her eyes to look at her aunt for further explanation.

Prudence's faded blue eyes were filled with tears, but not a single one breached her lashes. "He went off to battle that summer. It was his *duty*, he told me. And then he was killed exactly one year later in the battle for Quebec City, alongside his men, and General Wolfe himself."

Elizabeth felt tears rush into her own eyes. "And you have been—"

"Alone, ever since." She forced a smile of strength. "That is, until you and your sisters came to stay with me." She squeezed Elizabeth's hand as best she could. "What I want you to understand is that while our men will love us with all their hearts, when it comes to a matter of love or duty for country, a man's honor will always force him to choose . . . *duty*."

An aching tightness clutched at Elizabeth's heart. Quickly, before she dissolved into tears, she carefully settled the card and the rose between the pages of the book and returned it to her great-aunt.

"Thank you for telling me this," Elizabeth began, her voice breaking, "but I have to believe we will be together in the end. I cannot endure a lifetime without him. I simply cannot."

Curzon Street
Residence of Sir Henry Halford

The dinner planned by Sir Henry was more intimate than Elizabeth had anticipated. No one from the Royal College of Physicians was present, as he had told both her and Gallantine when he first offered his invitation at Almack's.

And no one, except for Sir Henry, and possibly his protégé Mr. Manton, seemed content with the seating order.

Lord Gallantine sat at one end of the great rectangular table, which seemed to greatly annoy him due to his inability to hear Sir Henry, who sat at the other end. Elizabeth was seated between the prince's cousin, Whitevale, and Mr. Manton, while Sumner and Lady Upperton sat directly across from them.

"It is no secret, Miss Royle, that rumors abound through Society that you and your sisters might be the illegitimate daughters of the Prince of Wales and Maria Fitzherbert."

Elizabeth fairly lurched in her chair. Sir Henry seemed to have no idea that he was labeling her a bastard at the dinner table.

"There are many who maintain that Prinny and Mrs. Fitzherbert were married, Sir Henry." Lord Gallantine tightened his grip so strongly around his knife that the blood seemed to drain from his hand. "Some have seen proof of that union."

Elizabeth forced a smile. "You knew my father, Sir Henry. He was a royal surgeon, like you."

"Yes, yes, but the *story*," Sir Henry prodded, "is there any evidence to support it? Rumor has it that Royle had proof of some sort."

Lady Upperton's expression left no doubt to Elizabeth that she did not like the direction the conversation had taken. "Sir Henry, please think about the implications of your questions. Miss Royle is a guest in your home this night."

Sir Henry grimaced, then applied a slick, oily smile to his lips. "I do beg your pardon, Miss Royle. The people do love a good story, true or not."

"Yes, they do, Sir Henry," Sumner answered. "But, I think I speak for most of us in this room this eve, gossip holds no place in educated society."

Sir Henry blanched slightly, and then his expression changed abruptly. "I prefer true stories of excitement, myself." He looked to Elizabeth quite suddenly. "Care for some salt, Miss Royle?" he asked. His heavy left eyebrow twitched in anticipation.

"No, thank you," Elizabeth replied, thinking in all her life no host had ever suggested she salt her food.

"Are you certain?"

"Quite." It was then that Elizabeth noticed that, unlike the other silver salt cellars at each guest's setting, hers was white, and while round, was not perfectly formed.

Sir Henry's gazed remained focused on Elizabeth, completely unnerving her. Finally, when it seemed that if she did not sample the salt he would not ever remove his attention from her, she lifted her hand to reach for the spoon in the cellar.

Mr. Manton's left hand shot out and caught hers. Then, gently, he pressed her palm to the table. "Please don't, Miss Royle."

Elizabeth saw Sumner's back straighten and his brow draw low the moment Manton touched her. For a brief instant she thought he would leap across the table for Manton, but he did nothing more. She turned and looked at Manton questioningly.

Sir Henry laughed aloud. "Now, now, Manton, you are spoiling my fun."

"If you continued, sir, I do not think Miss Royle would sleep at all this night," Manton replied sternly.

"Oh, I doubt that. Our Miss Royle was brave enough to attempt to save the prince's life." He leaned forward and seemed to be addressing Elizabeth alone. "I seriously doubt she would cringe from touching *a bone*."

"A bone?" Elizabeth's eyes shifted to the salt cellar. "Is that . . . oh, heavens, it cannot be." She looked at Sir Henry. "Is that . . . a vertebra?"

Sir Henry's eyebrows formed a hairy hillock. "She is Royle's daughter, isn't she, Manton? You have a keen medical eye. Indeed it is, Miss Royle—a human cervical vertebra."

"Oh, dear God!" Lady Upperton squealed, covering her mouth with her hands. "Why would you place such a thing on the table and before our young Elizabeth?"

Sir Henry lowered his voice to nearly a whisper. "Because I suspected she might be fascinated by what I will admit to you all next. But you must swear not to tell a living soul my secret." He looked around at everyone at the table and awaited their nods, which were given by all but one. Sumner merely rolled his eyes, which, it seemed, was good enough for Sir Henry, who looked to Mr. Manton and gestured for him to begin.

Manton sighed in annoyance. "In 1649, Charles

the First was beheaded and buried in the same vault as the great Henry the Eighth. The coffins, however, were lost—until two years ago, when they were rediscovered and the Prince of Wales demanded that an autopsy be performed to confirm the identity of the skeletons. The autopsies were performed by Sir Henry." Manton exhaled. He tightened his fist upon the table. His hand began to shake. "Sir, you must finish the retelling for I will not be party to horrifying the ladies."

"Very well, if you are unable to continue." Sir Henry glowered at Mr. Manton. "As luck would have it, I was left alone with the remains for a good deal of time before the coffins were sealed again. I was able to confirm the identities . . . but I was also able to secretly steal a single bone—payment for my services, if you will." He tilted his nose toward the salt cellar. "Charles the First's cervical vertebra, which, as you can see for yourselves, has been cleanly sliced by an ax."

Lady Upperton's face grew very pale and she began madly fanning herself with her serviette.

"Makes for a lovely salt cellar. Do you not agree, Miss Royle?" Sir Henry grinned at her.

Lady Upperton's eyelids began to twitch and

her eyes looked as though they would roll back in her head. Her head lolled suddenly and she fell forward, her forehead hitting the table's edge.

Elizabeth leapt from the table and raced around past Lord Gallantine to reach her. By the time she did, Sumner had already lifted Lady Upperton's small, unconscious body into his arms.

"I will take her to the parlor and allow her to rest on the settee, if I may," he said. Without waiting, he charged from the dining room, with Elizabeth trailing behind.

Elizabeth was kneeling at Lady Upperton's side when Mr. Manton rushed into the parlor a moment later with a dampened napkin from Sir Henry's table in his hand. She stepped out of his way and allowed the young physician to see to her.

He gave her a cursory examination and then sighed with relief. "Not to worry, Miss Royle. She's only fainted," he said soothingly.

"So, she will recover soon." Elizabeth gazed worriedly up at Mr. Manton.

"Oh, yes, yes. I have seen Sir Henry cause this same reaction in other ladies at least a dozen times before. I've counseled him against doing this time and time again. A vinaigrette will bring her around fully. I shall fetch one presently." With that, he hurried from the parlor, leaving Elizabeth and Sumner standing over Lady Upperton.

The moment he was gone, Sumner reached out for Elizabeth. "Will you meet me at the Serpentine tomorrow at sunset? Where we met my cousin and the princess—you know the place. We must talk."

Elizabeth nodded fervently. "Yes, but why—"

Sumner grabbed her into his arms and kissed her, with a desperation borne of need.

Suddenly, from outside the door, they heard the clink and roll of something dropping on the floor. A few moments later Manton entered the room with a vinaigrette bottle in his hand. "Forgive my delay. The vial slipped from my fingers to the floor, then rolled under a table. Didn't break, however."

Lady Upperton's eyes were half open, but a quick wave or two of the pungent vinaigrette fully revived her immediately. "Please, take that away,' she snapped, swatting at Manton's vial.

"I shall, Lady Upperton, but please keep the cloth upon your forehead for a while longer," he advised. "A small bump is rising, nothing to worry over. You thumped your head on the table's edge, I am afraid."

She looked up at Elizabeth. "You're a good dear. Fetch Gallantine, will you? I am afraid my head pains me and I should like to return to my home. You will join me in the carriage, won't you, sweeting?"

"I will, Lady Upperton, I am sure by *tomorrow evening*, if not before, you will be completely yourself again." Elizabeth flashed a quick glance at Sumner, and shot him a slight nod. "I shall inform Lord Gallantine as to our amended plans for the evening. Please excuse me, Your Royal Highness, Mr. Manton." She dipped a curtsy to each, and then hurried back to the dining room.

She tried to hide the confident smile that tugged at her lips as she made their excuses to Sir Henry and informed Lord Gallantine of their early departure from Curzon Street.

It was even more difficult a feat to conceal her joy as the carriage conveyed them both home, for Lady Upperton's ability to read a face was second only to Lord Lotharian's.

Still, the lady's nerves were in frays and tatters after Sir Henry's ghoulish game, and she seemed not the least aware that Elizabeth's demeanor had changed at all.

But it had. For after Sumner's passionate kiss, Elizabeth knew that before the glittering waters of the Serpentine tomorrow night, Sumner would tell her that his only duty was . . . to their love.

Chapter 14

Hyde Park
Rotten Row

"**T**his isn't wise, Leopold." Sumner reined his horse protectively closer to the prince's as they guided their mounts down Rotten Row through the thick fog. It was if the clouds had descended from the sky and settled eerily upon the road. "We can too easily be taken unaware."

"I can't stay corked up inside any longer," the prince replied flatly. "Aside from sitting in Sir Henry's parlor, riding at this early hour through this miasma of gray is probably the safest place I could possibly be. If we cannot see the approach of another, I doubt we can be seen, either."

"But we can be heard. You are so close to

securing this match. Why do you risk all by needlessly venturing out?" Sumner knew that his frustration with Leopold was plain in his voice, and he did not try to conceal it. He was putting a halt to his life while Leopold worked to diplomatically manipulate this marriage to a woman he did not love.

"I cannot abide living like a prisoner during my stay in London."

"Then let us return to Paris." Sumner knew it was too much to hope for Leopold to leave before the Prince of Wales had given him a nod, formal or encouraging, but he had to try. "In Paris, you will be free to roam the streets while conducting the remainder of the campaign through dispatches."

"I cannot, because nothing is resolved. Nothing!" Leopold was silent for several moments after that, his chest heaving and laboring with his clear agitation. "I have taken a box at the Drury Lane Theatre for tonight," he finally said brusquely. "We shall be attending. I will not hear any argument to the contrary."

Leopold's voice was firm and steady. He was not suggesting a night at the theatre. He had already planned it.

"Tonight?" Sumner tensed. "You cannot consider this."

"Yes, tonight." There was a curtness to the prince's manner he had never seen except in the heat of battle. "I understand the implications for my security. But I must go. Charlotte will be in attendance. I have no choice."

"You cannot appear in public with the princess. It is far too dangerous." And it was, but there was more to his position against attending the theatre that night. Sumner had spent the night before girding himself, rehearsing, for the uncomfortable task of admitting his true identity to Elizabeth this very evening.

It was true that Leopold's security needs had not altered, nor had Sumner's own sworn loyalty and responsibility to the prince.

What was about to change was Elizabeth's need to trust him, to believe with all her heart that he would return for her despite appearances to the contrary.

But, for her to put such great faith in him, he must put his trust in her first, and admit that he was not Prince Leopold at all, but his cousin, sworn to protect him at all costs during the increasingly dangerous campaign to secure a union between England and Saxe-Coburg.

It had taken a good measure of time, but ultimately he had come to the conclusion that perhaps if Elizabeth knew his true duty, her heart would not be broken each time the *Times* reported movement in the romance of Prince Leopold and Princess Charlotte. And that she would understand that soon the prince must leave for Paris—but that he would return for her. As he had promised.

"I realize the danger. Charlotte will not be viewing the performance with me, but will be ensconced in a neighboring box within view. I will exchange glances of wistful longing with her. Nothing more."

"You are risking much for no gain." Sumner huffed at the very idea of the prince and princess trading moon-eyed glances—at the risk of the prince's life.

"The gain will be great, if I am successful." Leopold nudged his mount into a fast trot. "My intent is to provoke Charlotte into confronting her father about marriage."

Sumner drew his horse alongside, matching his mount's stride to the prince's gelding. "Do you think it wise to do this so soon?"

"I cannot wait any longer. I am not blind to the fact that Princess Charlotte is entirely infatuated with me . . . just as she was with several others over the past years. I must use her passionate feelings for me now, before they fade."

Sumner fell silent.

Leopold drew back on the reins. His gelding's bit and bridle jingled as the prince pulled his mount to a prancing halt. "My cousin, you are like my brother. I understand what I am asking you to do. By standing in for me, posing as Prince Leopold, your life could be in jeopardy."

"And yet you ask me to do it."

"I do." Leopold looked down at the wet earthen trail. "Saxe-Coburg was plundered by Napoleon because we lacked the strength and power to defend it. A marriage to Princess Charlotte will merge our families—and Saxe-Coburg will never be too small or powerless to defend itself again. I do not ask you to do this because you are my cousin, my blood kin. I do not ask you because no one else could impersonate me so well as you. I ask you to do this because I can trust you, above all, to do your duty to Saxe-Coburg. You are a soldier, my brother in arms."

"I know my duty."

"I know."

"The fog is lifting. We should return to Curzon Street," he said to Leopold, his words a cold and deliberate command. "If we are to attend the theatre this night, I must note all occurrences and contingencies, then prepare."

As the two reined their mounts around, Sumner noticed that Leopold was smiling. "Is there something else I should know about this eve?"

"Oh yes, there is one thing of note." Leopold lifted his eyebrows most innocently. "I have anonymously reserved the box to our left for Lady Upperton, Miss Royle, and Lord Gallantine—though I took care to ask Mercer to admit to the graciousness."

Sumner stared at Leopold. "You didn't."

"Thought you might wish to know . . . contingency planning, you know." Leopold laughed, then brought his crop down upon his horse's flank and charged down Rotten Row.

Berkeley Square

"Lady Upperton, I cannot go to the theatre with you and the Old Rakes this evening." Elizabeth paced the parlor, her arms wrapped around herself in a tight hug. "I must refuse . . . I have another engagement."

"Well, dove, unless you give me a fair and reasonable explanation why you must refuse this invitation, I fear you must break your engagement," Lady Upperton warned. "It is by invitation of none other than Miss Margaret

Mercer Elphinstone that our party has been provided a box at the performance this eve. Is it impossible for you to imagine that it is not she who truly wished that you attend the performance, but rather the princess, who is graciously extending an olive branch to you?"

Elizabeth spun around and looked critically at her sponsor. "How have you come to this conclusion? You told me that the card was not signed."

"It wasn't. But when I sent my footman around to inquire as to owner of the box, I was informed Miss Elphinstone held the subscription."

"Mercer is a dear." Elizabeth unfolded her arms. "She might have sent the invitation because she felt sorry over the way I was dismissed by the princess when the entire inciting event was in no way my fault."

"Yes, that might be one explanation except for one thing—the card noted that both Prince Leopold and Princess Charlotte will be present at this performance." Lady Upperton swung her short legs back and forth from the edge of the settee.

Elizabeth stopped pacing. "Prince Leopold will be at the Drury Lane Theatre this night?" Not at the Serpentine . . . where he had asked her to meet him?

"Yes, the prince as well as Princess Charlotte. Did I not make myself heard, gel?"

Elizabeth glanced down at Lady Upperton. What was the meaning of this? Had he changed his mind about her, or had he simply been unable to extricate himself from an invitation to the performance from the princess? Filled with nerves, Elizabeth bit into her lower lip.

Either way, Mercer had taken care to include the mention of the prince—and the princess—attending. Perhaps he bade her to do it. A message for her that he could not meet her at the Serpentine as planned. It was a possibility.

And that possibility, she had to cling to.

"Very well then, Lady Upperton," Elizabeth relented, "I shall happily join you and the gentlemen at the theatre this night."

While there, she would make it her mission to speak with Sumner. She would find a way if it killed her.

Drury Lane Theatre

Elizabeth leaned forward on the bench seat and peered as best she could down the tier of private boxes. The light from the chandeliers above was low, making discerning any individual's features almost impossible.

Her prince, dressed in formal military attire, and given his remarkable height, would stand out from the waves of gentlemen all dressed so similarly in their dark coats and tails, and starched white neck cloths. Only, she did not see him anywhere.

She leaned close to Lord Lotharian, who never missed anything. "Have you seen the princess . . . or the prince, for that matter? The play is about to begin and I have not seen either party arrive."

"And you shall not, until the play does begin." Lotharian gestured to two grand empty boxes a short distance away. "They will no doubt take their seats there or perhaps in that box beside it. It is a precaution for safety, that is all, so I would not elevate your hopes."

"Elevate my hopes?" Elizabeth crinkled her nose. "I do not know what you mean."

"Why, that Princess Charlotte does not arrive. I know seeing her here, especially in the company of the prince, will be most difficult for you."

"I do not give a fig if the princess enjoys the play this evening or not. The prince's attendance is my only interest." Elizabeth placed her gloved hand on the rail and peered at the rows of theatregoers below. Then, lazily, she allowed her gaze to drift to the box just to the right of their own. "Oh, Zeus," she whispered harshly. "*He* is here."

Lady Upperton caught the railing with both her hands and rose up from the bench to see past Elizabeth. "Who, dear?"

"Sir Henry. He is just taking his seat."

"Who did you say? I cannot hear you, gel." Lady Upperton bent over the rail.

"Shh. *Sir Henry.*" Elizabeth tipped her head to the right. "Just there."

"Dear, no one can hear what you are saying, especially me. There is far too much audience chatter." Lady Upperton raised her mother-of-pearl opera glasses and peered where Elizabeth had gestured. "Oh, yes, and he is with that dear Mr. Manton, too. He has such a kind heart, that young man." Lady Upperton grasped Elizabeth's wrist. "Did I tell you that Mr. Manton had sent a note that they would be attending this night?"

"No." Elizabeth grimaced. "I am sure I would remember had you told me that."

"Mr. Manton inquired upon his card if he might call before the play to be sure I was well after the incident . . . with that horrid bone salt cellar."

Elizabeth turned on the bench to face her

sponsor. "And did he? Surely, Sir Henry did not dare to set foot upon your doorstep."

"No, neither did. There was no need. I returned a card letting them know that we would be here. Pity that Sir Henry has come tonight as well, but I suspected he would." From her beaded reticule she withdrew a folded cloth and handed it to Elizabeth. "At interval, would you please return this napkin to Sir Henry? I cannot endure having anything to do with that man, and this cloth is a reminder of the dinner and his unctuous manner."

While Elizabeth had no desire to engage Sir Henry at all, she had to concede that Lady Upperton had endured the worst of last evening, and so she agreed and set the napkin on her lap until the interval.

The orchestra in the pit below began to play, and Edmund Keane stepped onto the stage, to be greeted by the deafening roar of rousing applause.

Elizabeth turned her head to the right, to see, just as Lotharian had predicted, the prince and his cousin, Whitevale, entering the box to her right and taking their places before Sir Henry and Mr. Manton.

Elizabeth leaned forward to see past Lord Lotharian to the prince. Just then, Sumner, looking so utterly handsome in his dark blue coat and cerulean sash that Elizabeth felt her heart swell, touched his lips, pretending to cough, and turned his hand toward her.

Twin blooms of heat rose into her cheeks, and she cast her eyes demurely downward. When she looked up, Mr. Manton was watching her. He gave her a warm smile, to which she politely tipped her head in acknowledgment, and then returned her gaze to her handsome Sumner once more.

Only a minute later Princess Charlotte, Mercer, and several older women—whom Elizabeth took to be Charlotte's aunts—entered the box to the right of the prince's. She took her seat in a cushioned chair, obviously placed there for her use, then leaned forward and smiled at the prince, who paid her absolutely no heed.

Elizabeth was elated. His gesture of touching his lips and tossing it to her—not Princess Charlotte—had told her everything. He did not wish to dispatch her in favor of the princess. The theatre event had merely made their meeting at the Serpentine impossible this night. It was clear by his ignoring Charlotte's attentions in the box next to his that he had made his choice.

He had chosen her.

Elizabeth's heart was dancing. She could not

wait to speak with him, lud, even accidentally brushing against him would be worth waiting through the entire tiresome performance on stage.

The play seemed to last an eternity, and though the audience quite enjoyed Keane's expressive dramatics, Elizabeth waited impatiently for the interval.

She tapped Sir Henry's napkin on her lap, then, in her boredom, shook it from its folds and set about refolding it again. In one corner she felt a small lump beneath her gloved fingertip.

Elizabeth glanced up to see if Princess Charlotte looked her way. The princess had propped both her arms on the rail and was turned completely in the direction of the prince's box, smiling sappily. Her devotion to him was blatantly obvious to all.

Elizabeth's finger distractedly worried over the lump on the napkin. Raising her eyes toward the stage, she did not dare do something so ill-mannered as to lift the cloth to her eyes to see what it was she was feeling, especially if the gift of the theatre box this evening was indeed provided as an offering of apology from Princess Charlotte. Instead, she slipped her glove from her hand and traced the raised stitching with her fingertip. She felt two sets of parallel lines that intersected.

And then it occurred to her. It was two letters H, one turned to cross the other. It was Sir Henry Halford's insignia, neatly embroidered in white on the napkin's corner. That made perfect sense.

Suddenly, the theatre was filled with clapping and the curtain closed. At last, interval. And Lady Upperton had supplied her with the perfect excuse to enter the prince's box—returning Sir Henry's embroidered napkin.

Sumner's body thrummed from his awareness that Elizabeth was so near. He had taken a chance by unobtrusively casting the message of a kiss her way. But to anyone watching, he assumed his action would have held no meaning.

But as long as Princess Charlotte was in close proximity to Leopold, he had to refrain from any other contact with Elizabeth.

From the moment Charlotte arrived, patrons and ministers of Parliament alike were turning in their seats and leaning from their boxes to see the prince and princess. He could see the eagerness in their eyes, waiting for some hint that the newspaper reports and clever caricatures of the two royal secret lovers were all true.

Sumner was not about to give them anything to gossip about. Not when Elizabeth did not yet know the truth of his identity. From the periphery of his vision he could see Elizabeth watching him. He knew, too, that he could not so much as a give the princess a glance without hurting Elizabeth.

He could not afford to delay much longer. He knew he had to confess his identity to her soon. It might have been tonight if Leopold had not needed the perfectly costumed false prince to be in place.

Leopold was sitting beside him, glancing mournfully from time to time at Princess Charlotte. He played the lovelorn suitor so well that had Sumner not known his cousin's heart was not truly engaged, he would have believed his performance.

Then applause swelled within the theatre, and Sumner rose at once, wondering how he might slip away to see Elizabeth, even for a moment, without drawing the attention of the entire audience.

And then she appeared at the opening to his box, holding a white cloth in her hand. She curtsied to him, gazing up through her thick lashes as she rose, a secret smile on her lips. But then she redirected her attention to Sir Henry.

"Sir Henry." She offered a clipped curtsy to him, and then to his protégé, Mr. Manton. "Lady Upperton wished for me to return this to you," she turned briefly toward Mr. Manton, "and to thank you, dear sir, for your assistance and concern." She raised the white cloth in her hand, but when Sir Henry reached out for it she pulled it back and looked more closely at it.

"It . . . is a crosshatch." Her eyes rounded and her head jerked up to look at Sir Henry.

Sir Henry shook his head. "No, it is my insignia. My initials, one H, and another overlaid on its side. But others have told me that my mark does resemble a crosshatch. You are not the first." He reached out again and took the cloth from her.

Sumner noticed that Elizabeth was now trembling slightly. Without a care to those watching, he took her arm.

When she looked up at him, he saw an unsettling blend of fear and anger in her eyes. "The crosshatch," she said beneath her breath. "It is the crosshatch from the bottles. It was *him*—Sir Henry."

"What is that you are saying, Miss Royle?" Sir Henry looked suddenly shaken himself.

"Do allow me to escort you back to your sponsor, Miss Royle," Sumner said softly to her.

He met Leopold's judging gaze as they started from the box, but he stared him down. He did not know what had startled Elizabeth so, but he was not going to abandon her when she so clearly needed his support.

Without wasting an instant, he whisked her from the box. But instead of returning her to Lady Upperton as he had promised, he pulled her down the outer passage and behind a thick crimson curtain at the end of the hall.

"Why are you so frightened? What has Sir Henry done?"

Elizabeth tried to reply. Her lips moved but no words came from her mouth.

Sumner crushed her body against his and held her tightly, stroking her copper hair until her body stopped shaking. Only then did he release her.

When she raised her head to peer up at him, her eyes were shining with unshed tears.

"The crosshatch . . . it was his mark," she murmured. "I saw it on two bottles labeled 'laudanum.' He gave the laudanum to Lady Jersey and the queen. He knew. I am sure he knew what they meant to do. Likely even counseled them in how to administer it to Maria Fitzherbert."

"Elizabeth, I have heard the stories surrounding your birth—and that you and your sisters may be daughters of the Regent. But this is the first I have heard mention of Sir Henry's possible involvement. You are certain of this?"

"Yes . . . no. How can I be certain of any of this? The bottles with the crosshatch were left behind by my father as evidence to help prove our lineage." A shiver slid down her spine, making her whole body shake anew. "But we'll never prove it, never know anything for certain—except that the laudanum belonged to Sir Henry, royal surgeon."

Sumner tenderly settled his fingers at her chin and turned her mouth up to his. His lips moved over hers softly and gently, quieting her, calming her.

"Your lineage doesn't matter, Elizabeth." Sliding his thumbs across her cheeks, he wiped the tears from her eyes. "Blood princess or orphan, it doesn't matter. I love you, he whispered. "I wanted to tell you . . . so you know."

Her breath caught and she stared at him as if not trusting her ears with what she heard.

"I love you," he repeated, his voice clear and resonant.

Tears rushed into Elizabeth's eyes again.

The sound of applause returned Sumner to

the moment. "Now, you have to stop crying, my dear, for we have to return to the boxes."

Elizabeth laughed through her tears. "I am just so happy. I thought . . . oh, never mind." She rose up on her toes and kissed him. "I love you, Sumner."

She pulled a glove from her hand and scrubbed the tears from her cheeks, then turned to leave. She glanced back momentarily. "The Serpentine, tomorrow at sunset?"

"At sunset. I will be there." Sumner caught her arm and pulled her into one last, heated kiss before releasing her through the curtain. He drew in a deep breath before he stepped out from behind it, taking care to straighten the sash that crossed his full heart.

Suddenly, something slammed against his chest, and then searing pain knifed through him. He fell to the floor, opened his eyes and saw a blade lying next to him.

Rolling to his back, darkness already starting to obscure his vision, he saw the silhouette of a man opening the curtain and walking away.

"Elizabeth!" he called out weakly.

Elizabeth was standing outside of her box, smoothing her hair and gown before entering, when she thought she heard Sumner call out to her.

She stepped into her box and sat down on the bench. Still, she felt uneasy. Leaning forward, she watched for Sumner. But he did not come.

His cousin shot a meaningful glance at her, to which she shook her head. Whitevale leapt from his seat and rushed from the box.

Something was wrong. Had Sumner indeed called out for her?

Elizabeth rose, tore from her box and raced down the passage. When she arrived at the end, Whitevale was holding Sumner in his arms.

Blood dripped down the brilliant medals pinned to Sumner's coat and was already saturating the blue sash at his chest.

"Get Sir Henry!" Whitevale shouted.

"Sir Henry? But—" Elizabeth stammered.

"He needs a physician! Go."

She whirled around, caught up her skirts and ran up the passage.

Mr. Manton was standing outside the royal box. "What is it? Can I help?"

"Yes, *please*. The end of the passage. The prince has been injured." Without another word, Elizabeth entered the box and grabbed Sir Henry's lapel. "Come with me now," she ordered. She yanked hard and he stood, but would not move a step more.

"Miss Royle, you are making a spectacle of us both," Sir Henry protested. A hush washed over the audience, and even the actors on stage did not move as they watched the display in the box.

"Come with me now." Elizabeth tried to pull him forward.

"I demand to know why," he said loudly, surely for the benefit of those around them.

"Because someone has tried to kill Prince Leopold!" she shouted back, not caring who heard or what they thought of her. Her prince needed help.

Princess Charlotte screamed from the neighboring box, and the audience roared with panic as word of the attack spread through the theatre.

At last Sir Henry relented and came with her. Elizabeth hurried him down the dark passage. When they reached the two men, Sir Henry knelt beside the prince.

Grabbing his hand before Sir Henry could touch the prince, Elizabeth looked him dead in the eye. "You will do what is right, Sir Henry. You *will* save him. You will."

Chapter 15

Berkeley Square

Elizabeth paced the parlor with unforgiving force, shaking the letter she held in the air before her. "It has been days upon days, Anne, and still, all I have is this note from Whitevale telling me that the prince will survive. Nothing more," she said, her voice quavering. She shoved the short missive toward her sister, then sat down upon the settee.

Anne took the letter and raised it to her eyes. She rose and took over pacing for Elizabeth. When she finished reading, she let her hand fall to her side. "It says that what might have been a killing thrust of the blade was deflected by the medals upon his chest. The wound is deep but superficial. His life is no longer in danger." She furrowed her brow. "What do you mean this is all you have? The report is very, very good. He was very fortunate, Lizzy."

Elizabeth nodded dumbly, then covered her eyes with a shaking hand. A sob slipped through her lips.

"He will recover, Lizzy. La, you should be in the highest of spirits." Anne sat down on the settee beside her. "Why do you grieve so?"

"Because of this." She reached out and pulled a folded newspaper from the tea table. "A source for the *Times* claims that the two attempts on Prince Leopold's life were directed by a faction within Parliament that supports a union between Princess Charlotte and William of Orange." She peered at Anne. "It is all about political advantage and power, isn't it?"

"I think it fairly obvious that it's in England's best interest to secure the most advantageous union for the princess. The support for Silly Billy has always been strong—even you must be aware of that. The Prince of Wales himself is even reported to back a marriage between Princess Charlotte and the Dutchman." Anne sighed. "I am afraid England will not gain much from a marriage between Princess

Charlotte and Prince Leopold—though the prince will stand to gain much."

"You mean, it is his duty to make advantageous marriage for the good of Saxe-Coburg." Elizabeth sniffled, not wanting her sister to confirm her statement.

"I did not say that, but nor can I deny it." Anne hugged her sister to her. "Lizzy, I am so sorry about what has been happening while we were away. We returned from Brighton the moment I saw your name printed in the newspaper. You can imagine how frightened I was that something had happened to you as well, but that it was not reported because of the high standing of the others involved."

"I know you, Anne. And I am sorry you felt the need to return from your honeymoon because of me. You did ask me not to pursue the prince." The edges of Elizabeth's lips turned downward. "I should have listened to the spirit of your warning, rather than the imperative I heard in your words. And now, see what happened to the prince. All because of me."

Anne took Elizabeth's shoulders and turned them so that she faced her. "What happened to the prince was not your fault."

Elizabeth began to sob harder. "Yes, it was.

He would not have been alone in the darkness had it not been for me."

"What are you prattling on about, Lizzy?" Anne squeezed her shoulders as if to force a reply. "I don't understand what you mean."

"I had been with him only a moment before it happened. He was calming me down, kissing me, and telling me that he loved me." She buried her eyes on Anne's shoulder. "It is all my fault."

"Lizzy." Anne moved Elizabeth away and focused a concerned gaze on her. "I think you must tell me about what happened while I was gone. Everything."

And so for the next two hours, while Great-aunt Prudence slept soundly in her chair, Elizabeth confessed everything, from Almack's, to Cranbourne Lodge and the river trail, to Sir Henry's ghoulish dinner party, the crosshatch insignia, and the Drury Lane Theatre. She left nothing out, though as she recounted the outrageous events of days past and witnessed Anne's increasingly shocked expressions, she wished she'd omitted one or two things.

When she was finished, Elizabeth felt completely drained in both body and spirit.

Anne blew a long breath through pursed lips. "I—I hardly know what to say, Lizzy."

"Just tell me what to do. Please," Elizabeth beseeched her.

"That, I cannot do. From what you tell me, he loves you—but that even he claims that his duty must come first." Anne squeezed Elizabeth's hand and stood. "Logic tells me that he must marry the princess if her father consents to the match. It is for the greater good."

"But what does your heart tell you?"

Anne gave a sad smile. "That sometimes your dreams do come true . . . and that this dream deserves a little more time. Wait for him, Lizzy. Talk to him. You will know what to do when the time to act comes."

Minutes later Elizabeth watched through the window as her sister walked out to the pavers and stepped into the gleaming town carriage that awaited her.

Wait, Anne had said. If only it were that easy.

Three days later Elizabeth decided she had waited long enough. Her patience was spent. After all, a full fortnight had passed and surely the prince could receive a visitor by now.

She dressed in a white cambric walking dress trimmed at the hem with treble flounces of French work that swished nicely when she walked. On her head, she placed a white satin bonnet, topped with white plume, that tied prettily with a celestial blue ribbon.

It was no coincidence that the dress she chose gave the faintest impression of bridal innocence, but to mute the effect, she draped around her shoulders a blue silk twill mantle with lilies of the valley embroidered at each end with shaded silks.

Luck seemed to be on her side that day, for a hackney had dropped a passenger not three doors from her great-aunt's house, and she was able to secure the driver's service without ever risking a speck of dust on her splendid ensemble.

When the hackney reached Curzon Street, she asked the driver to wait, in the event the prince was unable to receive her, but when she inquired about the prince's condition at the front door, Sir Henry's butler led her directly into the parlor to wait.

Only, it was not the prince who greeted her. A looming shadow fell over Elizabeth, giving her a fresh sense of foreboding. It was none other than Sir Henry himself.

"I am so pleased you have come to call, Miss Royle," he said, moving quickly across the parlor toward her.

Elizabeth sat up straight, realizing too late there was no retreat for her. He stood directly over her, too close for her to stand. "Sir Henry. I have come to inquire about the health of the prince. Is he well?"

"When I last saw him, a week ago, he was doing very well. There was no infection, and the wound was binding nicely."

Elizabeth blinked up at the baronet. "Excuse me, but did you say . . . a week ago?"

"I did." Sir Henry condescended to step back from her at last, but the change in position was not for the better because he took his seat next to her on the settee. "He and Whitevale were installed at Carlton House recently. You did not know?"

"Obviously, sir, I did not, else I would not have disturbed you." Elizabeth glanced around Sir Henry, plotting her escape.

"I am glad you did, Miss Royle, for I should like to talk more with you . . . about your father and some unbelievable tales I've heard of late."

Elizabeth's stomach clenched. She had to extract what information she could from the baronet, then go away as soon as possible. "You did say that the prince and Whitevale were installed at Carlton House . . . at the invitation of the Prince of Wales, I assume?"

"Oh, my dear Miss Royle. Then you truly have not heard." He grinned cockily. "After the attack on the prince, Princess Charlotte immediately charged the Prime Minister with an ultimatum to be communicated to her father."

"An ultimatum—to the Prince Regent?" Elizabeth did not wish to hear any more, but she had to stay, in the event the report was not as damning to her fate as she anticipated.

"Oh, yes. She was quite emboldened by the threat to Leopold's life. As I am sure you, yourself, understand all too well."

Elizabeth fought off a daggered glare. "Please, Sir Henry. Tell me about the ultimatum."

"Very well, dear. Lord Liverpool was to advise Prinny that the attempt on Prince Leopold's life was believed to be made by supporters of a union between her and William of Orange—a cause the Regent himself openly backed. Therefore, in consideration of Prince Leopold's safety, the princess demanded that the Prime Minister advise her father that she has selected Prince Leopold as her husband. If the Prince Regent rejected his name, she would not consider another, and will remain for all her years a spinster."

Elizabeth swallowed hard. "And how did the Regent respond to this . . . ultimatum?"

"No one knows for certain, of course. Though the Prince of Wales did command that the prince be moved to Carlton House until Prince Leopold returns to Paris." In a very bold and ill-mannered gesture, he patted Elizabeth's knee, completely disregarding her squeal of disapproval. "Now, perhaps he did this to ensure the prince's safety. Perhaps the Regent simply wished to become more familiar with the nobleman who may someday marry his daughter. Either way, the prince has the Regent's interest now, doesn't he? I believe a wedding between Princess Charlotte and Prince Leopold is inevitable. Do you not agree, Miss Royle?"

Elizabeth leapt from the settee, meaning to quit Sir Henry's presence immediately, but he was too quick and caught her wrist.

She tugged against him. "Do release me, Sir Henry."

"I wouldn't dream of you leaving so soon, my dear Miss Royle, not when we have so much more to discuss."

"I have nothing to discuss with *you*." Elizabeth twisted her wrist but could not free herself.

"That is where we disagree, we have *much* to talk about . . . beginning with your mention of laudanum bottles your father had and your belief that I had some connection to them."

"Let her go, sir." Mr. Manton stood in the doorway. "The lady wishes to leave."

"Manton. I didn't expect you back so soon." Sir Henry released Elizabeth's arm and she jettisoned toward the doorway, where Mr. Manton stood.

Mr. Manton lifted Elizabeth's wrist and peered down at it. "Are you injured at all, Miss Royle?"

She shook her head vigorously. "No, not at all. I just . . . must leave now."

"Please allow me to accompany you home," he said gallantly.

Elizabeth gave a hunted glance over her shoulder at Sir Henry before replying to Mr. Manton. "I thank you kindly, Mr. Manton, but I have a hackney driver awaiting my return. Good day, Mr. Manton." She smiled at the young man as she curtsied, then withdrew her hand from his gentle grip. Turning quickly, she dashed into the entry hall and bolted through the front door, ignoring Sir Henry entirely.

Chapter 16

When she reached the street, drat it all, the hackney was nowhere to be seen. Elizabeth hadn't really expected that it would be, but the comment had enabled her to extricate herself from Mr. Manton.

She glanced back at the door and hurried down the footpath before her gallant Mr. Manton could come to her rescue once again, for at this moment she couldn't endure having his compassionate eyes upon her. Nor could she return home, for the same reason. She would simply dissolve into tears.

The Prince of Wales would certainly give a union between Princess Charlotte and Prince Leopold his blessing now.

Tears already welled, unshed, in her eyes. Anne would understand. How she wished she could go to her. But her sister's home on Cockspur Street was but a stone's throw from Warwick House, where Princess Charlotte was now lodged, and Carlton House as well, where her prince had been installed.

If she went to Anne, she could not bear, even for a moment, knowing that the man she loved was but a few steps away—possibly being interviewed by the Prince Regent in consideration of marrying the princess.

She simply could not endure it.

And so she walked and walked, past shops and squares, lawns of green, until she found herself at the gates of Hyde Park and the Serpentine beyond.

Tears budded in her eyes as she realized where her troubled heart had led her. To the place where she and Sumner were to meet the very night of the fateful event that would scar her life forever.

Slowly she walked to the bridge and stood at the rail in its center, staring down into the depths of the Serpentine.

Elizabeth thought about her great-aunt as a young woman exactly her age, when duty had robbed her of her husband. Prudence had warned her. Had told her that in the end, duty would always come first for a man.

She should have listened to her great-aunt, she told herself, and spared herself the heartache of losing the man she loved.

She should have listened to Anne, who could not deny that Leopold would one day marry Princess Charlotte out of duty to Saxe-Coburg.

She should have listened to Mercer, who told her, in no uncertain words, that Charlotte had set her cap at Prince Leopold and meant to marry him.

She should have listened to Princess Charlotte herself, when she returned victorious after securing Parliament's support for a union between her and Prince Leopold.

But she did not.

Instead, she listened to her dreams. She listened to her own heart.

And where had that gotten her? Standing alone, staring down at the welcoming swirls of the Serpentine below.

Elizabeth thought back to the morning not so many days ago when she fell from the river trail into the Thames. She remembered the cold water rushing over her face and how the bright light on the water's surface dimmed as she sank deeper and deeper into the river's depths.

Only now, if she fell, Sumner would not be there to pull her from the depths.

A heavy tear rolled down her cheek and dripped from her jaw into the swells of water below the bridge. It caught the light as it fell, and for the briefest instant it glistened like a diamond, before being swallowed up by the blackness of the Serpentine.

Wait, Elizabeth. Anne's sage advice suddenly filled her mind.

"Wait." She heard it clearly now.

"Wait." The words were coming from her own lips. "He will come back. Trust him."

Elizabeth stepped back from the railing and rubbed the tears from her cheeks. He had told her that he loved her and that he'd come back for her.

And she believed him. Despite logic. Despite what others told her. Despite Parliament—and the Prince of Wales.

She believed in Sumner and what he had promised. She did.

Elizabeth grabbed up her walking skirt in her hand and ran from the bridge.

He would come back for her.

And when he did, she would be waiting.

Two days later
Carlton House

"Are you well enough to attend the fete, Sumner?" Leopold asked as the valet assigned to him brushed down the back of his coat.

"I have been fit for days, and yet the guards will not allow me to leave the grounds or even send a message to . . . anyone." Sumner allowed the valet to button his blue satin waistcoat shot with gold threads, and even to accept assistance with his coat, as a prince would permit. But when the valet began to pin row after row of shiny medals upon the breast of his dark blue coat, he cringed in pain, snatched the silver tray of medals from the dresser and set it aside.

"A mite irritable this day, cousin?" Leopold glanced at his sleeker coat, and smiled approvingly at his own elegant reflection. "You needn't be. I managed to send a missive to Mercer, asking her to ensure that Miss Royle attends the fete this day; that she should do whatever is necessary to get her inside the Carlton House garden."

Beneath his coat, Sumner's shoulders tightened uncomfortably. "I did not wish her here today."

"But only a moment ago you were fretting over not being able to send a message to her."

Leopold sat upon a tufted bench and allowed the dresser to comb his hair fashionably around his face. "I sent for Miss Royle because I thought you would wish it."

"I did not wish her at Carlton House because if there is another attack, I do not wish to risk her well-being."

"And you do not wish her to see you dancing with Princess Charlotte," Leopold added.

"And there is that."

"You have not told her—" Leopold glanced at the numerous valets, footmen, and attendants in the chamber and did not finish his sentence.

"No, I haven't. I had intended to explain everything to her the night that plans changed and we attended the performance at the Drury Lane Theatre." Sumner shrugged against the weave of kerseymere. The blasted coat was too tight. He could barely breathe. "But today at the fete is neither the time nor the place."

"Cousin, you cannot simply ignore Miss Royle. She will be in attendance." Leopold rested his palm on Sumner's shoulder.

"I must." When the dresser came at Sumner with a comb, the prince stepped away. Sumner dropped down into a chair and begrudgingly allowed him to coif his hair in Leopold's stylish mode. "I must, for her safety."

"It is likely that since the Prince of Wales is hosting this fete, and will allow you—as me—to dance with Princess Charlotte, that the William of Orange supporters will see their cause as defeated. For I believe it has been. The Prince Regent will grant his consent in time. I am sure of it."

"I may be safe from attack, in other words."

"Yes."

"But then, you could be wrong. If you were dead, Leopold, a marriage between William and Charlotte would still be possible."

"Though now that Prinny understands her ultimatum, I do not think I am incorrect in my prediction." Leopold walked a circle around Sumner, examining his attire. "A dark blue slipper," he said to the valet, "not the black. It is day. What do Englishmen know of dressing well? I ask you that."

Sumner caught a glimpse of the glare cast from the valet at the true Prince Leopold, and it was all he could do not to laugh.

Carlton House
The garden

At three of the clock, Elizabeth and Lady Upperton were ushered into the lush garden a scant moment before the Prince Regent and the royal family arrived.

Rolls of flesh were plainly visible beneath Prinny's clothing, and he was a startling sight without the aid of stays. Still, he lent his arm to the queen and led the rest of the royal family, including Princess Charlotte, into the garden.

As Elizabeth followed the queen's progress across the lawn—the woman who may have had her and her sisters left for dead upon their birth—she caught sight of Lady Upperton gazing ruefully at her.

"I know this day is difficult for you, dear one, but please do not make it harder by dwelling on the distant past and what may or may not have occurred." Lady Upperton reached out and squeezed Elizabeth's hand.

"Until the queen arrived, I would have said that I looked forward to this day from the moment I received the invitation to attend." Elizabeth shook off the dark image of the queen and Lady Jersey from her mind. "For I will see Sumner, and Fate will see to the rest."

Lady Upperton sighed disappointedly, but did not press Elizabeth to set her dream aside. "It is lovely here, you must agree."

"Indeed, I do." Elizabeth drew in a refreshing

breath and immediately felt her spirits lift high. The Carlton House garden was as beautiful as it was extensive. Huge trees and glossy greenery were set off by clusters of brightly colored flowers.

Ladies were in full dress, with feathers, diamonds, and gowns, exactly as if they were attending a drawing room. The gentlemen were wearing fitted coats and formal white knee breeches and buckles. It was a spectacle to behold.

Tents had been erected here and there, and beneath them, tables of sumptuous food and drink could be found. At one end of the garden an orchestra had been assembled, and dancing had just commenced on the lawn.

Elizabeth rose up upon her toes to search for Sumner, but Lady Upperton grasped her arm and pulled her back down into her slippers.

"He is here, somewhere," Elizabeth muttered to herself. "Surely, he would have arrived before the royal family."

Lady Upperton lifted her lorgnette to her eyes. "There. He is standing before the orchestra." She gestured with a flick of her ivory-handled eyepiece.

In an instant Elizabeth spied Sumner, and her breath collapsed in her lungs. On his arm was

Princess Charlotte, her head proud and erect as he led her to the center of the dancing ground.

Elizabeth tested her will, trying to look away, but she could not remove her eyes from the royal couple as they danced a spirited Scotch dance.

She stared, her heart feeling as though it were breaking as Sumner gifted Charlotte with the same knee-weakening gaze as he'd given her, the one he claimed to love, at the Drury Lane Theatre.

"He is a guest in her father's house. I am sure that is why they are dancing," Lady Upperton offered.

Elizabeth stood silently watching the prince and princess dance. Those standing at the dancing ground's perimeter were captivated by the sight of the two handsome royals dancing gracefully in a heavenly garden.

It was a vision straight out of a fairy tale.

To Elizabeth it was a horrid nightmare.

Her eyes began to heat, and before a single tear could be shed, she fumbled inside her reticule for a handkerchief. But before she could withdraw it, Lord Whitevale, the prince's striking cousin, caught her hand and without asking permission in any way led her to the dancing ground.

"Today is not one for worry and tear, Miss Royle," Whitevale told her. "It is a day for making merry." He spun her around, smiling at her all the while.

The music hummed inside of Elizabeth, but try as she might, she could not focus on the dance. Not with Sumner so close—and yet so far away.

Though she could not remove her gaze from him, Sumner did not even glance her way once during the dance, even when they were called upon to *chassé* around one another.

Her throat felt thick and every breath became as much a chore as remaining on the dance ground a moment longer.

As the orchestra played the final note, and the dancers and audience clapped their approval, Elizabeth searched the crowd for Lady Upperton. She had to find her for they must leave at once. This was just too difficult to endure.

Why had Mercer been so insistent that she come, when she had to have known this would happen?

Perhaps that was the reason she had been invited. So she could see for herself, understand, the choice that Prince Leopold had made for the good of Saxe-Coburg.

Elizabeth hoisted the most authentic smile she could muster and thanked Lord Whitevale for the dance. After dropping a curtsy, she turned to leave the dancing ground, but Whitevale caught her waist and spun her around—directly into the prince.

Her head jerked up and their gazes met for one long meaningful moment. His hand reached out and steadied her. The moment his fingers touched her arm, a dull ache formed in her belly and heat began to pool between her legs.

Everything about this moment was so wrong. *Wrong.*

He had undoubtedly made his choice. The only one he could have ever made. What she was feeling, with no more provocation than an innocent touch, was nothing less than sinful.

His fingers felt hot upon her arm, and she knew if she did not leave at once, she might do something rash, something to persuade him to slip away for a short while to assuage her craving for him.

Her lips all but burned for his kiss. Her arms longed to hold him.

Prince Charlotte, her cheeks all aglow, moved between the prince and his cousin, and graced Elizabeth with a smile. "I am so glad you could attend the fete, Miss Royle. I consider this a secret celebration, you see, for my father has consented to consider a marriage between myself and the Leo with all due seriousness."

Elizabeth forced a smile, but she could not maintain it and it withered on her lips.

"My grandmother admits, however, that my father will give his blessing soon enough. He only requires enough time to be given the impression that the idea was his own." Princess Charlotte began to laugh. "I do not mind a bit, as long as he gives his consent before I am too aged to enjoy being married to such a handsome man."

Lord Whitevale, likely feeling as awkward as Elizabeth did at the intimate course the conversation had taken, blanched. The orchestra struck a chord again, and couples scurried onto the dancing ground.

Lord Whitevale bowed to the princess. "Do you think it permissible that we dance, Your Royal Highness?"

Princess Charlotte, never being a strict monitor of protocol, laughed quite loudly. "What a dear man you are. Come, let us dance. What argument could my father possibly have against my dancing with *you*?"

Elizabeth wasn't sure what to do. She certainly didn't trust herself. Her prince was here, directly in front of her. She was liable to say or do anything to hold him to her.

"Elizabeth," he said, in such a low tone her ears barely registered the sound. "There is something I must tell you. But I cannot do it here. Not now."

"I do not know what you might tell me that has not already been said by the Princess of Wales." Her words sounded reed thin and just as brittle.

"I have much to say. Much to confess."

Elizabeth shifted uneasily from one slippered foot to the other. She did not much care for the term "confess." It implied deliberate wrongdoing.

She turned her gaze up and looked into his gray eyes. In the sunlight, the ring of blue around them was as bright and vibrant as the cerulean sky above the garden. She could deny him nothing. "When then shall we speak?"

"In two days' time." He appeared quite earnest. "At sunset. You know where."

"Will you truly come?" Elizabeth had not meant to say the words aloud. They had simply slipped from her lips unbidden.

Sumner appeared hurt by that comment. "I will come." He lowered the tone of his voice again and leaned close so only she could hear him. "I swear it on my love for you."

Her heart thumped double time, and she felt the sudden urge to turn her face up to him, wishing he would kiss her. To make her know, truly know, that swearing on their love would make it so. No matter the circumstances.

A group of curious ladies sauntered near, and it was evident they were trying to hear what the prince had to say to the outrageous miss from Cornwall. "In two days' time," she repeated softly, not knowing what else to say.

"It was wonderful to see you again, Miss Royle. And I do thank you for your prompt attention at the theatre." It was apparent that he felt the presence of the gaggle of gossipers behind him, but his movements gave no hint he was aware of them. He looked steadily, passionately, into Elizabeth's eyes, and all the while made appropriate conversation. "I might not have survived had you not acted so quickly and secured a physician to tend to my wound. You are to be commended, my good lady."

Elizabeth bowed her head demurely and dropped a low curtsy.

Sumner bowed to her, then glanced over his shoulder to where Charlotte and his cousin danced on the lawn.

"Good day, Miss Royle. Please send Lady Upperton my well wishes," he said.

"I shall, Your Royal Highness." *Sumner.*

As he turned, he touched his lips and cast a secret kiss to her once more.

Elizabeth didn't know what she was feeling at that moment. His eyes told her that nothing had changed. That he loved her as she did him. But his mention of needing to confess something petrified her.

At that moment, she realized she was looking blindly through crowd. Focusing her attention, and trying the best she could to pen her emotions, Elizabeth looked about until she saw Lady Upperton standing on the tips of her toes to see what delicacies might be found toward the back of a bountifully stocked table.

Elizabeth plotted a path through the undulating crowd to meet her sponsor. Every step was an effort, for it was moving farther away from her prince, but it would not be forever, she told herself.

She'd be with him again.

In two days' time.

Chapter 17

Berkeley Square

The front door flew open with such force that it nearly broke from its hinges. "Elizabeth, where are you?" Anne shouted down the passage.

Elizabeth leapt up from the table in the kitchen, where she had been sitting, reviewing Mrs. Polkshank's list for the butcher. She whipped her head around and looked at the staircase through the kitchen doorway. "Anne?" she called back. "Is something amiss?"

All at once it sounded like a herd of oxen were being driven down the stair treads and into the kitchen. She was greatly relieved when she saw it was only Anne.

"Lizzy, have you read the newspaper this day?" Anne was gasping for breath, shoving a copy of the *Times* toward her. Had Elizabeth not known better, she would have thought her sister had run all the way from Cockspur Street to Berkeley Square to hand it to her.

"I have not had a spare moment all morning." Elizabeth took the newspaper from Anne, then gave Mrs. Polkshank a confused glance.

Cook shrugged her shoulders, appearing as clueless as to the reason for Anne's surprise visit as she.

Elizabeth sat down at the table and unfolded the newspaper.

Anne grabbed it from her hands, slapped it to the table, and ran her index finger down the front page. "There. Read this."

Elizabeth picked up the newspaper and raised the article to her eyes. Again Anne grabbed the *Times* from her hands.

"Oh, I cannot wait for you to read the *entire* article." She drew in a deep breath then shook her hands as though drying them in the air. "He is leaving for Paris—*today!*"

"Who is, miss?" Mrs. Polkshank asked.

Anne turned her head at Cook, then back at Elizabeth. "Prince Leopold. Today. Did you hear me? He is leaving for Paris today."

Elizabeth was bewildered. "No, that cannot be. I just spoke with him yesterday."

Anne poked her finger at the newspaper. "It says as much right there. Read it."

Elizabeth bent her head and looked at the article, but Anne slammed her palm upon it.

"No, don't read it," her sister cried out with frustration. "You do not have time!"

"I am sure I do have time. Prince Leopold is not going anywhere. We are to meet tomorrow evening at the—" Elizabeth caught herself. "At . . . the . . . well, I am not at liberty to say. Safety precautions, you know."

"Lizzy, the prince is leaving Carlton House at noon today." Anne waited for a response, but continued when Elizabeth merely sat and listened. "A mole, inside court, has it on good authority that the Prince of Wales has asked Prince Leopold to confer with his Coburg family about the desirability of a marriage between their two families. Once he has received confirmation that the Coburg family supports such a union, he will give consent—if his daughter is still unmarried at that time."

Elizabeth crinkled her brow. "And so . . ."

"So the prince is returning to Paris, to resume his military duties, while sending urgent dispatches to his brother and family. Or, so claims this source." Anne frantically shook her hands again.

No. It wasn't true. She had seen the look in Sumner's eyes. He loved her and would be at the Serpentine tomorrow at sunset. She was as certain of it as she was that the sun would rise in the morning.

"Come with me. If we leave now, you may be able to speak with him." Anne caught Elizabeth's wrist and tugged at her.

"Why don't you go, Miss Elizabeth," Mrs. Polkshank said. "Prove that mouse in Carlton House wrong." Cook folded her arms over her ample chest and gave her head a firm nod.

"It was a mole," Anne snapped. "Not a mouse."

"I don't care what sort of vermin it is," Mrs. Polkshank replied smartly. "I learned a long time ago that you can't trust a rat no matter what he calls himself."

Elizabeth pushed up from the table. "I agree with Cook, and I shall accompany you for the reason she suggested. No other. For I do not believe for one instant that the prince is leaving England today."

Carlton House

Anne bade her carriage driver to hand them down at the far end of the gateway to Carlton House, then return to her home on Cockspur Street to wait.

"That way, if Prince Leopold spies us, from a window above or . . . possibly from a carriage . . ." Anne paused as she stepped to the street. ". . . we can claim we were returning from shopping on Pall Mall and walking to my home."

"Aren't you the clever one? You have thought of everything." Elizabeth sighed as the footman handed her down from the town carriage to join her sister.

"There is no need to be angry with me. I did not pen the article in the *Times!*" Anne's spine seemed to stiffen to such an extent that Elizabeth wondered how she managed to walk.

"I am not angry with you, dear, I am furious with myself for coming to Carlton House at noon." Elizabeth glanced at the high windows just below the rooftop. Once, she had looked up at these very same windows wondering if the Prince of Wales, her natural father in all possibility, was looking down at her at the same moment. Now she wondered if her prince, her future husband, was gazing through one of those many windows. How a few weeks made such a difference.

She sighed. She should not have come.

It was only a waste of time.

A transgression against trust.

In the distance, a clock sounded the noon hour. Without meaning to, Elizabeth held her breath and waited for the bell tower to strike twelve times.

Eight . . . nine . . . ten, and still no carriage passed through the gates.

Eleven . . . twelve.

Nothing.

She released her pent breath and smirked at her sister as they neared the guarded gate. "I told you, Anne, he is not leaving London."

"Must you always take everything so literally?" Anne stopped beside the gates and pretended to fish for something inside her reticule. "When a person says 'noon' they are referring to sometime *around* twelve of the clock. Not exactly twelve."

Elizabeth leaned against the gate while Anne prattled on, quite obviously stalling for time to prove the rat inside Carlton House had the right of it all along.

Suddenly, the gate began to rumble and she leapt away from it.

"Stand aside, miss!" the guard yelled. "Stand aside."

Anne rushed up and stood beside Elizabeth as the Prince of Wales's glittering closed carriage rolled to a halt at the guard stand. As the team of six pranced in place, Elizabeth ignored the guard's warning and took a step forward to look inside the carriage. She could not help herself. She had to be sure.

A chill as cold and biting as ice ran up her spine and through her heart. There, inside the carriage, was Princess Charlotte, and across from her the prince and his cousin.

"Step aside, miss!"

The warning call of the guardsman drew the notice of those inside. The prince's eyes grew large and round as he saw Elizabeth standing there.

Ruefully, she touched her fingers to her lips and then opened her hand fully and released her kiss.

Princess Charlotte looked from Elizabeth to the prince and said something. The prince nodded once in Elizabeth's direction and then the carriage drove through the gates and down Pall Mall.

Elizabeth's heart pounded like a kettle drum in her ears and her skin became cold and damp.

"Lizzy?" Anne took her arm. She pressed her mouth to Elizabeth's ear. "Stay on your feet, sister. Dignity, remember? Just a minute more, that's all, and he will be gone from sight."

Elizabeth wavered as she numbly watched the carriage move down the street until it turned and disappeared onto St. James.

"Take me home, Anne."

"Too far. We'll go to my home." Anne slipped her arm around Elizabeth's waist. "It's just around the corner. Not far. Just a short walk . . ." Anne was clearly worried about her. She always chattered when she was tired or her nerves were stressed.

"I can manage." Elizabeth pulled away from her sister's arm and concentrated fully on walking. "I am perfectly fine."

He will come back.

He will.

Berkeley Square
The next day

Great-aunt Prudence did not leave her room that morning. Instead she sat before the small writing desk in her bedchamber scribbling notes and drawing pictures that she refused to allow anyone, except Cherie, to see.

Elizabeth worried about her elderly great-aunt when Prudence did not come down to join her for their noon meal. And so she waited, since noon, according to Anne, was not a precise time.

But at half past the hour, worried that something was wrong with her aged great-aunt, she started up the stairs to inquire how Prudence was feeling.

Cherie was just leaving Prudence's bedchamber and gestured to Elizabeth that her great-aunt was sleeping.

"Is she well? Shall I call for a physician?" Elizabeth asked.

Cherie shook her head vigorously, then waved off her concerns with a silly smile.

"You will call for me if you have any concerns about her, won't you, Cherie?" She was not leaving the passage until she had some assurance from the silent maid.

Cherie nodded, then turned Elizabeth around and gave her a good-natured push down the passage.

"All right, all right." Elizabeth grinned, and as she descended the stairs realized that it was the first time she'd smiled since yesterday noon.

She had purposely kept herself busy all

morning, and had even attempted to join Mrs. Polkshank as she departed for the butcher—although Cook told her that assistance was not necessary. Then Mrs. Polkshank added that if she did not trust her to purchase the beef, maybe she ought to haul the butcher home with her to review the price per pound of flesh with Miss Can't-trust-anyone. It was then that Elizabeth decided to stay at home.

Now, however, she was running low on ways to engage her mind and hands until sunset. Already the small house staff was growing quite exasperated with her and she could not seem to occupy herself with reading or writing letters. And resorting to sleep to pass her time was not an option. "To sleep, perchance to dream—ay, there's the rub." She should have listened to Shakespeare, too, for a dream had cursed her with a heart rent in two.

Rounding the newel post at the bottom of the staircase, Elizabeth had just turned for the parlor when the brass hammer came down upon the front door.

Instead of waiting for MacTavish, who was no doubt hiding from his annoying mistress in the kitchen with Mrs. Polkshank, Elizabeth went to the door and opened it.

Her knees were suddenly transformed to

melted beeswax and she found herself sitting upon the floor—looking up at the prince.

Sumner stared at Elizabeth, who was sitting on the entryway floor, her arm still raised, her hand tightly holding the door handle.

He bent and scooped her up, but she made no move to settle her feet on the floor and stand. She said nothing, but stared up at him, her mouth fully agape.

"I could not wait until sunset to see you," he said to her as he reached down and removed her hand from the door handle, then kicked the door closed behind him.

Elizabeth lifted her finger and pointed, mutely, to the parlor.

"This way?" he asked.

She nodded, and so he carried her into the parlor, settled her gently upon the settee, and then returned to close the door opening to the passage. He turned the key in the lock. "I cannot afford another interruption, if you do not mind."

Finally she found her voice. "I can't believe you are here." Her eyes welled suddenly. "I thought—the newspaper reported that you departed for Paris yesterday."

"I promised I would come back for you."

He sat beside her, unconsciously tapping his

pocket where a small emerald ring lay in wait.

"Elizabeth, I told you that there was something I must I confess, and I must do so now."

She raised her hand feebly. "I do not know that I can bear a confession this day. Seeing you standing at my front door, after I had watched you leave Carlton House for what I thought was . . . forever, is about the limit of surprise I can manage in one day."

Sumner bowed his head. He was wicked to allow her to suffer the way she had. But Leopold had safely departed London and was on his way to Paris.

Now was the time to admit everything to Elizabeth.

He opened his mouth to begin, but at once she was in his arms, her lips pressed against his. *No.* No, he had to tell her. He pulled back. "Elizabeth, please. I must confess."

"I can't hear it. Not now. Just let me pretend for a little while longer. Please." She reached out for him, but he caught her wrists and held them.

"Pretend?" Sumner lowered his head. "There is no need to pretend. I am not going to marry Princess Charlotte." He could see she did not believe him, and after what had come to pass, he did not fault her.

"Princess Charlotte said her father would consent." Elizabeth tugged against him, visibly needing an end to any talk of this subject that pained her so. "The *Times* reported that you were returning to Paris to resume your duty and to petition your family for support of a union."

The tears battered the wall of her lashes, threatening to spill. She struggled feebly to pull away from him, but Sumner knew that if he released her, she would run, and he would face another delay to admitting what he must to end her pain.

"You have to hear me, Elizabeth. I need so much for you to understand."

"I cannot." Her emerald eyes flashed and she threw her weight forward to break his grip, but he held fast and they both tumbled onto the thick rug.

She tried to roll away, but he threw her onto her back and leaned his body against hers, holding her prisoner to his coming words.

"I never meant to deceive you, Elizabeth. I never meant to hurt you, or cause any pain." He lifted a heavy copper curl from her shoulder as he leaned close and kissed her calmingly. "But before I say what I must, know that I love you, and I want nothing more than to be with you."

A tear slipped from the corner of her eyes and trickled over her temple, where it disappeared into her long, thick hair. "Please, do not linger. Tell me what you must and then let me grieve."

"There will be no grieving. There is no need, for I will not marry Princess Charlotte . . ." He drew in a deep, fortifying breath. ". . . because I am *not* Prince Leopold."

Elizabeth blinked several times in succession, releasing her tears in steady streams down the side of her face. "What did say? I vow, I must not have understood you. I could not have."

"You did, but I will say it again so you may be certain. I am not Leopold."

Confusion was plain in her eyes as she stared at him, as if she was seeing him for the first time.

"When I first met you and your sister in the jewelry shop, I was on an errand for Prince Leopold, my cousin. I introduced myself as Lansdowne, the Marquess of Whitevale. I am he. Sumner Lansdowne, Lord Whitevale."

Perplexed eyes peered up at him. "But I saw you—everyone knew you to be Prince Leopold. How can what you say possibly be true?"

"Not everyone knew me to be Prince Leopold.

Princess Charlotte, Mercer, and of course the Prince of Wales himself all knew me as Leopold's cousin, his confidant, and his guard."

Elizabeth had long stopped struggling against him, but holding her this way as they talked was far preferable to the way he had imagined this moment, with her hugging herself for comfort against the cold rail of the Serpentine bridge.

"H-His guard?" She furrowed her brow, but as the moments passed, gradual understanding smoothed her features. "Are you telling me that you posed as Leopold . . . to draw off the attacks from your cousin?"

"Yes." Sumner's response came as a relieved sigh. He closed his eyes briefly and then continued. "On our first day in London, a shot was fired from a crowd. We couldn't be sure it was meant for the prince, but he had received letters in Paris, before we journeyed here, warning Leopold that if he persisted in his quest for Princess Charlotte's hand there were those who would ensure he would never be successful."

Her eyes were large and round. "The backers of William of Orange?"

"Yes." Sumner felt the faceted emerald in the ring in his pocket pressing between them, distracting him. "But there were no further letters.

No words of warning. Still, for the sake of Saxe-Coburg, Prince Leopold's safety became my only priority in London."

Elizabeth lowered her eyes from his.

"Until I met you," he added.

Her green eyes swept up to his, and he knew at last that she would forgive him.

Chapter 18

Elizabeth squeezed her eyes tightly closed, inadvertently pressing from her damp lashes a single remnant tear.

This was a dream. It had to be.

In her boredom, she had fallen asleep on the settee—and now she was dreaming. But . . . once, she had been told that if you realize you are dreaming, the dream ends at that moment. As far as she knew, however, it hadn't. She could feel Sumner's warm body against hers even now.

She opened her eyes quickly to be sure, knowing that if this was just a dream, Sumner would be gone and she'd likely find Mrs. Polkshank's huge, marmalade cat sleeping against her, sharing his furry warmth.

But Sumner wasn't gone.

He was leaning over her, kissing her softly, passionately. She felt him nudge her body as he slid his hand between her back and the carpet, and then pressed his palm against the small of her back, pulling her body firmly against him.

He broke their kiss then, and though she hungrily pursued his mouth with her own, he escaped her and instead swept his lips across her cheek and then down her throat to the shallow hollow beneath her shoulder bone.

She sighed as his mouth moved lower still, tantalizing her with his achingly slow progression as she realized his ultimate destination.

Sumner lifted his head to see as he pulled at the thin satin ribbon that cinched her bodice closed. She couldn't endure this any longer. She could not.

Elizabeth slid her fingers through his thick, dark hair, then cupped her hands behind his head and struggled to urge his mouth back to hers. "Kiss me," she whispered as she pressed her lips to his.

She felt him smiling against her mouth as his fingers at last released her ribbon cinch and her simple cambric gown opened to his touch.

His hands were rough but warm against her

skin as he lowered her chemise and a slight chill of pleasure drew goose bumps across the skin he had bared. Her nipples hardened in her anticipation.

Being slender of form, she rarely wore a corset for a day at home, and now, as his lips moved over the swells of her breasts, she was grateful there was not another layer of clothing between her and his moist, searching lips.

Laying her hands on the muscled slope of his shoulders, Elizabeth blindly trailed her palms down his chest and fumbled between them to catch the lapels, hoping to coax his coat, and more, from his body.

Sumner received her silent message and leaned up to shrug his coat from his broad shoulders. His desire for her pressed up hard against his breeches, forming a tautly drawn tent. Her body responded with a rush of heat between her thighs.

But then, to her great surprise, given his ardor and obvious state of arousal, he carefully folded his coat and placed it on the settee beside them.

He did not show such care with his cravat, nor with his waistcoat or the shirt he very nearly tore from his form. It was as if he could not peel the layers from his body fast enough.

As he bent over her again, she could not help but skim her fingers along the shallow trenches of his bare, rippled abdomen and up over the firm mounds of his chest.

Sumner closed his eyelids and sighed with pleasure as her fingers skipped lightly over his nipples, turning them to stone beneath her soft touch.

He leaned over her and brushed her mouth with his lips. Not kissing, but rather teasing her, making her chase his mouth. But he did not surrender despite her assertive advance.

Elizabeth groaned as his hardness pressed against the place she wanted to feel him most. It was maddening. She wanted nothing more than to at last feel him, not his fingers or his mouth, *him,* inside of her. Her thighs parted slightly as she raised her hips, forcing him against her.

"Sumner," she breathed, "I need you."

His eyes sparkled mischievously as he grasped her and, without a word, eased her summer gown and her chemise from her shoulders. Then he yanked it down to her waist, making her gasp with the sudden rush of air on her skin. His mouth settled over one breast and suckled it roughly while he lowered her gown farther, to her hips.

He broke the bond between them to slide one hand behind her, clasping one side of her bottom and lifting her, just long enough to pull the gown to her knees. A moment more and her gown puddled beneath her feet. She kicked her slippers off. Her body was lit with excitement of what would come. She was ready to feel herself joined with him. Wanting so badly for him to ease inside of her, to feel their bodies merge into one . . . at last.

He did not touch her for several moments more, and she lifted her eyelids to see that he was looking appreciatively at her naked body. She flushed at once, and even saw the color of her embarrassment rise in her breasts, then felt it journey upward to heat her cheeks.

She crossed her arms over her naked, pinked breasts, but Sumner would not have it. He caught her wrists and lifted her arms away, settling them on either side of her head, shaking his head slowly. He would not allow her to hide her body from him.

Sumner's gaze fell from hers as he ran his palms down her wrists, her arms, and over her nipples, making them harden almost painfully. His fingers drifted onward, trailing down the sensitive skin at her sides, sending waves of shivers over the entirety of her body. His hands continued their leisurely exploration of her form, slipping to her hips, then down her stocking-sheathed legs.

There was only one place he had not touched, and knowing this gave Elizabeth a throbbing twinge of excitement.

Leaning back, Sumner surveyed her hungrily. He said nothing as he traced the curve of her quivering leg up her silk stocking. Then he cupped his hand behind her knee and lifted it so he was now kneeling between her spread thighs.

His fingertips brushed the furl at the apex of her legs, making her body tremble with delicious anticipation. *Oh, please, please, let me feel you. Now.*

Elizabeth leaned up just enough to catch the back of his neck with her hand and pull him hard down atop of her, feeding at his mouth as they fell back against the soft carpet together.

She clung to Sumner as he kissed her, touched her, drove her into a frenzy, made her writhe in sweet sensation. But there was something more she needed. "Sumner, please, make me yours."

He paused for a moment, then seemed to glance at his coat folded neatly on the settee, but whatever thought had been in his mind was fleeting, for he turned back to her and knelt lower between her spread thighs.

His body seemed golden, his abdomen, his hips, almost dark in contrast to the whiteness of her inner thighs on either side of him. Bravely, Elizabeth reached out her hand and fumbled with the buttons of his breeches until his front fall opened at last. His hard length bounced into her hand. His erection pulsed and twitched in her palm, exciting her as never before.

She did not know exactly how to touch him, how to please him, but her daring welled much like the heat within her and she stroked him with eager fingers, pausing as she neared his plum-shaped tip, exploring with the ring of her thumb and index finger the thick ridge beneath it. His penis jerked, in a way that seemed to please him. And so she let her instinct guide her further. Twisting her hand around, she all but closed her hand over him before sliding it down his length to the light nest of hair at its thick base.

Sumner shuddered and leaned over her again to kiss her deeply. "I love you," he whispered against her lips. His erection pulsed. The urgency was his now, and he nudged her knees wider apart with his body.

He slipped his hand between her thighs and

stroked her, dipping his finger into the heat of her. She arched against him.

Elizabeth clung to his broad shoulders. His firm penis prodded gently between her legs until she thought she would go mad if she did not feel him inside of her.

Sumner closed his eyes as he moved his tip just between her engorged nether lips. He groaned as he skimmed her wetness. He pressed into her, only a small bit, and her body cinched around that part of him, wanting to draw him fully inside.

"I love you, Elizabeth," he said again as he leaned up on his arms and positioned himself to drive into her.

His eyes were questioning, but her reply was sure. "I love you, Sumner, with all my heart. I want you and I need you."

Elizabeth tensed as he moved into her. Still, there was no pain, as with the first time he touched her deeply, only a slight sting as her body slowly stretched to accept him fully. She slid her hands along his outer thighs to his hips, and then grasped his hips and pulled him deeper inside. She sighed as she felt him nudge against her, deep inside of her.

Sumner slowly pulled back, then moved into her again, pushing harder, deeper, with each rocking motion. She felt her body contract around him, tingling, filling her with the undeniable urge to raise her hips to him, press down against him. To meet his every thrust with one of her own.

She felt as though she'd had too much wine, and her mind began to spin. Thought was beyond her. There was only the feeling of Sumner joined with her. She closed her eyes and let herself become lost in the wildly spinning center of molten heat growing within her where their bodies met and became one.

Sumner supported himself and rose up to watch her as he thrust into her, harder and harder each time. Beads of perspiration erupted on his forehead as his rhythm grew faster, his pumping into her making her body bump and nearly leap from the carpet with each thrust.

Elizabeth closed her eyes and bit into the flesh of her lower lip. She could no longer meet his movement. He was driving too fast, too hard for her to keep pace. Her legs were shaking, and she drew them up around his hips, pressing down against his hard buttocks with her heels, holding him inside of her, turning just a bit to control the depth of his thrusts, his pressure.

She bucked against him and cried out as something inside of her flared, sending wild licking flames through her core and outward to every part of her body.

Sumner squeezed his eyes tightly. She felt him strain, and a whisper of damp heat spread across the plane of his back as she clung to him. He groaned once and then again before leaning down to kiss her tenderly, then rested atop of her.

They lay that way, bodies bereft of energy, resting in each other's arms, for several languorous minutes. Sumner finally rolled onto his back and Elizabeth turned on her side and nestled against him, resting her head on his shoulder. He wrapped his arm around her body and held her there. And what she felt then . . . well, it was perfect. It felt like destiny.

She turned her head just enough to look up at him. Bliss filled his eyes and he was smiling down at her.

"Tell me it will always be this way," she whispered, never wanting the moment to end.

He edged up and rested his weight on one elbow. "It can be. If you will have me." He flung an arm behind him and reached up to the settee. He fumbled with his coat and then tossed the garment he had taken such care with earlier, allowing it to fall in a crumpled heap near the cold hearth.

She laughed, not grasping at all what he was about.

He kissed her softly, then his ardor seemed to grow and his kisses became more persistent as he claimed her mouth. "I do love you, Elizabeth, and I wish to always be with you." He leaned back, lifted her wrist and slid onto a finger on her left hand a gold ring emblazoned with a sparkling cut emerald. "And I hope you wish the same. If you do, I desire that you wear this ring, that so matches the love I see in your eyes, as a symbol of my troth."

Elizabeth held her hand up before her face and blinked up at it. "Are you asking me to—"

"I am asking you to marry me, Elizabeth." The look in Sumner's eyes, so wanting yet so unsure, moved her deep within her heart.

"I have never wanted anything more than to be your wife . . . to be with you forever." She wrapped her arms around his neck and their lips met and locked.

Her dream was coming true.

Hyde Park

The sky was red with licks of brilliant gold as the sun set. The darkness of the Serpentine reflected the vibrant colors of the evening sky, making it look like an endless swath of rippling crimson silk.

Sumner stood with his arm around Elizabeth at the rail of the bridge, gazing at the bright pink sun as it gracefully bowed closer and closer toward the horizon.

He looked down at her.

Sensing his attention, Elizabeth turned her head and looked up at him. "What is it?" she asked.

"I was a damn fool. I should have told you who I truly was long ago." Sumner removed his arm from her shoulder and leaned forward to rest his forearms on the rail. "I put both of us through so much needless heartache."

"Why do you dwell on that?" She wrapped her arm around his biceps and stepped closer, the side of her body pressed against him. "We are here now, and we have each other and always shall." She cocked her head. "And besides, you would not be the man I love were duty something you could simply set aside when circumstances became too difficult. But you didn't do that. You couldn't. You guarded Prince Leopold and ensured his safety for Saxe-Coburg, even when it meant possibly sacrificing your own life. How could I ever fault you for your bravery and sense of responsibility?"

Sumner threw his head back, drew in a long, deep breath, then exhaled. "There is something more you should know. Something that only two other people are aware of—and Leopold is not one of them."

Elizabeth looked up at him quizzically. "Tell me."

He paused a moment, since he'd never once spoken these words aloud and was not quite sure how or where to begin. "I have heard of your possible relation to the Prince of Wales, Elizabeth. And I know that, as much as you tried to discount Sir Henry's comments at the dinner party, there may be some truth to Society's chatter. You may be Prinny's daughter."

He could feel Elizabeth tense.

"And, I wish for you to know that whether or not you are of royal descent matters not to me. I believe I have loved you from the moment I saw you walk into the jewelers . . . looking a bit drowned."

Sumner looked to her and smiled, then gazed out over the water. "I hope my background, my true history, does not affect how you feel about me, either."

Elizabeth relaxed. "Unless you are my secret brother by Prinny, nothing you could tell me would change my plans to marry you at our earliest opportunity. I love you, Sumner. *You.*"

He swallowed hard. It was time. "Leopold's family took me in when I was but an infant. No one ever spoke of the circumstances of whose child I was or how I came into the Coburg family. Soon, I learned not to speak of it since the subject seemed to upset my adopted parents. All I knew, after years of searching for the truth, was that my mother had died in childbirth and my father had not been able, or perhaps willing, to care for a baby."

"But you and Leopold always refer to one another as cousins."

"Yes. All my life I was always referred to as a cousin. Who would ever dispute it? Leopold and I looked so much alike. But there were always whispers that we were not so much distant cousins . . . as half brothers."

"Is it true?"

"I do not know, exactly." Sumner sighed. "But when I reached my majority, I was informed that my supposed father, Lansdowne, had died and I was to become the Marquess of Whitevale."

"So you never knew your natural father?"

"No. I never even knew *if* he was my natural father. The similarities between Leopold and myself are striking. We were raised together, schooled together, fought together. To me, Leopold is my brother."

"And this is why protecting him was so important to you."

Sumner sighed yet again. "Yes."

Elizabeth turned him toward her and, not caring who might see, kissed him. "None of this matters at all, Sumner. But I thank you for explaining your extraordinary bond with Prince Leopold."

She was right, Sumner decided. Circumstances of birth did not matter.

What did was that he would soon marry the woman he loved with all of his heart. He felt buoyant to have shed the weights of his past from his shoulders.

"I was thinking," he began, turning Elizabeth for a stroll from the bridge. "I may leave the military and retire to Whitevale. I have never seen it, can you believe it? You will be my wife, so the decision is truly ours together."

Elizabeth laughed as they stepped off the bridge and into the grass. "As your soon-to-be wife, I would choose anything that will remove you from the line of gunfire ... and knife points. But I wonder," she added, "how you will adapt to the staid, calm of life in the country when you are used to dodging bullets and cannonballs."

"With you, my dear, I do not think life will ever be 'staid.'"

There was a flash of light from the shadows of the trees, and Elizabeth heard the chilling, all too familiar whiz of a bullet passing between her and Sumner.

"Get down!" he shouted. Instead of retreating for cover, he charged directly toward the flash, disappearing into the darkness of the trees.

Elizabeth gasped and brought her fingers worriedly to her lips. She remained crouched for only a few moments and slowly came to her feet. The sun had just settled behind the treeline, the light in the sky rapidly dissolving into night.

Her whole body tensed as she waited for Sumner to emerge. Her ears were primed for any sound, any hint that her love was safe. But there was nothing.

She started walking at first, then running toward the trees, worried for Sumner.

And then there was another flash of light and the sound of gunshot. "Sumner!" she cried out, ducking under branches and pushing leaves from her face as she ran toward the sound.

She heard thrashing ahead, grunts and the smack of landed punches, then the sound of footfalls coming directly toward her.

"Sumner?" she whispered feebly, knowing that if it was not him, she was in grave danger. "Sumner, please answer me."

"I am coming. Go back to the bridge," came his voice from twenty or so paces beyond where she stood. "Go!"

Turning, she did as he asked and hurried in the relative light at the water's lapping edge.

A few moments later Sumner's large, distinguishable form stepped from the cover of trees. From her position, it appeared that he dragged another man, whose arm he'd pinned behind his back. As they approached, she saw who the other man was.

"Mr. Manton?" Elizabeth sputtered. "It cannot be."

"It is," Sumner confirmed.

"He was the gunman? Dear Mr. Manton was the man trying to kill us?"

Manton jerked his head upright. "Not both of you. *Him*." He looked up with disgust at Sumner.

"B-But why?" Elizabeth asked. None of this made any sense to her. Mr. Manton had always seemed such a gentle soul.

"He supports a union between Charlotte and William of Orange, I suspect." Anger sparked in Sumner's eyes as he looked at this man who had relentlessly tried to kill him. He wrenched Manton's arm higher behind his back, making him groan with pain.

"I don't give a damn about William of Orange," Manton cried.

"Then why did you do it?" Elizabeth stepped closer. Despite his violent display, she could still see tenderness in Manton's eyes.

His expression softened. "Because of *you*."

Sumner loosened his hold so he could turn enough to face Manton. "What do you mean, because of her?"

"From the first time I saw her at a ball a year ago, I knew I loved her," he admitted, his eyebrows drawing close as he peered coldly at Sumner. "And recently she expressed fondness for me. But then *you* came into her life. How could I ever compete, when it was clear that a prince sought her affections?" His expression changed abruptly and he looked longingly at Elizabeth. "I never meant for you to be hurt. That was an accident. You must believe me, Miss Royle. I would never harm you. Not intentionally."

"You were the shooter at Pall Mall as well,"

she said flatly. Of course he was. And then it occurred to her that she had come upon him in the passage just after Sumner was stabbed. "*And* in the theatre."

"Yes." Manton lowered his gaze, defeated.

"And the shot in the crowd when we first arrived in London?" Sumner prodded.

Manton shook his head. "That wasn't me, though I did read of the incident in the *Times* and the suppositions about the supporters of William of Orange being at fault. So, when I saw you, I realized who the man was who had so captivated Elizabeth. I knew that if I . . . if you were dead, the blame would be settled upon the supporters of the Dutchman, a group with which I have no affiliation. It was so clear to me what had to be done." His faced pulled into a frightening scowl. "Only you don't die, do you?"

"And he shall not for a very long time, now that you have been apprehended," Elizabeth fairly spat.

"Come with me." Sumner yanked Manton forward and began to march him up Rotten Row. "We will let you answer to the authorities." His voice grew firm. "And do not dare speak to Miss Royle again. Do you understand?" He jerked his arm. "Not one word."

"Yes, Your Royal Highness," Manton wailed.

"Lord Whitevale, if you please, sir." Sumner's face remained impassive, but at his words, a small smile tilted the edges of Elizabeth's lips upward.

Chapter 19

Berkeley Square

When Elizabeth entered the house, she heard Great-aunt Prudence loudly calling her name from the parlor. She hurried inside, since her aunt rarely raised her voice . . . unless her claret goblet was empty.

When she came into the parlor, the old woman smiled broadly. "I saw you leave with *him*."

Elizabeth lowered her gaze and smiled inwardly, though she could feel the whisper of a blush on her cheeks. "I did."

"You're going to marry him." Prudence pointed a bony finger at her left hand.

Elizabeth raised her finger and showed her

the glittering emerald he had given her as a betrothal ring. "I am."

"When?" The old woman had something in that mind of hers, but what it was, Elizabeth had no notion.

"In two weeks time." Elizabeth looked suspiciously at her great-aunt. "Though we still have to discuss it with the Old Rakes and Lady Upperton, of course."

"Good. We shall have enough by then." Her great-aunt sighed happily.

"Enough of what?" Elizabeth scrunched her brows. Just what was Prudence going on about?

"Enough of *everything*." She gave her head a good, hard nod, then flashed Elizabeth a broad grin.

Very well then. Elizabeth turned to retire to her chamber but thought better of it. She wanted to tell someone about Sumner. "He is not a prince, you know. I just learned."

"Oh?" Prudence replied. "Is he a gardener?"

Elizabeth laughed. "No, he is actually the Marquess of Whitevale . . . but why would you ask if he is a gardener, Prudence?"

"Because you have leaves and sticks in your hair, dear." She pointed at the top of her head.

Elizabeth's hand flew to her crown, where

she felt a small twig. She pulled it from where it had tangled in her hair and looked at it. This was all quite mortifying for she had been let off on Cockspur Street to tell her sister Anne and her husband Laird of her wonderful news. Neither of them had said a word about the twig and leaves in her hair. But now their vaguely amused stares made more sense. "It is not at all what you think, Prudence. It is actually quite innocent." *This time.*

"Oh? And just what am I thinking, my dear?" Her great-aunt lifted her snowy white eyebrows. "I do wish you would tell me. I should like to know."

"That . . . it is oak." She gave Prudence what must have been a discomfited expression. "But it is not. It's birch. Simple mistake to make. I've done it myself once or twice." Elizabeth slapped a hand to her forehead and turned around. "Good evening, Prudence. Clearly I am in need of rest," she mumbled as she quit the room and took the stairs up to her bedchamber.

Early the next morning, Elizabeth went belowstairs determined to solve the mystery of the rising food expenses. When she married Sumner, she would leave Berkeley Square and not allow Great-aunt Prudence's house funds to be stolen away from under her nose.

When she reached the kitchen, she expected to see Mrs. Polkshank. Instead she found Cherie, holding a very heavy case of wine, and Prudence, eyes widened in surprise, with a smoked ham under her arm.

"What is this?" Elizabeth asked, taking the ham from Great-aunt Prudence, and then the wine from Cherie, and setting them on the scrubbed pine kitchen table.

"We have enough now," Prudence replied. "Plenty."

Mrs. Polkshank, who had obviously heard the exchange, was just coming up from the cellar with a lamp in her grip. "I'd say she has enough contraband champagne and smoked meats for your prince's entire regiment—or for a wedding breakfast." She beckoned to Elizabeth. "Oh, come on, come on, Miss Elizabeth. You'll be wantin' to see what you've been pinching me about for two months."

Elizabeth was completely befuddled as she descended the stone and earth stairs. Mrs. Polkshank held up the flickering lamp, illuminating the large room. There, filling the root cellar, was case upon case of contraband French champagne, a case of prime claret, and smoked meats of every kind. "So the food expenditures have been so high because—"

"Of your wedding!" her great-aunt called down into the root cellar.

Elizabeth hurriedly climbed up the shallow steps, with Mrs. Polkshank behind her holding the candle high so her mistress would not trip in the dim light. When they both emerged, Cook closed the trapdoor and dragged a tiny braided rug over top of it.

Elizabeth's gaze went straight to Prudence. "But how did you know I would be getting married?"

"Because you dreamed it, gel. And your dreams do come true. Mostly." Prudence smiled. "Once I heard, I knew I hadn't long to prepare, but Cherie and Cook helped me collect what we needed for a fine wedding breakfast."

Tears came to her eyes. She had been so hard on Mrs. Polkshank about the cost of food. And she, Cherie, and dear Great-aunt Prudence had only been planning for the wedding they believed in—even when she herself had given up hope. Spreading her arms wide, Elizabeth clasped them all together in a heartfelt hug.

Two weeks later
St. George's, Mayfair

"We're not going to have enough," Great-aunt Prudence said as she leaned on her cane and peered into the crowded church. "How much do you think they will drink?"

Elizabeth laughed. "It is a breakfast, Prudence. They will not drink so much as you suppose." She looked at Anne and Mary. "I think I am ready."

"You are not the least filled with nerves?" Mary set a comforting hand on her shoulder, then fluffed the frilled tulle that ornamented her wedding gown's short sleeves.

"Not in the least. I have been witness to this wedding so many times in my dreams and in my mind that even Prudence's worry of there being too few bottles of champagne does not concern me at all." Elizabeth leaned toward Anne and whispered to her, "Have you seen him? He is here?"

"Standing near the nave with Prince Leopold at his side." Anne swallowed hard then.

"What is wrong? There is something you are not telling me."

"Nothing of importance, only, when you walk down the center aisle, do not look to your right when you reach the front." Anne scratched nervously at her neck.

"Why ever not?" Elizabeth adjusted the flounce of rows of tulle at the foot of her white satin petticoat, while Mary tightened the snowy full ribbon bows at her back.

"It is only . . . oh, blast, you must know. Princess Charlotte has come." Anne cringed.

"Why would that bother me? Sumner was never going to marry her, and she was never in love with him." Elizabeth smiled. "Besides which, she may be our sister. Family is always welcome."

"I suppose you are right, Lizzy." Anne still did not seem quite convinced.

Elizabeth drew her kid gloves up to her elbows while Anne settled a wreath formed of tulle edged with white satin upon her head.

"Beautiful!" Anne and Mary chimed as one.

Elizabeth turned and looked to Lord Gallantine, who did look quite the gallant in his dark frock coat and silk twill cravat. He offered her his arm and together they began down the long center aisle of St. George's.

Lady Upperton's snowy white hair topped with a bonnet sporting an overtall white ostrich plume called Elizabeth's gaze to the front of the church. She could see from the family box pew that Lord Lotharian was gazing proudly at her, and Lilywhite, already dabbing his eyes with a lacy handkerchief.

Elizabeth turned her gaze toward the nave and at once her eyes locked with Sumner's. She gasped, for she had seen him standing just like this before . . . in her dream.

He was a sight to behold in a crimson red coat, with golden epaulets enhancing his broad shoulders. Across his chest was a sash of white satin ornamented with several medals of honor.

As she neared, he lifted his hand briefly to his mouth, then opened his palm and cast a kiss to her, sending a warm flutter through her elegantly gowned body.

When they reached the nave, Lord Gallantine handed Elizabeth to Sumner. Her eyes met his and suddenly it was if the world dissolved around them. She could hear the rector, responded appropriately, but never once did her gaze leave Sumner during the ceremony. Everything was just as she'd dreamed it.

Until something happened that she had not expected—had not dreamed even once.

At the moment the rector pronounced Sumner Lansdowne, Marquess of Whitevale, and Miss Elizabeth Royle, husband and wife, Prince Leopold stepped up beside his cousin.

There, on a crimson tuft of velvet, she saw a sparkling tiara. Confused, Elizabeth peered closer, and recognized it as the very same bejeweled tiara that Sumner had placed on her head on the day they met.

Prince Leopold smiled at her. "His heart chose it for you, my dear, so you must have it." His gaze shifted, and Elizabeth followed it to Princess Charlotte. The princess was nodding her head and smiling at her.

Elizabeth looked to Sumner.

"You are my love, my wife, and my princess, and will always be," he said.

Anne quickly moved forward and whisked the tulle headdress from Elizabeth's copper locks.

"I love you, Elizabeth." Sumner lowered the tiara down upon her head and bent to kiss her.

A moment later applause echoed through St. George's, restoring Elizabeth and her husband to the moment. Together they turned to face the congregation, and began to make their way down the center aisle.

When they passed the box where the princess and Miss Margaret Mercer Elphinstone stood, Princess Charlotte reached out her hand and touched Elizabeth's arm.

Elizabeth paused to look at her.

"He has always been a prince among men," the princess whispered. "He never pretended otherwise."

Elizabeth smiled and nodded her understanding, but she did not require the Princess of Wales to tell her this.

She had always known it.

Sumner was her fairy-tale prince and always would be.

Chapter 20

~~~ ⚬◯◯⚬ ~~~

Berkeley Square
The next day

Elizabeth peered into the mirror in the entry hall as she tied the bonnet's lush, green satin ribbon and fluffed the bow at her throat. MacTavish handed her a rose-hue twill mantle fringed with tiny white tassels and then opened the door for her.

She had just stepped through the doorway when she heard Lord Lotharian's deep voice coming from inside the house. Elizabeth ducked back inside and followed the low tones into the parlor, where she was surprised to find him speaking, quite animatedly, with Great-aunt Prudence. They both turned, appearing equally surprised when they saw her standing, mouth agape, before them.

"I did not realize you had called, Lord Lotharian." Elizabeth looked suspiciously at him. Nothing was ever as it appeared with the clever old rake. "I was under the impression that my sisters and our husbands were to join you at Cavendish Square—in Lady Upperton's library. Am I incorrect?"

Lotharian flashed a charming smile at her. "No, no, not at all, dear Elizabeth. Since your husband is coming from his meeting at Carlton House, I thought that you may be in need of conveyance."

"Why, thank you, my lord. MacTavish has a hackney waiting outside, but I shall ask him to release the driver. Do excuse me." Elizabeth smiled, then stepped around the corner and waited a moment for the conversation inside the parlor to reconvene.

"I daresay, is she absolutely sure?" Lotharian was asking Prudence. "Once I do this, it will be very difficult to be undone."

"This was the plan all along, Lotharian. Once the gels were happily married, they would be told . . . the appropriate *truth*." Prudence's voice was strong with conviction. "You will tell them this day, won't you?"

"Yes, yes." Lotharian sounded, for the first time, as though he were overcome with nerves. "I will ask you to undertake arrangements for my funeral, for once they hear what I tell them, the gels and their husbands will no doubt throttle me to my end."

Great-aunt Prudence chuckled at that. "You will do quite well Lotharian. My faith is in you."

There was the sound of heavy steps on the carpet. Lotharian was coming. "If there is any change—you will send word immediately."

Elizabeth scrambled down the passageway on the toes of her kidskin boots to ask Mac-Tavish to dispatch the hackney. She could just hear the two elderly dears beyond.

"I shall," Prudence said. "Good-bye and good luck, Lord Lotharian."

"Thank you, Mrs. Winks, for I shall need all the luck I can obtain."

Cavendish Square
The library

Additional seating had been set up in Lady Upperton's large library for the occasion. What occasion that might be, no one but Lord Lotharian knew. And quite possibly Great-aunt Prudence.

But Elizabeth had overheard enough to know that whatever he said would once more change their lives forever. This unnerved her no little amount, for Lord Lotharian did nothing by half.

Mary, Anne, and Elizabeth sat nervously, side by side upon the settee, while three large chairs had been positioned behind each of them for Mary's husband, Rogan, the Duke of Blackstone; Anne's new husband, Laird, Earl of MacLaren; and finally Sumner, Marquess of Whitevale, who had only just arrived.

Lady Upperton sat before her mechanical tea server and amused the gathering by setting it into motion, efficiently pouring dish after dish of tea. Lady Upperton glanced up at the hidden door in the bookcase nearest the hearth. The tiny woman was visibly agitated, and judging by the way her small hands shook, had she not invented the mechanical tea server, she would not have been able to take the role of mother herself this day and pour the tea herself.

Suddenly there was a metallic click, and the flames of every candle in the room pointed toward the hearth as the hidden door opened, drawing enough air from the library that the tendrils of copper hair at Elizabeth's hairline lifted toward the door.

Lilywhite waddled through the doorway first, followed by the tall, bewigged Gallantine, and, at last, Lotharian, who wore a very serious expression on his hawkish face.

Lilywhite and Gallantine took the tufted chairs lined up parallel to the Royle sisters, but Lotharian remained standing.

"Dear Lotharian," Mary began, "please do not make us endure the torture of waiting any longer."

Anne was nodding. "I was not able to sleep at all last night, for when you ask for a meeting, someone's life changes completely."

"And now that we three are blissfully married, which was the promise you made and kept to our father," Elizabeth said, keeping in mind the exchange she overheard in Prudence's parlor, "I can only assume you have something new to report—or another scheme in the works—to prove our birthright."

Lotharian's brows fluttered at that. "You are quite clever, Elizabeth. All of you are." He glanced at each individual in the room in turn, as if purposely trying to delay his oration. "But, it seems, not quite so wily as . . . *I*."

Everyone looked to each other for understanding, murmuring among themselves, but no one—even the other two Old Rakes of

Marylebone—knew what Lotharian was about.

Only Lady Upperton did not move or speak. She simply stared down at her quivering hands.

Sumner came to his feet. "Enough games, my man. Tell the ladies what you mean to say. Elizabeth and I must leave for Whitevale before the sun sets."

Lotharian waved Sumner down, not deigning to speak another word until everyone was seated and silent. When at last everyone was settled again, he began. "The Royle sisters are *not* the daughters of the Prince of Wales and Maria Fitzherbert. The story of their birth is all a grand ruse, contrived by me alone, to stir interest within the *ton* and confidence in the gels."

"Wh-What is this? Why would you say such a wicked thing?" Rogan demanded, reaching forward and settling a comforting hand on Mary's shoulder.

"I promised Royle I would see that his daughters were happy and married well. I achieved that." Lotharian began to pace as he spoke, his voice not so even and calm as it normally was in the company of friends. "How else would three gels from Cornwall with no money and no true connections gain entrée into Almack's and into the finest drawing rooms in all of London? If I did not achieve this, how could I hope to match the Royle sisters with gentlemen of quality," he gestured to the sisters' husbands, "like yourselves? Sumner, here, was the only match I could not foresee, but then you, Lord Whitevale, were in the midst of your own ruse of secret identity, weren't you? Lady Upperton and I did not realize who you were until Elizabeth mentioned the name Sumner. Prince Leopold is known for his formality, elegance, and superior manners. From first we met, you, sir, did not reflect the refinement I expected, but rather the qualities of a warrior—strength and loyalty."

Gallantine was incensed. "Damn you, Lotharian! You have been lying to us all, even to Lilywhite and to me—your trusted brothers of the Old Rakes of Marylebone. And you did this . . . why?"

"For my plan to work, everyone had to believe it completely." Lotharian withdrew the document box that belonged to their father.

He must have gone to Berkeley Square to retrieve it, Elizabeth realized, not to convey her to this library as he'd claimed.

"Thankfully, your father did have many connections in court and Parliament. He did favors, and kept secrets . . . in this box."

Lady Upperton spoke at last. "Lotharian asked me to create a mechanical false bottom in the document box—which I did. In it, he hid several items from your father's belongings—items from which he could weave the dark, yet fanciful story that you three young ladies were the secret daughters of Maria Fitzherbert, the prince's illegal Catholic wife."

"So, Lady Upperton, you knew of this plan all along?" Laird asked.

She nodded. "I confess did. Most of the time, I did."

Mary shook her head fiercely. "I do not believe it. The cashmere shawl—it did belong to Lady Jersey."

"Yes, it did," Lotharian admitted. "Royle saved many things. Among them was a shawl that Lady Jersey had used to stop Prinny's bleeding after a bloodletting. Just as she said."

Elizabeth studied Lotharian closely. His usual cool demeanor was absent. He had to be lying.

"The page from the wedding register that we found inside the book?" Anne asked impatiently.

"I only placed the *Book of Maladies* inside the box because Royle had written all sorts of cryptic notes in the margins. The letter opener, and what was inside the book—both a complete surprise to me," Lotharian ruefully conceded. "Clearly, you and your sisters have a knack for deductive reasoning, as well as a good deal of pure luck."

"Why, if this is true, did you include the bottles of laudanum?" Elizabeth probed, still not quite believing Lotharian's new story. "They were marked with Sir Henry's insignia."

"Your father had a great number of bottles and potions. He was a royal physician, as was Sir Henry. I had no notion the bottles bore the baronet's mark. I included the laudanum bottles because they worked so well with my contrived story. If Maria Fitzherbert was drugged, she would not know whether the babies were born alive or dead. If she did not know, and you truly did have conclusive proof of her lineage, I doubted any of you would dare approach her with such an outlandish story."

Everyone, except Lady Upperton, his willing cohort in this monstrous lie of all lies, glowered at Lotharian.

"What I do not understand, Lotharian," Anne said, "is why you went to so much trouble to create a fantastic history for us, a mystery to be solved."

"Because if I simply told you the story, you would not be so convinced," Lotharian explained. "If you uncovered proof of your supposed past yourself, you would be far more likely to believe that you were . . . princesses by birth. Worthy of the company of the *ton*."

Elizabeth stood up and set her hands firmly on her hips, the way she'd seen Princess Charlotte do so many times. "Why should we believe you now? This tale is as fantastic as the first."

"Because your father asked me the favor of seeing you happy—he knew who I was. What I was. That is why, when he first became ill, of all of his many friends, he came to me first. He knew I would do *anything*. I would not stop until the three of you were happy and married. He knew, because of what I was, he could rely upon me to fulfill his dying wish."

The room was very still.

"I do not know what to believe," Anne said.

"What is easier to believe, sister?" Mary asked. "That we are the secret daughters of the Prince of Wales and Maria Fitzherbert? Or that some poor farm maid in Cornwall left three babies on our father's doorstep?"

Elizabeth thrust both her hands outward. "It does not matter what the circumstances of our birth were." She glanced at Sumner and smiled. "Don't you understand that? We are all married to the men we dearly love. And, la, Mary, you have already been blessed with a baby born of that love."

Lady Upperton looked up then. "Elizabeth has the right of it. What matters is not where you come from, it is where you have come. The gift your father left you is ensuring, by whatever means, that his daughters each had love in their lives. Lotharian, though his methods were not the least bit orthodox, made your father's grandest wish for the three of you come true."

Lotharian stood at the edge of the gathering, his lean arms folded protectively over his chest.

Elizabeth walked across the library and embraced him. "Thank you, Lotharian." She turned and looked to Anne, who rose and came to Lotharian as well.

"Though there were times I would have wrung your neck had I known what you were doing, now I can only thank you. For you achieved my father's goal. I am in love, I am loved, and I am the happiest I have ever been in my life." She hugged Lotharian tightly.

Mary stood, arms folded, and looked Lotharian hard in the eyes. "What you put us all through . . ."

"Love is worth the most to you, and its chances are greater of lasting, if you have to work for it," Lotharian said. "It was a lesson that both you and Rogan needed to learn."

Mary exhaled a small laugh. She closed the space between her and Lotharian and embraced the old man.

"All is forgiven?" he asked tentatively, then looked to the Old Rakes, who came and reached out their hands to him.

Then Lotharian silently turned to the three young men. "I suppose the three of you will take me outside now." He grinned nervously.

"Only if we cannot shake your hand here, good fellow," Sumner said.

"You brought us each a great gift," Laird added. "I am grateful."

"A rake is a rake . . . until he marries," Rogan said. "I ought to know. So, how could I possibly fault you for your less than wholly honorable methods?" He clapped Lotharian on the back.

"Exactly, lad," Lotharian replied. "But I have come to believe that I have lived my life as a rake long enough." It took some doing for his old bones to manage, but he knelt down before

Lady Upperton. "Will you, dear lady, do me the honor of becoming my wife?"

"Oh, my goodness." Lady Upperton's eyes rounded and she clapped a hand to her chest. The old woman took a moment to steady her breathing before replying. "Have you got my father's consent?"

Lotharian blinked in confusion for a moment and then grinned. "I have not, my lady, so I suppose it will be a Gretna Green wedding for the two of us. But I must know, my dear gel, just how fast is your father's horse and how is his aim?"

Everyone laughed.

That is, until they realized Lotharian's proposal was no ruse.

And that in two days time their presence would indeed be required in Gretna Green, for the long-shot marriage of the season—that of the old rake, Lord Lotharian, and Lady Upperton.

Epilogue

The rain trickled down the window panes, squirming and wriggling like the earth worms Mrs. Prudence Winks had flung with her cane from the walk into the sodden garden bordering her niece's residence as she arrived for her visit.

Her niece sat very still. Her expression was as somber as the afternoon sky.

"You can change your mind, Maria," Prudence said. "The fact that the gels are all married means nothing. You can always come forward—and tell them."

Maria Fitzherbert raised her blue eyes to Prudence. "No, I cannot. There is no need."

"There is." She had posed as the sisters' great-aunt for two years, and had come to love them

351

as though they were her own. "They would wish to know you."

Maria shook her head slowly. "It would do no good. *He* would hear of it, the Church would learn of their existence, and their lives would never be their own again."

"But if they could choose between knowing you and a life of normalcy—"

"They shall never have the need to choose, Prudence. I have chosen for them." A lone tear trickled down Maria's cheek. "I made my decision more than twenty years ago. And we all must live with that choice."

"But Maria—"

The corners of Maria's pink mouth lifted. "They are happy, you say?"

Prudence smiled gently. "They are."

She turned her gaze to her folded hands upon her lap. "Then, I do not regret my decision."

Heat stung Prudence's eyes. There was no more to be said.

Maria turned her eyes back up to Prudence. "Cherie has requested that she remain with you. I gave her my blessing."

"Truly?" Prudence swiped at the tear catching in her lashes.

"I have managed well enough without her

services as a maid, but I will miss our weekly chats about the sisters," Maria admitted softly.

"There is no reason those cannot continue. No doubt she and I will see the gels often," Prudence said. "Though they may have to adjust to the knowledge that Cherie can speak, and is only very quiet by nature."

Maria chuckled silently. "Isn't it something that when someone does not speak, those around forget she can hear."

"Even when she is . . . sleeping." Prudence grinned.

How sad that her part in Lotharian's grand scheme was at an end. But the relationships she had enjoyed were not.

Prudence pressed the tip of her cane into the Aubusson carpet and slowly came to her feet. She faced her dear niece one last time before departing. "Thank you, Maria."

The thin skin around Maria's eyes crinkled. "Thank you, Prudence? For what?"

"Never mind, my dear. Just . . . thank you."

As Prudence caned her way through the front door, tears blurred her vision, but she was smiling.

In becoming, in all ways, the sisters' great-aunt, she would be loved and cared for into her late years, just as she had been for the past two seasons with the Royle sisters.

She would never be alone again.

And for that she would always be grateful for the gift Maria had given her.

Author's Note

Because my stories often include a concoction of real and fictional characters, one question readers often ask me is, "Did this really happen?" Well, this is a difficult question for me to answer . . . because the answer is both yes and no. While the heart of *How to Propose to a Prince*, the romance of Elizabeth and Sumner, is fictional, the rest of the story is a complex blend of historical fact and my own imagination.

For instance, George IV and Maria Fitzherbert, a Catholic, were secretly married until the Crown decided the marriage was illegal and therefore never happened—leaving the prince free to marry Caroline, Princess Charlotte's mother. There was also speculation, even during the Regency period, that Maria Fitzherbert may have secretly birthed a child from this union. This rumor was bolstered by the fact that during her lifetime Maria Fitzherbert repeatedly refused to sign a document swearing that she never had a child by the prince.

Prince Leopold's family did lose vast holdings to Napoleon, and his pursuit of Princess Charlotte very likely arose from the need for him to marry strategically. It is also said that after his marriage to the unruly Princess of Wales, he did come to care for Charlotte and mourned deeply when she died in childbirth a short time later.

The beautiful Miss Margaret Mercer Elphinstone was indeed Princess Charlotte's only intimate friend. She became a close friend of Prince Leopold's as well and is credited with being instrumental in bringing the two royals together.

Sir Henry Halford was an influential surgeon to both members of the royal family and to many powerful personalities in Parliament. Most notably, he was physician extraordinary to the mad king, George III. He did, in fact, perform the autopsies to confirm the identities of the skeletal remains of King Henry VIII and King Charles I. He published his findings in

An Account of What Appeared on Opening the Coffin of King Charles I, in the Vault of King Henry Eighth in St George's Chapel at Windsor (London, 1813). Reports exist of the baronet frightening and awing his dinner guests by using the severed cervical vertebrae of the beheaded Charles I as a macabre salt cellar. His was a story too outlandish to be a work of fiction. I had to merge it with my own story.

Other than the bridge over the Serpentine, which did not yet exist when this story took place, every scene was set in locations that existed during the Regency period, many still existing today.

As for the Royle sisters and their quest to prove their royal bloodline, sadly, the heroines are completely fictional, but their quest is not. Even today I know of at least one family searching to prove—through DNA instead of clues beneath the false bottom of a document box— that they are descended from a child born to George IV and Maria Fitzherbert. This book is dedicated to that family.

Cheers,
Kathryn Caskie